BEAST UNDER YOUR BED

A YA HORROR ANTHOLOGY

BEAST UNDER YOUR BED

A YA Horror Anthology

Curated by Megan Guilliams

Dark Moon Rising Publications | Virginia

70 Foxwood Drive
Rocky Mount, Virginia 24151
Tel: (540) 257-2861

ISBN: 978-1-972596-04-3

10 9 8 7 6 5 4 3 2 1

Printed in the United States of America

Contents

BEAST UNDER YOUR BED

A YA HORROR ANTHOLOGY

SCAREDY-WOLF

BY JOSHUA LADD

April was a little girl who had a secret garden all to herself. Her parents, who owned the massive brick house with its pointed black gables and towering chimneys, were too important to society to spend much time at home with their beautiful daughter. She had only Mrs. Bott, the caretaker, to keep her company, a wretched woman whose warty face reflected well her abysmal disposition. To distance herself from her unpleasant steward, April spent her afternoons wandering the estate gardens—through endless rows of kaleidoscopic flora, herbs that grew wild in untamed bushes, the labyrinthine hedges that encircled a mildew-green fountain.

The garden was an organized if overgrown sprawl of land at the foot of forest-covered mountains. On one early fall morning, April was trotting down the garden's stone paths, eating some berries she had picked. She merrily sang her favorite rhymes around mouthfuls of the sweet fruit, the dark-red juice of the luscious berries running down her chin and staining her white dress, until her skip came to a stop at the pumpkin patch. The pumpkins were plump and bright orange in the morning sun, but it was not these bulbous children of autumn that had grabbed April's attention. There, sitting among the blanketing pumpkin vines, was a giant black wolf, whose shiny yellow eyes were as startled to see April as April's blue eyes were at seeing them.

They stared at each other a moment before the wolf asked, "Well? Aren't you going to scream and run away?"

"Why would I do that?" asked April, who was not familiar with wolves because her evasive parents had never been around to read fairy tales to her at bedtime.

The wolf guffawed. "Because I'm the big bad wolf. Aren't you afraid of me?"

"Well," replied April. "You do have strange eyes and long, sharp teeth."

"Yes," said the wolf. "You know, the better to eat you with?" He grinned, showing all his pointed teeth jutting down like stalactites from his cavernous mouth.

"Eat me? Wouldn't you rather eat some delicious berries instead?" April took a step forward, offering a small red mound of berries in her outstretched hand. The wolf suddenly jumped back, flaring its black tail and growling menacingly.

"My, whatever is the matter?" asked April.

"You stay away from me. I don't trust you."

April went aghast at this insult. "Whatever reason have I given you not to trust me?"

"You're not afraid of me. What strange creature are you to not be afraid of the big, bad wolf?"

April giggled. "I'm a girl."

"Exactly my point."

"Oh, you're just being silly," said April as she walked toward the nervous beast who shuddered at every approaching footstep. "There, there," she said, petting the wolf's massive head. "There's nothing to be afraid of."

Then, quite suddenly, the wolf erupted into tears. He half-howled as he whined to April. "Nothing to be afraid of? Aroo-hoo-hoo! If there's nothing to be afraid of, then I have no purpose in life! Aroo-hoo-hoo-hoo!"

"Come now," consoled April. "Surely we can find someone for you to scare."

"You mean you'll help me?" The wolf looked up at her with hopeful, teary eyes.

"But of course. I can't stand to see such a beautiful creature cry. Besides, I know what it means to not be wanted. Come, we'll go to the fountain, maybe you can scare the fish."

The wolf blinked away his tears, jumped up, and began trotting down the winding stone path with April skipping along beside. A stately row of hedges stood ahead, their green leaves splotched with brown as they gave way to the season, capped by a coterie of charcoal crows who cawed the coming of the two comrades.

"Caw!" said one of them. "Lil April is covered in berries! Caw! Lil April has found a wolf!"

"Caw! Caw!" the chorus concurred.

"This is the big, bad wolf," said April.

The wolf let loose a tremendous snarl and bared his fangs as his fur stood on end.

"Caw!" said a crow. "Why does it make such a monstrous sound?"

"He's a wolf," said April. "Why shouldn't he be loud?"

"Be-caw-se it's rude."

April wasn't aware of this because her ambiguous custodians had never been there to teach her.

"You-you're not afraid of me, either?" asked the wolf shakily.

"Afraid of you? Caw! Wolves are the least of our problems!"

"Caw!" agreed another crow. "Mrs. Bott swats us with her broom when we try to eat the berries. Caw! Besides, if you're not afraid of him, why should we be? You're only a little girl, after-caw!"

"Hey, I'm not so little," said April. "You could have at least pretended to be afraid. Come, wolf, let's visit the fish in the fountain to see if we can scare them."

"Caw! Good luck!"

"Aroo-hoo!" howled the wolf. "Not even crows are afraid of me! Aroo-hoo-hoo!"

"Come now," said April. She placed her small hand on the distraught creature's head and led it through a wooden door and into the hedgerow labyrinth. As they started down the winding path, April explained to the wolf how they would negotiate the maze.

"I'm going to yank out tufts of your fur to drop along the path in case we get lost."

The wolf looked up at her with his fearful, yellow eyes. "You're going to do what?"

"Here's a good place for our first marker," she said as they reached their first intersection. She grabbed a fistful of the wolf's sheer black fur and tore it from the quivering beast's back.

"Yoowwll!"

"I think the fountain is this way." April trotted down the path to the right and once again began singing a favorite rhyme, cluing in the less-than-enthusiastic wolf on certain lines in case he wished to sing along. They gradually traversed their way to the center of the labyrinth, where the fountain stood, with a tearing howl from the wolf at each intersection as chunks of his fur were left as hairy guideposts.

The towering fountain was carved into an effigy of a man with a regal hat, clutching the neck of a wretched-looking sea-creature with stringy tentacles and three horns sprouting from its head, highlighted in green by the carpeting algae. The two friends approached this watery sculpture and bent over the blue pool in which it stood to see a frenzied group of long, black fish swimming frantically in circles. The fish immediately froze when the wolf threw his front paws on the rim of the stone pond, shoved his giant snout as close to the water as possible without getting it wet, and erupted into a cacophonous blare-horn of barking, flinging sudsy saliva into the fishy faces and baring his terrible teeth.

When this canine tirade was over, the largest of the black fish swam to the surface and stuck out its scaly face. "What the devil is going on out here?"

"Good afternoon, little fish!" exclaimed April. "Please, meet my friend, the big, bad wolf."

The wolf flashed its eyes and growled at the slimy fish, which was turning blue.

"Excuse me a moment," the fish said as it dunked beneath the surface and took a breath, expelling a tremendous bubble.

"Where did it go?" asked April, whose withdrawn wellsprings were never around to teach her that fish can only breathe underwater.

With a soft splash, the fish reappeared and said, "We have no time to entertain guests, right now, especially none as noisy as yourselves."

"You mean," began the wolf. "You do not fear me?"

"Wolves are the least of our troubles! Er, excuse me," it said as it dashed back under to take another breath. With a small splash, it reappeared. "Mrs. Bott snatched one of our friends today. He was a prominent member of our pond, and now he's a prominent ingredient in the old hag's dinner. Be wary, friends, or you too could wind up in her gullet." The fish, unable to hold its breath any longer, submerged and swam back to the waiting school.

There came a mighty buzzing then as a black cloud funneled up from beyond the labyrinth's borders.

"Oh no!" yelled the wolf. "A tornado!"

"A tornado? I don't know what a tornado is—," (her bygone babysitters had not been around to teach her), "—but those are the keepers of the flower garden, the Bee Queendom, and someone has riled them!"

They quickly made their way back through the green labyrinth and trotted down the stone path to the floral rainbow of the tightly organized flower garden. The herbaceous kaleidoscope of softly colored petals swirled hypnotically, while the antagonized column of frenzied bees buzzsawed a blizzard of noise above their heads.

The wolf, convinced that such measly creatures as insects would fear him, once again let fly a barbarous barrage from his big, bad mouth. From the twisting tower above, one large bee, the queen herself, flew down to meet them.

"Vat iz the meeening of thiz?" she asked. "Haven't wee beeen troo eeenough alreadeee?"

"Aroo-hoo-hoo! Not even little insects are afraid of me!"

Ignoring the crying canine, April asked the queen bee, "What do you mean?" She did not know how rude it was to address royalty without a title, such as "Your Highness," because her wayward watchguards were never around to teach her.

"Vat devvaztating mannerz you humanz have. First, Mizezz Bott steeelz our honeeey and now you treeet mee like a common beee!" The offended insect huffed at April and the Wolf, sticking out her tiny chest and angrily buzzing back to the towering whirlwind.

"I must say," said April, "that mean old Mrs. Bott seems to be wreaking havoc in my garden. She swats at the crows and steals the fish right out of their home to make for her supper. Then she riles the flower-keeping bees by stealing their honey."

The wolf, who had begun his beastly bawling once more, howled in response. "Aroooh! Everyone is afraid of Mrs. Bott instead of me. Aroohoohoo! I have no purpose in life."

April looked down at the sad creature. "Don't worry, wolf. I know how we can make everyone fear you."

"You have a plan?" the wolf asked, around sobs.

"I do. We're going to scare Mrs. Bott! If the other animals see that she is afraid of you, then they will be afraid of you, too."

"Scare Mrs. Bott?" said the wolf. "But what if she tries to swat me with a broom?"

"It's almost noon. She should be having her tea in the rose garden. Come, wolf, we'll teach that mean old hag a lesson she'll never forget."

"But what if she tries to cook me for supper?"

April led the pitiful beast down another stone path that curved toward the brick house. She scooped another handful of wild berries that grew along the path, and as she made her way to the rose garden with her trembling friend, she sloppily shoved bunches into her mouth, creating explosions of red juices that cascaded down her white dress.

April's vacant custodians were never around to teach her that sneaking up on someone and then jumping in front of them, making a loud noise, was not good behavior, and this is exactly what April did, with berry juice gushing from her mouth, down her chin, and all over her dress, and her fur-torn, teeth-bared wolf growling beside her. Mrs. Bott, sitting under an umbrella and sipping tea from her dainty cup, sent forth a shattering screech as a crooked white streak shot through her black hair.

Before the wolf could unleash a volley of vociferation at the cruel housemaid, the ugly woman fell over dead, her hairy, jagged warts standing up like tombstones, and the wolf frowned, disappointed that he couldn't show off his verbal vexations.

"You did it, wolf!" said April. "You scared Mrs. Bott right to her grave!"

"Arooo!" he howled in excitement, wagging his huge, black tail. "I scared her to death! I feel so much better!"

April said, "You look better. Your fur seems blacker."

The wolf turned his massive head to the young girl.

She continued, "And your eyes seem brighter. And…oh my. Your…teeth look sharper."

Indeed, the wolf's teeth gleamed in the afternoon sun as hot saliva boiled between them. The wolf stared at April and licked his massive jaws.

"Do they, April?" He growled, creeping toward the girl.

"Um, Wolf?" was all that April could say before the wolf pounced.

It was a shame that April's absent stewards were never around to tell her that it is not a good idea to make friends with wild animals, especially when the wild animal is none other than the big, bad wolf. Poor April was eaten all up, and the body of mean old Mrs. Bott followed her into the wolf's stomach before the evil beast retreated to the deep forests on the mountain. From that day on, the animals of April's garden lived forever in fear of the wolf's return.

LOSING EVERYTHING BECAUSE THEY JUST DON'T UNDERSTAND

BY JASON ROGERS

Have you ever wondered what the worst thing to happen to a teenager can be? I will tell you.

Tonight is going to be a bad night. Horrible. And, it's all mom's and dad's fault. They just don't understand what they are doing to me.

Let me go back to earlier in the night. Mom got off the phone with one of her friends and instantly yelled.

I lie here in my bed right now. The night is heavy, and the darkness is thick. There could be something horrible right above me, and I wouldn't know it easily. I'm sweating, and I am wide awake.

I have school tomorrow, and I must face a whole day without my life.

I was in the living room, and she was in the kitchen. The stairs going to the second floor were all that separated the two rooms, so her voice was crisp and clear – and scary.

"Braedon Amir Sanderson! Come here right now!" My mom said earlier that day. She used my whole name, so I knew she was angry, and when she gets angry, it's time to face the Loud Monster. Her yelling is worse than the Big Bad Wolf. It's like a police siren.

I did what I had to do. I lowered my head and walked really slowly to the kitchen, where she waited. My dad, my older brother, and my younger sister waited in the living room. My younger sister, who didn't like me, smiled in evil happiness. My brother just shook his head in shame. My dad looked at me like he was staring at a lazy employee. I had to walk through the maze of couches and chairs, which made me pass by all of them.

"What did you do? You're ruining this game. I can't hear a thing with your mom screaming." Dad gave me the evil eye. He was angry that I made her yell.

I entered the kitchen.

I don't want to say what happened in the kitchen in detail, because that was not the scariest part of the night. It was bad, don't misunderstand me. But...my mom thought I did something that I didn't do. She thought that I had taken part in some bullying of a girl. She said it was cyberbullying. But I didn't. I wouldn't do anything like that because I would lose something very important to me. I would have my life taken away. Really. I'm not joking.

My friends would be lost. My whole world would be taken away. The whole thought really scares me. Nothing really scares me more than that. There isn't a demon or a monster or a ghost that could take everything from me like that.

I stared at the white tile with the black grout as I got yelled at. I saw a crumb that she missed when sweeping the floor, but I didn't dare point that out. She would think I wasn't listening.

Mom said she was going to think about my punishment. She didn't believe anything I said. The girl who suffered from the bullying – cyberbullying...um, her name is Sara. Her mother knows my mom. They go to the same church. I don't know if Sara blamed me or not, but Sara's mother sure did. I promise. I swear. I didn't do anything.

I went upstairs and took a shower. This gave me some time to think about things and have an imaginary conversation. You know, a conversation in your head about how things should have gone.

I was focused on the yelling, so I didn't even check my phone.

I'm thirteen, and I know some classmates and people at my middle school who do things like that, but, as I said, if I did anything like that, I would lose everything in my life. And losing my life is worse than dying.

I can't say that around my mom or dad. They say that I'm exaggerating. They don't understand. They grew up in a different time. Popularity depends on certain things now.

As of this moment, I still have what is important to me. It wasn't taken away, but there was going to be a punishment.

I'm brushing my teeth right now. The bathroom is pretty big. I share it with my brother and sister. She has one side, and I share the other side with my brother. My parents' room was almost right across the hall. My mom sits on the bed, and she can see right into the bathroom. She's worse than a dentist about me, my brother, and my sister brushing my teeth. But, she doesn't just tell or instruct. She yells and lectures.

So…I always brush my teeth against the far wall on my side so she can't see me.

I am just finishing up when my younger sister comes into the bathroom. She sees me and gets a mischievous smile on her face.

"Mom, Braedon's taking too long. I need to use the bathroom."

Her name is Shannon. She fits the stereotype of every younger sister and the youngest sibling: the universe revolves around her.

Shannon didn't even look back at Mom when she spoke. She just said it really loud so that Mom could hear.

"Braedon, let your sister use the bathroom. Stop playing games."

I say: "I'm not playing games. I'm just brushing my teeth. Just a moment."

Instantly after I said that, my mom jumped in.

"It's been a moment. Now get out."

Shannon laughs just loud enough for only me to hear.

"Braedon, go check that the doors are locked downstairs," Dad says – or..."

"Okay."

I go downstairs. It's all dark. I can hear Mom and Dad watching TV, my older brother – Elton – talking on the phone, and Shannon complaining about something to mom as she brushes her teeth.

The main door is locked. The whole area around that door is very dark. For years, it has scared me. Even now, at thirteen, I don't really want to turn on the lights because of what I might see. There are coats hung up and the washer and dryer in this room. I sometimes imagine there are some dark figures that will pop out. Maybe they just stand there and wait for someone to get close with curiosity. Maybe I will get lost in some creepy backrooms. There's even a musty smell and a stink of old paint that hasn't been used.

These thoughts – these fears – have me frozen for a few moments. We live in the country, so the outside is very dark. There's a difference between city dark and country dark. The country also brings silence over the whole area.

Hurrying, I leave the room and go to the door that leads out into the backyard and our porch. It is not locked. Makes sense because this door is used often. Elton goes outside to get privacy while on the phone. And I wouldn't put it past Shannon to unlock it just to get me into trouble. Because of that, I make sure the locking sound is loud and pronounced.

I can hear my mom's footsteps heading in the direction of my bedroom. She tries to be sneaky and quiet, but her footsteps are like elephants stampeding. This has been beneficial to me sometimes. It's given me time to hide things as she approaches my room.

"What are you doing?" I say to myself – just loud enough so I can hear it.

I look up towards my bedroom. From the stairs, I can see my light turn on for a few moments, and then it goes off. Mom goes back to her bedroom and shuts the door. For the millionth time today, I gently pat my pocket. Everything I need is right there. Even when I walk, I can feel the weight of it, which makes me comfortable.

"Honey, I got it here…I think." Dad says loudly to her.

"The man showed me how." She replies.

What in the world's going on? Is that about me and my punishment?

When I get to my bedroom and get comfortable, I will check it. There's a good chance I will be able to quickly after getting into bed, because Mom and Dad already have their door shut.

The last two doors are locked. I checked them even though we never really use them. I'm really just wasting time to make sure mom and dad are asleep. I can hear my mom talking to my dad about something. They are trying to figure something out together from the sound of it. Dad types on the keyboard on the computer in their room.

"Come on, go to bed," I say – again, quietly.

I wait downstairs in the darkness of the kitchen. I don't want to give them a reason to talk to me at all. They can't see me coming up the stairs, but they can hear me because I will be right next to their doorway when I get to the top of the stairs.

My mind wanders as I lean against a wall and face the stairs so I can see who comes down, if anyone does.

The fact that I am a loner in my family is something I don't really have a problem with. I mean, I don't really like sports or cars or building things. Elton does, though, so he spends a lot of time with Dad. Shannon is the only daughter, so she and Mom spend a lot of time together. Also, I did get into some trouble here and there since I was, like, ten or eleven, so our parents are always on edge about anything I do. I wish they would leave me alone, but I know that's not going to happen. My grades aren't very good in school, which makes Mom pretty upset. A "C" is average. That means that most students will get it. It's not bad, and it's not great. It's average. But, to mom and dad, it's failing. Elton gets the same grades, but they don't get onto him about them. It's not fair, but I'm not going to say that my parents hate me. I just want more freedom.

I always look forward to seeing my friends at school. Stephen, Johnny, Lindsay, and Paulie. They are always fun. I'm sure they've messaged me since I last checked my phone. It was before I went into the bathroom to brush my teeth. Oh, it has been a long time, but I didn't want to have it out in front of Mom or Dad. I would get into more trouble. If I check it while checking the door locks, Mom and Dad may catch me. I get really focused on it sometimes. What new memes have my friends found or made? What's going on with them at their houses? Did they get to work on our music on Bandlab? Stephen made a really cool beat a few days ago. Did he make an ending yet? I needed to know. This wasn't about wanting to know. This was about need.

I head up the stairs quietly. Shannon and Elton are still on their phones in their rooms. They talk pretty loudly behind their closed doors. I sneak a peek at mom's and dad's bedroom door. The lights are off. No light shines from the bottom of the door. Good. They are asleep.

As you can see, this night is already terrible, but it gets even worse.

Very quietly, like a naturally talented ninja or a highly trained spy, I go into my room. I shut the door and turn on the light for a moment. Everything in my room is the same. The queen-size bed is on the right, and my desk is on the left. My dresser is against the wall next to the door, and the closet is next to the desk on the far side. My room's pretty barren of anything. Nothing has been moved or changed. My computer is still on my desk. My guitar hasn't been touched. What did Mom do when she came into my room? What was she looking for? What did she want to take? If it were my smartphone, she would've just yelled for me to bring it to her. No. It was something else. But…nothing looked amiss.

I turn out the light and crack my door open. I am not supposed to keep it closed unless I am changing my clothes. That is one of many rules that just apply to me. Shannon's and Elton's doors are closed right now. And, they are talking on their smartphones. They will be awake most of the night, which will cause them to be really rude in the morning.

Oh well. I just need to focus on myself and not get into trouble.

I get into bed and put myself into a position where I can look at my phone but not let the screen light bring any attention to me. This involves some particular positioning of my sheets and comforter.

My smartphone lights up, and my world opens up. Happiness hits me again.

I put in the pattern, which is pretty complicated.

The first thing I always do is go to my second 'calculator' app and make sure it's secure. Of course it is, but I like to know. I can't have my parents seeing those pictures I keep secret. Then, I check my app that blocks the surveillance app Mom had the smartphone salesman put on Elton's, mine, and Shannon's phones. The app I downloaded blocks the app the salesman installed from collecting some things from my phone.

Everything is good.

The whole time I check those two things, I see that a bunch of messages came in on the group chat I keep with Stephen, Johnnie, Lindsay, and Paulie. I smile and get ready to have a conversation with my friends. This night is looking up.

Little did I know, though.

I read over the messages. Lindsay has an idea for a new song. Paulie's got some lyrics to show everyone, so he posts them on the group chat. And Stephen signed off early so he could work on the ending of the beat he was working hard on.

Oh, everything's good.

From the corner of my eye, I see…

Oh, dang.

I see…

And this makes me worried.

I see that the battery life of my phone is at 23%. That might last all night. Even if it does, I will have to find a way to charge my phone at school. I'm not allowed to bring my recharger cable to school. Mom checks my backpack every morning, too. And…Paulie has an iPhone, Johnnie has an iPhone, and Lindsay has an iPhone. But I have a Samsung phone. I won't be able to use their chargers.

My mind races. I don't want to get up and out of bed, but I will need to if I want to be part of the group conversation. My battery life will go down to 10% before I know it. The plug-in (and where I keep my charger cable) is on the wall on the other side of the room.

Okay. I'll just say a few things and then say that my battery level is low.

I type in a comment, hit send, but that little red circle with the red exclamation point pops up under the message. Undeliverable. Message failed.

What in the world?

I try again, but it's the same thing.

My stress level is on the rise. I am cut off. I can't connect.

I look up at the top right corner of my phone, and I see that I have no bars. There's no service.

Is it everyone? No. It can't be, because Elton and Shannon are on their phones right now.

I turn my phone off and restart it.

But the same thing is happening. I'm sweating right now, and my heart is racing. What's going on?

My battery is down to 17% now. Two problems at the same time. I need to get over to the outlet, but...my room's really dark. And...those evil things that might be near the washer and dryer might be in my room. I get scared to roll over sometimes. Maybe something's right behind me, and if I turn around, I will be face-to-face with it.

Is there something under my bed? A robber? A monster of some sort? Probably not. But I'd believe that there are ghosts around in the dark.

I close my eyes and see those little balls of light we all see. I think they're called phosphenes. Shut your eyes really hard, and you can see them. Sometimes those phosphenes take on the shapes of skulls, which scares me.

I throw the covers off me, but I don't roll over. What if the Slenderman is standing there watching me? I know he doesn't actually do anything, but...I don't know what I would do if he's there. If I scream and he vanishes, Elton will never stop making fun of me. What if someone is doing the Blue Whale Challenge and they are under my bed?

Oh...the Momo Challenge! I clench up and can feel my racing heartbeat in my head. It's loud and makes it so I can't hear anything. And without the use of my phone, I wouldn't be able to record any of these things? Who would believe me with some kind of video evidence? I will look crazy.

I glance at my phone. It's down to 13%. How is it going down so quickly?

Still NO SERVICE.

I roll over but keep my eyes closed for a moment. *There's no such thing as ghosts. There's no such thing as ghosts.* I tell myself over and over.

My eyes open and...

Is there something there? My eyes are playing tricks on me, maybe? The room is darker than usual. The pictures of my family and some famous people look at me. I dart my vision to all corners and crevices. I need to make sure nothing's hiding.

I thought I saw something a moment ago – right in the corner of my eyes. Something moved? It might have been a shadow or a cloak or whatever it is that ghosts wear. But it disappeared just as fast as I saw it.

Sometimes, my mind plays tricks on me when I'm already scared like that.

I focus on the outlet, but something seems off with it. Is something missing?

Before I can get over there, I ease my head over the side of my queen-size bed and look down.

Nothing moves or pops out from under the bed. I take a deep breath and lower my head down so I can look under the bed real quick.

Nothing. Under the bed is empty, but this doesn't stop me from looking all around.

I roll off the bed like a gymnast and end up in a sitting position on the floor of my room.

I stand and walk quietly over to the outlet. I then noticed what was off about it. My recharger is gone. Did I put it somewhere else? I think hard to myself as I also look around the room.

The charger is nowhere.

My breathing is harder, and my heartbeat is so loud that it drowns out Elton's conversation in the next room.

I look all around. I'm frantic.

When I look far to my right, I catch a glimpse of mom's and dad's bedroom door. Then, I remember.

Mom came into my room when I was checking the locks downstairs. I didn't know what she took, but it must have been my recharger.

My phone is now down to 9%. It's like a time bomb, and I can't let it get to zero.

I turn around to make sure nothing's right behind me. My eyes move quickly to every part of the room.

My stress combines with anger. Mom took my charger, and…

Oh! That's what they were trying to figure out earlier. Mom and Dad cut the service to my phone! I am cut off from my friends. I will miss them so much.

My charger is right behind that door. If I try to get it, Mom will surely wake up. She's such a light sleeper. I will get caught, and I will lose my phone for sure. Right now, it's the service and charger, but I still have the phone. Losing service and the charger is like losing a finger, but losing my phone would be devastating.

But now…what's going on out there? Did Stephen finish the song? Are they listening to it right now? What is Lindsay's new idea? I NEED to be online to hear what they have. I NEED to help out.

What if there's a Challenge going on and someone is coming to my house? How will I be warned? I am like a shipwrecked sole survivor on a deserted island. I'm cut off. I'm in Hell and cut off from God.

My battery life is 5%. The number is flashing now, telling me that I need to charge it now. I won't even be able to use my camera now.

Why wouldn't Mom believe me earlier? I had nothing to do with that cyberbullying. I would never do something like that, especially to Sara. I like her. I know that some guys say she's not good-looking, but she is to me. I can't tell Mom because Elton and Shannon might hear and make fun of me. She has to know that I didn't have anything to do with it. I just focus on music.

4%.

I can't explain anything to Mom right now. I can't contact my friends to see if they know anything or if they did something. I'm lost in a silent wilderness. Mom is wrong in her thinking, but I can't do anything until tomorrow. I will only have a short time to explain to her before I need to catch the bus. And she won't let me take my charger to school! Oh…who can I borrow a charger from?

3%.

There's nothing I can do right now. Nothing. I'm helpless. It's like I'm face-to-face with the Slender Man and I'm tied to a tree. I can't fight. I will just lose more. I'm powerless. I am friendless. The night is moonless. The air is soundless. I'm literally in a horror movie, but this is real life.

2%.

I'm still standing in the middle of my room. I haven't moved. My breathing and heartbeat are the loudest things in the world right now, and mom and dad don't care. They are sleeping calmly, but I'm fighting a horror inside me. I'm surrounded by huge brick walls, and I can't see or hear anything on the other side. My friends are there, and they don't know what's going on with me either.

I go back to bed. My desire to throw my phone is strong. You know, just throw it against a wall in anger. If I can't use it for anything, what's the use of it? It's just a lump of electronics. I don't think I've ever been this angry or stressed before. I'm being punished in the worst possible way for something I didn't do.

Lying down, I stare at the screen.

1%.

The blackness will come soon.

Death will come soon – for my phone and me. I will not literally die, but I might as well. It's the same thing.

I can't call. I could scream into my phone, but it would be like yelling into space. No one would hear me. I'm just here, and I am losing out on things.

0%, and the blackness comes.

The light from the screen has gone out, leaving no light in my room. I am surrounded by darkness. The only light is what escapes through the cracks of the closed doors of Elton's and

Shannon's rooms. The light makes the shape of an "L," like the universe is calling me a Loser twice.

"Why are you making all this noise?" Mom says, which makes me jerk in fear.

I didn't hear her get up or walk over to my room. I didn't know she was watching me. My heartbeat and breathing covered the sound of her footsteps.

"Sorry," I say.

I want to ask her, but I can't. It will just make her angry, and I will lose my life, my love, my hope – my smartphone.

"Did you see what I did?" She asks.

"Yes," I answer.

She waits. I don't say anything else. I'm not even looking at her. My eyes are closed, and I'm lying on my side.

"Go to sleep. We will talk about it tomorrow," she says.

"Tomorrow morning?" I ask.

"After I get home from work. Now, get to sleep."

She walks away.

When she gets home? That is later in the day. It will be almost five o'clock. Will she be able to switch my phone back on then?

One whole day with no phone?

Please, take me, Slender Man.

Please, someone doing a challenge, take me.

Please, someone or something, come from the backrooms and take me.

This is my worst night ever, and it's all Mom's fault.

The Nothing Monster has taken me. I can do nothing. I have nothing now. And, I will have nothing for at least a whole day.

ROGER AND THE GHOST

BY PAUL LONARDO

She heard the laughter of the trespassers as they made their way across the lawn and headed up the walkway. The three boys who mounted the steps to the front porch were not wearing costumes, but she knew instantly that it was Halloween. She strongly disliked the annual pseudo-holiday and avoided it at all costs, but it caught her by surprise this year. It had been a milder and wetter autumn than normal, and even the ash trees were still holding onto their leaves.

"Let's go inside and divide up the take," said the boy carrying two pillowcases filled with candy.

"Just as long as you divide it equally this time," another boy spoke up.

"I'll decide what's even," the first boy shot back.

A sudden pounding on the door rattled the walls and ceiling, dislodging a layer of standing dust inside, which drifted down around her like dirty snow.

"Trick or treat, Dead Girl," the boy shouted.

She quickly ducked behind the couch when a shadow appeared in the window across the living room.

"I think I saw her," the third boy screamed.

"Where, where?"

"I don't see anything."

The window filled with silhouettes.

"Over there. Behind the couch, near the fireplace. See her ponytail?"

There was a tapping on the glass as the cell phone camera lights penetrated the pitch-black interior. It was the only window in the entire house that wasn't broken. Because it was entirely concealed by dense, overgrown hedges, it was protected from the stones that the local teens frequently hurled at the old house for fun. She had plugged up the other windows with some cardboard, though it was more for privacy than any sort of hindrance. Anyone could access the vacant property if they really wanted, but the children in the neighborhood had always been too afraid to set foot inside the abandoned house. Halloween was different, however. It had a way of making some kids brave, or at least daring enough to act on things that otherwise scared them, just for the thrill of it. On this particular night of the year, mischievous children and even adventurous adults would wander closer to the house than usual, walk around the grounds, and occasionally knock on the door. They wanted to see a ghost. However, if any of them had ever found themselves in the presence of an actual ghost, she couldn't be sure how they might react to her, so she would always spend Halloween night locked in the basement. That's why she hated Halloween.

Now, she felt trapped. She would already have been in the safety of the cellar behind the steel-reinforced door if she had realized that it was October 31. Her only hope was to make a run for it before the teens got inside. There was a large open space between her and the door in the kitchen that led to the basement. She was sure to be seen, but she didn't have a choice. She dashed toward the kitchen, hoping the shadows would conceal her movement.

"There she is. Come on. Let's get her."

As she entered the kitchen, the back door started to open.

Oh, no, she thought, remembering that she'd left the door unlocked after coming in from the backyard that afternoon. She stopped and quickly dove under the kitchen table as someone entered the house.

"Is anyone here?" The soft whisper was followed by the sound of the door closing and the *click* of the deadbolt lock.

She crawled on her hands and knees across the floor to the far end of the table as the intruder came further inside. The legs of the boy stopped directly in front of her, between her and the cellar door.

"It's okay. You can come out." The boy's voice was kind. "I don't mean you any harm. I just want to meet you."

She didn't move for a moment, then she slowly crawled out from under the table and stood facing the boy.

"Hi," said the tall boy with a gentle smile. He wore a white robe with a separate oversized hood that was pulled down behind his head.

"Hello."

"My name is Roger. What's your name?"

"I don't remember."

The house was dark, but she was glowing with a low, throbbing luminescence. "You don't seem surprised that I can see you."

"This is the only night of the year that just about everyone can see me," she said. "I'm not really sure why. I think it's because people expect to see ghosts on Halloween, and their minds are more open to it than any other time of the year."

"I see you all the time," Roger told her.

"You do?"

"Yeah. Out on the back porch. Sometimes in the back yard."

"There used to be an old tire tied to the branch of a giant sycamore tree that I used to like swinging on," she said. "It's gone now, but I still like to go outside and try to remember what it was like then."

"What else did you like to do?" Roger asked.

"I don't know."

"You don't look like a ghost," he told her. "You seem like a regular girl."

He smiled at her, and she blushed.

"What's it like to be..." he began. "You know?"

"It's not bad," she said.

"Aren't you lonely? Do you miss being with your friends?"

"I never had any friends when I was alive," she said.

"I don't have any friends, either."

"What about those boys outside?"

"Oh, that's Dennis, my older brother, and his friends, Jaden and Alex. I was out trick-or-treating with Dylan. He's my little cousin, so I don't think that even counts as a friend. Those big boys came along and took our bags of candy. Dylan ran home crying, and I came here to get our candy back from them. I thought maybe you could help me."

"*Me,* help you?"

"Sure."

"What do I have to do?" she asked.

"Do you ever scare people?"

"I try not to scare anybody."

"But you could? I mean, if you wanted."

"I guess so." When Roger smiled at her, she couldn't help but smile back. "And you'll be my friend if I help you?"

"We're already friends," Roger told her. "Besides Dylan, you're the only other kid who will talk to me."

"What do you want me to do? she asked.

When he finished telling her his plan, the sound of shattering glass from the living room caused them to look up.

"Okay," Roger said. "It's time. Let's go." He paused briefly and looked her in the eyes. "Thanks."

A moment later, they disappeared into the basement together as the three teens entered the house through the broken window.

"Whoa!" Dennis exclaimed, shining the light from his phone around the vast living room. The sparse furnishings were festooned with cobwebs and covered in a half inch of dust, which rendered the room colorless, like an old Black & White TV show.

"This place looks like it belongs in one of those bad horror movies you like, Alex."

"Yeah," Alex agreed. "I don't think anybody's been in here for years."

"Except for the ghost," Jaden added. "Let's just divide up the candy and get out of here."

"Don't wimp out on us now, Jaden." Dennis stepped in front of him, looking down on the boy, who had a half-foot advantage over him in height. "I don't see any ghost. Do you?"

"I *did,*" Jaden told him. "It was right over there." He pointed toward the faded antique camelback sofa.

Dennis reached into one of the pillowcases and removed a candy bar, tossing it behind the sofa. There was a shrill squealing as it struck the floor, followed by the sound of tiny nails clicking on the floorboards as a rat scampered off into the darkness, carrying the chocolate in its mouth. Jaden jumped and let out a shriek as Dennis and Alex laughed and mocked him.

"There goes your ghost," Dennis said.

"This place is giving me the creeps," Jaden said. "Just divvy up the candy between you two. I don't want any of it."

"Fine by me," Alex said.

"Me too. Give me some light here."

Alex fixed his phone on Dennis as he opened one of the bags and reached a hand inside. Suddenly, his eyes widened as something attached to his hand. He would have looked pale if everything around him wasn't already a monochromatic moonscape. The LED lighting revealed the lower part of his arm swarming with cockroaches.

"What the…" he withdrew his arm from the sack and shook it vigorously to dislodge the vile insects before they made it above his elbow.

Dennis dropped the pillowcase, and the roaches spilled out, disappearing under the sofa and into the nearby walls.

Just then, a small figure in a white robe appeared out of the gloom and stopped near the boys. The hood was pulled up, concealing the person's identity, but Dennis recognized the homemade costume as the same one that his younger brother had been wearing.

"Roger?" Dennis stepped closer to the hooded figure. "What are you doing in here?" He reached down and pulled the hood back. When it dropped down, there was no face, no head, nothing at all inside the costume. It was completely empty. Then the robe fell to the floor, and there was nobody inside.

"What's going on here?" Alex asked.

Dennis was too shaken by what he had witnessed to respond.

"Can we get out of her now?" Jaden begged.

Something moved inside the other pillowcase Dennis was holding, and he released it from his grasp. It struck the floor with a heavy THUD, and out rolled a bloody, severed head. It came to a stop face up, and when Dennis saw his brother grinning up at him, he took a step back and yelped. "Let's go," he said breathlessly and set out quickly in the opposite direction. The other boys followed.

"Where's the window?" Jaden asked, his voice shrill and full of panic.

"It's got to be here," Dennis said, more of a demand than a statement. But as they continued along, there was only an endless dark wall.

"We must be going in the wrong direction," Alex suggested. "Let's double back."

They headed back the other way, but there was still no window to be found. Their frantic movement released clouds of dust particles into the air, which swirled all around them, diminishing their vision even further.

"We're trapped," Jaden bellowed. "We never should have come in here."

"You better shut up," Dennis warned him. "We must have missed it, that's all. Keep looking."

All at once, the lights on their phones went off at the same time and it became as black as a tomb inside the old house.

"My phone battery just died," Alex said.

"Mine too." Jaden shook his phone vigorously and struck it with his other hand to try to get it to work. "What are we gonna do?"

"We're gonna stay calm," Dennis said evenly. "This house isn't that big. There are other ways out."

A loud bang, like the tailgate of a dump truck opening, was followed by the sound of some granular substance being emptied nearby. All around them, heavy, damp soil began to pile up rapidly. It ran over the tops of their feet and continued pouring in.

"We're being buried alive," Jaden croaked.

They maintained their position atop the rising tide of earth, riding it like a dense wave. Higher and higher they went, well beyond where the ceiling should have been. Completely blind and terrified, their pleas and cries for help did not resonate. It was as if they were underground, and no one could hear their anguished screams. Soon, they were at the peak of a high mountain of dirt, where they were no longer able to maintain their balance. One by one, they fell, tumbling down the steep slope. In an uncontrolled descent, their faces impacted the dirt and chunks of soil lodged in their ears, noses, and mouths. Sputtering and coughing to keep from suffocating, the boys thought they would continue to fall forever. Then, without warning, they rolled to a stop, their bodies collecting in a heap. It took a moment for them to get their bearings, and to their collective astonishment, they found themselves lying on the ground in front of the abandoned house. It was a moonless night, but there was considerable ambient light for them to see that they were not in any danger whatsoever. No one said a word as they surveyed one another's faces, which were caked with mud and blood.

Dennis was the first to get to his feet. "We don't tell anyone about this," he warned his friends. "Ever. Or you'll answer to me."

Alex and Jaden nodded, and then all three boys quickly strode away from the house at a brisk pace, almost running.

Watching from the broken window, she and Roger laughed.

"That was awesome!" Roger said. "You're pretty good at that. Especially for never having scared anyone before." He looked down at the pumpkin lying on the floor and nudged it with his foot. "I really liked that trick. Did you see the look on my brother's face when he thought it was my head?"

"It was nothing," she said.

"*Nothing*? It was nothing short of spectacular."

She blushed.

"Thanks again," he said.

"I should thank *you*," she said. "That was fun. I probably used to like Halloween a lot. I do now, at least."

"I meant, thank you for being my friend." He stepped close to her and gave her a hug, and even though she did not have a physical body, she felt his embrace.

THE ARTIST

BY MEGAN GUILLIAMS

Original Short Published in The Dark and Chilling Tales of Murdock Monroe

"When will you be done?" the little boy moaned.

"The more you complain, the longer this will take." Marcelle had been dealing with this little puke for weeks now. His parents had commissioned a life-sized portrait for his tenth birthday, which was coming up in just a week or so. They had put the little brat in a blue sailor's suit, complete with knee-high socks that couldn't have been very comfortable.

"I wanna go get ice cream. Mama said I could get ice cream if I were a good boy." Marcelle couldn't help but rub his temples. The only thing that made this job worth doing was the vast amount of money the mother had offered him and the chance to try out his new paintbrushes, which he had won in a silent auction. They were breathtaking. The handles were made of Dalmatian Jasper and silver and had fascinating runes engraved at the base. Many people had bid on the brush set, but he swooped in and got them at the last second. He could still hear one of the men who had bid right before him try to threaten him as he picked up the set, saying something like

"You're gonna regret this," and "Do you even know how to use them?" Marcelle rolled his eyes and quickly responded with, "Oh, I don't know; I only paint portraits for a living." He could still remember the man's face as his eyes widened with wonder. He looked like he was going to say something else to Marcelle, but the man was ushered out of the room before he could do so. Marcelle finally put down his brush and looked at the little boy, who had a little fat finger shoved remarkably far up his left nostril.

"Okay, Lewis, you finally finished. I think your mother is going to love it." Rolling his eyes, Lewis got to his feet and wandered around to look at the finished piece. For the first time in the weeks that the little man had darkened Marcelle's doorway, he finally saw a look of wonderment cross the boy's face.

"You did this?" He asked, eyes as big as a saucer.

"I did," Marcelle said, putting a hand on the boy's shoulder.

"It's amazing!" Marcelle couldn't stop smiling, and when the mother came to pick up the boy and the painting, she couldn't have been happier and paid the man handsomely. It wasn't until later that evening that things started to take a turn for the worse.

Marcelle returned to his cabin a little later than he had wanted. Working in the big city and living in the countryside sometimes poses that problem. He could hear impending rain falling in the distance and knew to get inside and buckle down for the night.

Living so far from humanity sometimes posed disadvantages, such as if the rain got too intense, his internet would go down. He never thought of getting a landline because his cell phone was always reliable when he worked in the city, but when he came home, his phone had no service. On the other hand, though, Marcelle wouldn't consider moving closer to his studio. Waking up every morning to the sight of the wild horses and fresh air brought him back to his Native American roots.

Fumbling with his keys, he could feel the first drops of cold rain hit the top of his head. Opening the front door, Marcelle put his art kit inside and slipped off his shoes. It had grown rather cold in the house, so Marcelle ventured to the back to load the wood-burning stove and put on a large pot of vegetable soup. He had a modest garden outside and grew all his own food when it was viable to do so.

He had just started the fire when he decided to pull up his emails for the day.

"That's odd," Marcelle said when he noticed Lewis' mother had sent him three emails. He could see the lights flicker overhead, and he knew it wouldn't be long before he would have to get out the oil lamps. The rain outside was unforgiving, and the lightning lit up the night sky.

Opening the first email, he began to read.

Dear Mr. Corrend

We couldn't be happier with the portrait you painted of our son, Lewis, and have decided to hang it over the mantel by the fireplace. Unfortunately, as the evening progressed, my husband and I noticed a grey stain in the top right corner of the painting. We were hoping you could look at it and maybe touch it up.

With Regards, Lauren Cloud

Marcelle couldn't think of a single reason the painting would have a grey streak on it, but because the Cloud family were such generous people, he didn't mind clearing a little time to fix a smudge. Opening the second email, though, he felt like maybe he was being punked.

Dear Mr. Corrend,

I don't know how to put this, but the stain is growing, and it has now almost taken on a human form. I don't know what kind of crazy paints you used, but I now have to request a refund. The painting is disturbing, and we have decided to put it in the guest room on the other eadside of the mansion.

With Regards, Lauren Cloud

Again, the lights flickered overhead, and Marcelle wasn't sure if he could respond to the email, but against his better judgment, he opened the last email. *Dear Mr. Corrand* was all he read before the electricity went off. Marcelle shut the laptop and rubbed his face. He knew he had to get the oil lamps out before the sun went down and make up some excuse for why Lewis' painting began to change abruptly. There was no way he would give them back his whole commission; that was a month's worth of work, and he couldn't take that kind of loss.

Making his way to the kitchen, Marcelle pulled two large oil lamps from the cupboard and removed the glass lids. He couldn't count how often he had to do this in the spring. The sunrise, though, would be breathtaking, and the rain would be good for his fall harvest. He hadn't lit the second lamp and had only just put the lid back on the first when he heard a loud rapping on the front door. Marcelle couldn't feel anything other than confusion because he had never had visitors in the fall. The weather was far too unpredictable. Picking up the lamp, he returned to the living room and looked through the peephole. Outside in the pouring rain, there was a hooded figure. Only then did the lightning hit again, and he could make out the silhouette of a man in a hooded raincoat. Even though Marcelle only made out the bottom of the man's face, he had a sinking feeling he had met him somewhere before.

"Can't I help you?" Marcelle asked. The man on the other side of the door didn't hesitate; the expression on his face remained unmoved.

"My car broke down a little way back. Can I use your phone?"

"I hate to break it to you, man, but I don't have cell service, and we just lost power. I can only offer a warm place to wait out the weather." The man nodded, and Marcelle let the man inside. Walking inside the living room, the man stopped dead in the center of the room and allowed Marcelle to shut and latch the door behind him.

"What brings you out here to the countryside?" Marcelle asked. His back was turned to the man, lamp in his right hand.

"I'm sorry," the man began, "I didn't know what to say to get you to let me in." As Marcelle turned to face the man, he pulled down the hood, and Marcelle's eyes grew large.

"It's YOU!" Marcelle hissed, "You're the man who razzed me at the auction just because I outbid you for those brushes."

"Yes," the man began, "It took me almost a month to find out where you live, and I sorely hope I have caught you before it's too late, but by the looks of your popularity, I highly doubt I have." Marcelle looked at the man curiously,

"Well, if you're going to stand in the middle of my living room, the least you can do is tell me your name." The man turned around, went to the couch, and sat down.

"My name is Howard Smith. I'm an antiques dealer from Wisconsin. I have been following the history behind the paintbrushes you purchased. I don't know how this always seems to be the result, but anyone who gets a painting done with those brushes dies in some crazy way. I can only assume that the brushes make the owner insane." Marcelle scoffed and rolled his eyes.

"Well, I just finished a painting for a lovely family in the city, and nothing happened to them or me." In the back of his head, though, Marcelle couldn't help but think about the grey stain on the portrait. Were the Clouds slowly going insane? No, that couldn't possibly be. "Are you insinuating that these brushes are cursed?" Howard shook his head and ran a wet hand over his face.

"No, not necessarily; the fact that these brushes were originally made in the late 1700s could indicate that they were fashioned with chemicals that could be absorbed into the skin, causing hallucinations or temporary insanity. I don't know why it doesn't happen immediately, but it will happen. Now, if you don't mind, I would like to take the brushes and have them examined thoroughly. If nothing comes back, I will return them to you." Marcelle scoffed again and put his lamp on the table beside his recliner.

"How am I supposed to know you're not just going to run off with them, Howard? You did seem a little too interested in my brushes at the auction."

"Your brushes?" Howard got to his feet and began to walk towards Marcelle, who instinctively stepped back, knocking over his paint kit. One of the larger brushes in the collection rolled out onto the floor and stopped at Howard's feet. Howard bent over and picked up the brush; his eyes were excitedly bright. "I've never been able to look at one of these up close. Please let me see the others." Marcelle hurried to pick up the art kit, shoving the remaining brushes inside the leather briefcase.

"I won't let you get your grubby little hands on my brushes!" Picking up the lamp, he brushed past the man, hurrying into the kitchen.

Howard was bathed in darkness; holding the brush in his left hand, he covered his head with the raincoat hoodie and walked towards the flickering light in the kitchen.

"Come on now, Marcelle; you're making things a lot harder than they have to be." Howard lumbered into the kitchen, where Marcelle had pulled out the other five brushes and held them against his chest. He couldn't figure out exactly why he felt the need to protect them, but he knew for a fact that the man in front of him shouldn't have them.

"Give me back my brush, Mr. Smith." Marcelle hissed, and this got Howard laughing maniacally.

"I figured you were too smart for that old antiques dealer bit. I used to own these babies long ago, and it's time they come home." Lunging at the man, Howard swung the brush handle at Marcelle's face, cutting his cheek. Marcelle couldn't believe how sharp the brush was and how strong Howard seemed to be; Marcelle had at least 30 pounds of lean muscle on the man who seemed to have no problem attacking him. Howard swung again, and this time, Marcelle jumped back, hitting the open and unlit oil lamp and knocking it to the floor with a crash. The oil seeped into the wooden floor, getting between the cracks and moving towards the wood-burning stove. Slipping and sliding, Marcelle made his way to the back of the room, where he had left his soup to cook, and grabbed the handle.

"Where do you think you're going?" Howard shouted as he rushed the man, swinging the pot with all his might. Marcelle threw its contents at Howard's face. Screaming in agony, he stumbled back, dropping the brush on the ground. Marcelle swooped in and picked it up just in time to see Howard fall back and knock the lit lamp from the table. The kitchen went up in flames. Marcelle ran back through the kitchen and managed to reach the back door before the gas main ignited and his whole cabin went up in flames.

"It's a damn shame what happened to that artist, fella." Mr. Cloud said as he sat down to watch the evening news with his wife and son.

"Oh, yes. I'm glad that I didn't demand a refund…how could I when everything the poor man worked for went up in flames? All over, some crazed fan."

"Indeed." Mr. Cloud had just lit his pipe when the doorbell rang. It was a clear, crisp fall evening, and he couldn't fathom who it could be. Looking through the peephole, he could make out the silhouette of a man in a grey raincoat. The top half of his face was hidden from view.

"Can I help you?" Mr. Cloud asked. The man didn't flinch, and his mouth showed no emotion.

"I'm sorry, sir, my car broke down a little way back, and I was wondering if I could use your phone." Mr. Cloud opened the door and let the man in. Pulling back his hood, Mr. Cloud knew immediately who it was.

"Marcelle, what can we do for you?" With a little smirk, Marcelle pulled out his largest brush and quickly slit the man's throat without hesitation.

"Nothing personal, Mr. Cloud, but seeing as my art supplies have been depleted, I am in great need of new paints, and a tall man in a top hat gave me the recipe…but the ingredients, well, that can be a killer."

It was almost a week before the police found the bodies of the Cloud family, each one with their throats slit, but the little fat boy who gave Marcelle such a hard time had his tongue cut out as well. Upon further investigation, the police discovered the large painting in the guest bedroom. The one with the little Cloud boy and the man in the grey hooded raincoat holding the paintbrushes, only the bottom half of his face could be seen.

CAPTAIN TIDE'S NEW HOOK

BY PIP PINKERTON

The legend of the ruthless Captain Tide, the vicious, infamously brutal pirate, who sailed only at night, stretched far and wide among the various ports along the seven seas. The barbarous pirate captain apparently had a penchant for slitting throats, just not deeply enough to kill, then throwing his enemies (or victims) overboard, into waters heavily frequented by hammerhead sharks, in particular. He was also known to thoroughly enjoy killing the old, the young, women, and the defenseless.

When David Rice, a self-proclaimed master apprentice to the famous silversmith, Roquelaure, had first heard that Captain Tide was looking for new pirates to fill his ranks, he was profoundly excited. The call had been for preferably young (weak-minded, strong-backed) men who could take care of most of the maintenance on the ship, as well as fit the bill of menacing and intimidating marauders. David followed the rumors quickly, tracing them to a man named Willy, a one-eyed pirate and Captain Tide's right-hand.

David, who looked about seventeen but was as tall as any man and who was built thin and wiry, displayed his violent prowess adequately by taking on two drunk sailors who were at least his size or bigger. Willy saw this and was immediately drawn to the boy. The two conversed over a few drinks; Willy bought David a rum or three, and David told Willy how good a silversmith he was. Next thing he knew, David found himself part of the crew of The Calamity Catcher, Captain Tide's infamous pirate ship.

After that first night, however, David's abilities as a silversmith had never again been mentioned, possibly because there had been very little silver aboard the ship to smith. That is, until one day, a few weeks into their voyage, Captain Tide ordered, seemingly out of nowhere, for David to craft him a new hook, an elegant hook which he could wear to dinner, as he sometimes had to meet with reputable persons to unload his pilfered booty.

David took what silver he was given, the absolute minimal amount needed to make a sufficient hook, and that was only if he didn't mess up even once. He got started immediately. The captain afforded him a small work desk that he was to be set up in the galley of the ship, right near the chef, whose malodorous stench could have killed a dog. There was a sickness going around the ship, a slow, vitality-draining illness that was gradually killing off the crew, and many wondered if maybe it had something to do with what the chef was feeding them.

After half a dozen days of appearing to work nonstop on the hook, David finally had a finished product that he was ready to present to the captain.

A short while later, David found himself waiting patiently, in a tight chair, in the small meeting room outside the captain's quarters, next to the bejeweled box in which he had placed the finished hook. Captain Tide, a talk, dark, rugged, and moderately greasy man, whose mere glance made you want to be working or just plain somewhere else, anything to avoid having him come over and talk to you, walked into the room and immediately stared with piercing intensity, directly into David's eyes.

"I believe you have a new hook for me," Captain Tide stated expectantly. "Grab the box, follow me."

They entered the captain's quarters. Tide closed the door behind them.

"Here you are, sir. I did the best as I was able. I crafted it down as good as my master taught me, and with just what you had on this here ship, sir," David replied with what seemed like nervousness.

"You wouldn't be trying to tell me that my tools are inadequate, would you?" Tide asked, a hint of devilish delight in his voice.

"I-I don't know what you mean, sir, but I don't mean to insult your tools, no sir, not one bit, sir," David answered, now beginning to fidget in his seat.

Captain Tide opened the box he had given the boy for when the job was completed, and from it, he removed an elegant hook that appeared to be crafted of the finest pure silver. The captain marveled at his new possession, examining it meticulously, before fitting it snugly onto the stump of his long-amputated left wrist. After staring intently at the final result for what seemed like an eternity, the pirate captain let out a disappointed "hmmph" sound.

"Everything okay, sir?" David asked in a voice barely above a whisper.

"Not quite straight, is it?" Captain Tide observed with a casual, almost regretful melancholy.

"The hook is straight, I swear to it," David assured him confidently, yet his posture and gestures suggested more than just a hint of desperation.

"No. I do believe it's slightly crooked," Captain Tide concluded with a sigh of disappointment, as if he were a young child who hadn't gotten the gift he had wanted on his birthday.

"The hook is straight, Captain. I tell you it is!" David stated again, fear and panic now prevalent in his voice.

"Well, now, David, I take it that what you are telling me is that my eyes are maladjusted, which I don't believe to be the case, either that, or you are calling me a liar. Now, which is it, David, which is it?"

"I never did hear the word maladjusted before this day, sir, but you can't be a liar, my captain, how could you be, the word of a captain is always true in the eyes of his men," David answered shakily.

"Indeed, how right you are, David, and now, I say to thee that this hook is crooked," the captain stated calmly as he drew his flintlock pistol and aimed it point-blank at the innocent deckhand.

"The hook is straight!" David shouted, knowing that it was.

Captain Tide pulled the trigger and shot David right in the chest, dropping the poor lad instantly to the ground.

"Pity, this is a well-made hook," Captain Tide commented regretfully, then adjusted the hook on his wrist just a little. "Oh…I guess it is straight after all."

Captain Tide began to laugh. Behind him, the floorboards began to creak.

"I told you it was straight. Too bad it's not real silver, though," David's voice spoke, only it wasn't the same as before. Now, not only had confidence and strength replaced his feigned timidity and meekness, but the tone of David's voice was more gravelly and more guttural than it had been just moments earlier.

Captain Tide turned around and was immediately startled into a gasp. His tongue could not form words, nor could he will his hands to go for either his flintlock or his cutlass. He couldn't scream. He couldn't even tremble. Captain Cornelius Tide was, for the first time in his whole miserable existence, truly paralyzed with fear.

Standing before the flabbergasted captain was David, who just stood there, fully erect and seemingly unhurt. He wasn't straining or wheezing or struggling to stand or giving any indication of pain as he stared intimately into the pirate captain's eyes, staring right into the blackness of his pupils, into the deepest depths of the man. Captain Tide tried to avert his gaze, but when his eyes moved down to David's chest, he watched in horror as the gory hole in the man's chest stopped bleeding and rapidly began to close right before his eyes.

"W-What are you?" The words stumbled from Tide's lips as if they were stones too big to fit between his teeth and had to be turned and twisted until they could be forced through, scraping the bottoms of his teeth along the way.

David only smiled, no longer looking anything like a young cabin boy. His body now seemed tense, poised, like a spider waiting to strike. He had transformed from a malleable, naïve young boy to a cunning, devious man of experience, all without changing his appearance.

Captain Tide knew he had to act swiftly and intelligently, knew that his life depended on it. "You were right after all, David, the hook is straight," the captain murmured nervously, then a little louder, but without true bravado, added. "There's no hard feelings now, your captain commands it."

David continued to stare at the pirate captain intently, cocking his head from side to side: the predator sizing up its prey.

The stare unnerved Tide instantly and completely. He felt weak; his insides felt fluttery. He had killed many men before, and many men had tried to kill him, but he had never once felt fear like this. It was a most unadulterated dread. Even when he had his hand cut off and fed a hammerhead shark for cheating in a poker game against his brother, who would likely have killed them had they not been kin, even as the shark snatched up his fingers between its endless rows of teeth, when it seemed to smile delightedly in that half-a-moment they locked eyes before it swam away, almost as if to let Tide know that it now had a taste for him, even then, had he not felt the dread he felt now.

"You have been quite the bad man there, Captain Tide, and now you just shot an innocent, unarmed, mind you, naïve young cabin boy for what essentially amounted to nothing. Your reputation as a dirty, ill-playin' scoundrel precedes you veritably."

"Extra rations at dinner time," Captain Tide offered uncertainly, trying to keep the panic out of his voice. "No more swabbing the deck. You're better than all those poor slobs out there. No more hard labor for you. Captain's honor. I swear to it."

"You shot me, Captain Tide. I was right, the hook was perfect, and still you shot me," David said, seemingly as incredulous of the whole situation as the captain. "And now you want to make amends by a meager amount of extra vittles at meals, and no hard labor? You figure those poor slobs out there, the men I bunk and eat with, the men who I spend most of my time with, the people I know far better than I know your pretentiousness, you think they will be happy with me eatin' and sleepin' alongside them and not working? You must be trying to get me killed, Captain?"

"No. No. Not at all. How about a promotion? You can command the other men, and they will have to respect you, or they will taste my blade. First mate sound good to you? I'll demote Willy. Consider it done. He's only had that one eye anyway."

"You know, I was afraid at first. I've never been shot before. I knew I wouldn't die, but I really did think that it would hurt a bit more," David said, a smile broadening across his face, his canine teeth elongating to twice their normal size.

"Willy! MEN!!!" Captain Tide screamed, racing for the door.

David moved with lightning speed and slammed the door shut in front of the captain, forcing the handle inward and toward the doorframe itself, bending the whole mechanism in such a way that the door would have to be pried open from either side for anyone to open it.

"What do you want? Treasure? Gold? Women? I can get you whatever you want," Captain Tide pleaded. "The ship is all yours, Captain David, and I'd be your first mate if you'd have me at all."

"Do you like your hook?" David asked almost inaudibly.

"Yes," Tide practically shouted. "It is the best hook I ever did own. Can I pay you for the job? I will get you treasure, boy! You can be rich, rich beyond your wildest dreams."

"Did you really like it? Did you know it wasn't real silver?"

"What? No?" Captain Tide replied, confusion spreading across his face.

"Yes," David answered. "Real silver hurts us. That is why I was posing as a silversmith; then, everyone would give me their best weapons against me, and I would return to them well-made fakes. I do mean well-made, too. I take quite the pleasure in the art of creating things with nickel silver. I learned it from an ancient alchemist when I went to China to eat a Geji. You ever hear of a Geji?"

Captain Tide shook his head almost dumbly, his lip trembled like that of a small, whimpering child.

"They're quite beautiful maidens. See, that's a little hobby of mine, eating exotic people and such. Anyway, had the hook been crafted of authentic silver and not nickel silver, then you could maybe have hurt me. Silver hurts vampires. Too bad you noticed a minute imperfection, one that wasn't even really there, and not the big imperfection that was there."

"V-V-Vampire," Captain Tide stuttered, his eyes widening from coming hysteria. The terrified pirate captain turned and started rapidly across the room, aiming for the cross hanging above the head of his bed.

"Don't worry, Captain Tide, I am sure Willy will make a great successor to the rank of captain. Too bad you didn't like my hook," David said calmly, just before springing forward and latching inexorably onto the frightened pirate captain.

Captain Cornelius Tide screamed.

Willy shouted wildly as the other men tried relentlessly to pry open the captain's door and enter the cabin.

David fed well, until every last beat of Tide's heart had pumped down his gluttonous gullet, and when the pirate captain finally lay dead in his arms, he dropped the corpse to the ground and escaped nimbly out of an open porthole window, just as Willy and the other pirates broke into the room. He had never drunk of a pirate captain before and was glad he could now mark it amongst his exotic repertoire of victims. Dawn wasn't for seven or eight more hours, and David knew of a few islands not far away. He started to swim rather quickly.

Willy and the men burst into the room just in time to see the last vestiges of David's shirttail disappearing out the porthole window. Three shots were fired wildly, but all they managed to do was put holes in the side of the ship.

Willy bent down to examine the captain, even though he could tell right away that the man was dead. He grabbed Tide's flintlock and aimed it at the others.

"I say I be captain now," Willy told them.

No one disagreed, nor did they seem to hold any grudges or claims to the title. They had all worked under Willy on orders from Captain Tide, and now that Willy was captain, they didn't expect him to do anything any differently than Tide had.

"Oh, and we are no longer to be known as The Calamity Catcher, when ye ride under Captain Willy, ye ride upon the decks of Inferno!"

The men, with the flintlock still absently pointed in their direction, all unanimously cheered.

David washed up on the shore of an island he had seen before but never set foot upon. He was about to get up when he heard people nearby heading his way. David feigned being a drowned sailor, consciously forcing his lungs to pump just a little, to give his rescuers/captors an impression of weak life.

Minutes later, two men found him and immediately brought him back to their village. They put him in a small, dark, secluded tent in the corner, away from everyone else, getting him inside just as the sun was coming up over the horizon.

A short while later, an intricately painted, bone-studded bulk of a witch doctor came through the tent opening and examined him. After a moment, the witch doctor began to sprinkle some unknown powder all over David's body while mumbling something that may have been a chant. He then lit leaves that smelled strongly of a foul scent that David was entirely unfamiliar with, before beginning to waft the noisome smoke all throughout the room.

David Rice, well, at least as he was currently known, found the powder and the smoke to be irritating, but it would all soon be worth it for the payout. Last night, he had eaten a pirate captain; tonight, he would feast upon a witch doctor.

Doll's House

BY D. WINCHESTER

It was only when the movers had left, and the house was quiet again, that she could finally play with her toys. Her parents had never approved of such things, of course, so they'd been kept in the attic, in the old brass buckled steamer trunk that was tucked behind the brick chimney that dominated the center of the dusty room.

The stuffed animals they'd been fine with, so that was why Bill, the ragged old dog, and Jeffers, the one-eyed bear, lay on top of the blocks and wooden puzzles that were missing pieces, but if you dug past that, and checked under the moth-eaten quilt that lined the bottom of the chest, you'd find her figures – her *collection*.

Oh, she wasn't supposed to keep them, and honestly, they weren't really hers to begin with. Not really, but she loved each of her little figures so, and so she'd slowly collected them over such a long time. They were Mary-Anne's secret joy, and she'd never let them go. That's why she had to hide them. No one else was going to get to play with them. Not until she was done with them, of course, but that could take decades.

By day, the house sat empty, but when it was dark out and all the neighbors had gone to bed, she'd bring them out in twos and threes and play little games. Sometimes she would make Dave and Jillian playhouse, and other times she'd use Jason instead. She thought that Jason and Jillian sounded like a dumb name for a couple, though, so that was rarer.

Of course, none of them had ever known each other while they'd been alive, but that didn't matter. They could be whoever she wanted them to be, whenever she wanted them to be, as long as no one was around to tell her mother. They could have little tea parties and fights. They could go on adventures. They could do lots of things, at least until they started to remember who they really were.

Dave hadn't been married, and Jason's wife had been named Tanya, but she'd managed to escape, so she wasn't part of Mary-Anne's collection. That happened sometimes, but she didn't mind too much. There would always be another family to play with. How could there not be? Every time someone moved out, they offered such a good deal that another family simply had to move in.

The eight-room Victorian on Ogden Lane was her own personal dollhouse. It had been since…well, since forever, and she loved to play games with the people that dwelled within almost as much as she loved to play with her toys once they were gone.

Tonight, she was going to her favorite game of all: Murder in the Dark! It was a simple game, and much better than some of the others. When they were playing house, her figures always had time to remember that this wasn't their couch, that wasn't their dog, and actually, their husband was already dead.

Figuring out little details like that ruined the whole thing as far as Marie-Anne was concerned. She'd seen this house decorated a hundred different ways, and trying to remember what furnishings went with what doll was just tedious. Those details weren't important; all that mattered was that her dollhouse was full.

So, every night it sat vacant, the whole house came to life as furniture and draperies conjured from the memories of three dozen different families that had occupied the place over the last century and a half appeared in an instant. It was a delightful little trick that made her dance with glee because it was different every time, depending on who she played with.

It was the very best present she could have hoped for. Well, except for watching them suffer slowly in her richly decorated wonderland, of course.

Even in such a large house, though, Murder in the Dark could take hours and hours. Especially if Cleo or Patrick picked a fantastic hiding spot, or someone bigger like Martin was the murderer. Then she could look forward to hours of entertainment as all of her little toys scampered to and fro, looking first for a way to escape, then a way to defeat the monster that was hunting them, before finally settling for someplace they could hide and try to avoid another painful death.

It never worked, of course. Marry-Anne always won. She should. She'd been playing these games longer than any of her toys had been alive, and she'd still be playing them long after she wore these figures out and replaced them with new occupants.

It turned out that you could only play with a human soul so much before its features were worn smooth, and they forgot who they were. Toys weren't fun to play with after they got like that. Not to her anyway. She needed someone who could struggle and play, not someone who could only be propped up for a tea party.

***

As soon as her daddy opened their new house's front door, Michelle darted inside, just beating her brother Ryan inside as they scampered up the stairs to see who would claim the larger room. "I'm going to win," she teased as she raced up the steps to the second floor, a half a dozen steps ahead of him, but that wasn't true. She was a great big sister, and she was going to let him choose instead.

She just wanted to make him feel like he'd won. At thirteen, she was four years older than the younger boy, so there was nothing to be gained by beating him. Plus, Daddy had told her they'd go out for ice cream after the movers got started if they didn't fight, so she'd be on her best behavior.

Still, as she raced down the hallway on the second floor, just slow enough for Ryan to pass her, she looked around, focusing on how pretty this place was. Their daddy had shown them pictures, of course, but this was much nicer than their house on the West Coast had been. Even though he'd called this place a fixer-upper, it looked pretty fixed up to her, with dark wood floors and old light fixtures.

"I win!" Ryan shouted, getting into the larger bedroom just before her.

"Nooooo!" she cried out with pretend irritation, "I was so close!"

With that out of the way, they started exploring some of the other rooms. Eventually, Michelle said, "You know - I think you claimed the master bedroom. Where is Daddy going to sleep?"

"I don't care!" Ryan yelled, trying to figure out the correct answer. "How about…the closet!"

They laughed at that as they walked through the whole house, one room at a time. Well, the whole house, minus the basement. They took one look down the stairs into the darkness and decided that wasn't happening without an adult and some flashlights.

Once their father had gotten the moving truck sorted and the boxes started to pile up in the living room, he showed them all the places they missed, though. He showed them that the basement wasn't so scary and that the house was so old it had something called a coal chute, even though she was sure that was bad for the environment. He even showed them the detached garage and the attic.

"I didn't even know we had an attic!" Ryan shouted as he charged up the stairs ahead of them. "This room is bigger than our old house! What are we going to do with it?"

"Well, I thought we might let your sister have it," he said, making Michelle's head spin in surprise. "She's getting to that age where girls need a little—"

"Really, Daddy?" she said, ambushing him with an unexpectedly tight hug. "Thank you so much. I love it!"

And it was true. She did, even if it was a little creepy. The fact that she got to have a whole floor to herself made up for that, though.

"Awwww! No fair!" Ryan pouted. "I wanted the big room!"

"Well, in a few years, when she moves out to go to college, you can live up here next," Daddy said. "How about that?"

Michelle didn't care about her dad's attempts to placate Ryan's whining. Instead, she tuned them out and looked around the room, taking in every last detail. When they'd first come up here, something had made her feel like she should leave as soon as possible, but now that it was hers, that feeling vanished, and she needed to explore every inch of the place.

What she found wasn't very interesting. Some of the windows were cool because of how old and weird-looking they were, but mostly the room was just kind of creepy, and slanted walls meant there were very few places to put her bookshelves. At least, that's what she thought until she worked her way to the far side of the room. It was there, on the other side of the chimney, that she found an old steamer trunk with a little doll sitting on top of it that the previous family had left behind.

Excited at the prospect of a find like that, she eagerly opened the thing as different options flashed through her mind about what could be inside. Treasure, money, garbage, or even the bones of the people who had lived here before were distinct possibilities for a moment.

She was disappointed when she found that it was locked. The doll was interesting, though. It was ancient and had a porcelain face with a knitted body that made it hard to tell if it was supposed to be a girl or a woman.

For a moment, she was going to tell her dad about the chest, but something about that made it feel like it would be better if she kept it a secret. So, instead, she said, "Look at this, Daddy, someone forgot their toy."

"Well, then, I guess it's yours now," he said with a smile. "What will you name her?"

"Ummmm…" Michelle exaggerated, pretending to think. She would have picked a name like Jojo, Billie, or Taylor after some of her singers, but in reality, the name had popped into her mind as soon as she'd picked up the doll. "How about Mary-Anne?"

"I think Mary-Anne is a great name!" her father said with an embarrassing amount of enthusiasm. "Now we just need to find a Ginger, and they can go find the professor."

He laughed at his joke, but both children just looked at each other. And shook their head.

Michelle said, "You're so old, Daddy," and at the same time, Ryan said, "You're so weird, Dad."

Everyone laughed at that.

"Well, I think it's ice cream time," he said with a caring smile. "We wait any longer, and it's all gonna melt. Does Mary-Anne want to come?"

"Dolls don't eat ice cream," she said, rolling her eyes as she walked to the nearest windowsill and set the doll down. "She'll wait right here until we get back."

"That's good thinking," her daddy agreed. "She can keep an eye on the movers and make sure everything gets where it belongs."

With one last look at the strange doll, Michelle joined her father and brother as they descended the stairs. While she'd been willing to let her brother win their first race, riding shotgun was serious business, and there was no way she was letting him beat her again.

When the room was empty and the lights were off, Mary-Anne slowly turned her head to watch the children run out the front door to the car.

This was going to be a lovely family to play with, she thought to herself. She didn't know if she would keep any of them yet, but she knew that they would all enjoy the games that lay ahead, whether they wanted to play them or not.

CAO

BY MAWR GORSHIN

"Timmy, you're a very special little boy," his teacher told him as she cupped her hands over his cheeks. "You can…feel things, hear things, sense things, understand things that few other people can, and all at the tender age of six. Oh, sweetie, you're so sensitive, all those gifts you have."

"But, Ms. Cavanaugh," he said to her, the tears still rolling down his cheeks, "I hate being so different. It always gets me into trouble. I get picked on so much by my classmates for crying all the time. My mom and dad are always getting mad at me. I try telling them what I tell you, about the waves I feel all around me, and in me, and they never believe me. Nobody but you believes me. Everyone thinks I'm crazy when I talk about it." He sobbed some more.

"Those…waves…you feel around you," she said, now hugging him. "You say it's like electricity, or like water sometimes?"

"Yeah," he said, no longer sobbing. "The waves go up and down, inside and outside me. When they're up, they feel good. When they go down, they feel bad. I don't know if I should like them or hate them. Should I feel good, or feel scared?" He started sobbing again.

"Oh, baby," she said, taking him on her lap and rocking him back and forth. "I'd say what you're feeling is God, that's all, and that's a wonderful thing. Don't be scared of God. Fear Him, and you'll have nothing to fear."

"So, when the waves feel good, they're God, and when they feel bad, they're the Devil? When they go up, they're God, and when they go down, they're the Devil?"

"Oh, I don't know about that, but I'd say when they feel good, that's God comforting you. When they feel bad, that's when God is challenging you."

Though he wasn't sure if she was right about the energy he felt being God, he was sure that Ms. Cavanaugh was the only person he could talk to about his oh, so strange thoughts and sensations. One time, he tried talking to his mom and dad about them. His mom just sneered at him.

"You're such an idiot," his dad said to him.

Thanks to his teacher's encouragement, though, he didn't stop believing in those waves. He couldn't stop believing in them if he tried. Sometimes they seemed…to be talking to him, not in words, but he *felt* the meaning so clearly that he was convinced it was a kind of language.

That language was making him worry more and more. In recent months, he was getting this message vibrating in his brain, often at night: *Cao is going to take you away, Timmy.*

He was convinced that 'Cao' was all those waves of energy, the electricity that was everywhere—inside him, outside him, even as far away as outer space. Cao made everything. Cao was and is the whole universe. What his teacher called 'God,' Timmy knew was Cao.

And Cao was going to take him.

Where?

Cao promised he'd go to a better place, but why should Timmy have believed that? Though his mom and dad weren't very nice to him, at least they made him feel safe in their home. Like Cao, his parents were sometimes good, sometimes bad—like God at one time, and like the Devil another time.

'Cao' is pronounced like 'cow,' but it's nothing like the farm animal, or the sacred Hindu animal…though it promises to feed us as cows would. Timmy often felt, though, that it just wanted to make him *cow* in fear.

One night, after feeling Cao whisper the vibrations, *Cao is going to take you away,* far too many times for comfort, he went out of his bedroom and saw his mom and dad watching an old black-and-white movie. Two men were running through the jungle with something they had—was it stolen from other people? They fell into some mud and started sinking in it. They tried to reach for something to grab onto and pull them out, but they just sank further and further into the mud, until their heads went under. One man's upper arm was still above the surface, his hand reaching and struggling…until it just stayed still, never to move again.

Timmy began bawling in pity for the two men.

"Timmy!" his dad shouted after looking behind his chair.

"What are you doing out of bed?" his mom asked after looking to her right from her chair.

"I couldn't sleep," Timmy sobbed. "Cao won't let me sleep."

"Oh, not that ridiculous 'Cao' nonsense again!" his mother said.

"Did those poor men die?" Timmy asked.

"*You're* gonna die in a minute if you don't get back to bed," his dad said.

Timmy was crying louder now.

"If you don't get back to bed now, *I'll* give you something to cry about!" his dad yelled, raising his hand to threaten the boy with a spanking.

Timmy hurried back to bed.

He lay there under his brown bedsheets, with his night light on so he wouldn't be too scared of the dark, and he continued sobbing. He kept on…*feeling*…Cao's message as if he were hearing words:

Cao is going to take you away from here.

"To where?" he sobbed.

Away from your parents. To a much better place, where no one will bully you ever again.

"But there *is* no better place without Mom and Dad."

Isn't there?

Timmy sobbed himself to sleep in an hour.

***

The next day, some kids in the playground at school were pushing Timmy around and laughing at him. He was crying again. Ms. Cavanaugh broke it up.

"Leave him alone!" she shouted at the bullying kids, who went away right after that. "Come with me, Timmy." They went inside the school. "We should tell your parents about what those kids were doing."

"Why?" Timmy said. "They won't help me."

"Why wouldn't they?" she asked. "They love you and care about you, don't they?"

He shrugged.

Her eyes widened.

Then she noticed a bruise on his arm.

"Did those kids give you that bruise?" she asked.

"No," he said. "Daddy did."

Her eyes widened again, as did her mouth.

***

She called his home phone number and got his mother.

"Do you know his father gave him that bruise on his arm?" she asked his mother.

"Oh, nonsense," his mother said. "That boy's a liar."

"That's a very sweet boy," Ms. Cavanaugh said. "I find it hard to believe he goes around lying."

"Well, he *does!*" the boy's mom snapped. "He's been a misery to us ever since he was born. My husband knocked me up when we were dating, *Roe vs. Wade* was overturned, and our families forced us to get married! That kid ruined our lives, and he's nothing but trouble and heartache!" She slammed down the landline phone.

Ms. Cavanaugh just sat there with her phone in her hand for several minutes, stunned.

***

That night, the vibes of Cao made Timmy want to get out of bed and see his parents again. They were watching another scary movie on TV.

Timmy saw a young, blond-haired man lying on a cot, smoking. Then a hand appeared from under the cot all of a sudden. It held the man's head firmly on the pillow of the cot. The man's eyes widened. Unable to bear watching another death, Timmy turned his head away from the TV.

He ran back to his bedroom, sobbing. His dad heard him.

"Are you out of bed again, you little twerp?" his dad growled. "Get back in there!"

Again, Timmy lay under the brown sheets, trembling and sobbing. He kept feeling Cao's vibrations.

You're coming with Cao, far away from here.

The boy wondered if the 'voice,' the presence, was under his bed, just like the hand in the movie. He wanted to look down there so badly.

He needed to.

But he didn't dare.

You're coming…whether you want to, or not.

He pulled himself closer to the side of his bed, inch by reluctant inch.

Cao is taking you…

He reached the edge…but he couldn't look over.

Far away…

It took all the effort of the weeping boy to look over the edge. He finally did. He saw no one. No hand.

You will *come with Cao…*

Now he tried to pull himself down to see under the bed. He was trembling and sobbing, his nose running.

Cao will *take you, Timmy…*

The boy was amazed, in his terror, that he hadn't wet his pajamas by now. Daddy wouldn't beat him for that. Millimetre by millimetre, he moved his head lower and lower to see if Cao was there.

Finally, he saw under the bed.

No one.

He went back up to lie on his bed, relieved.

Cao is coming for you, Timmy.

He yelped with a jolt.

"Am I just imagining it?" Timmy whispered. "Is Cao just in my head, as Mom says?"

He thought about how Cao had no reason to be under the bed specifically…because Cao was *everywhere*. There wasn't any place where Cao was not. Timmy could never escape from Cao, no matter how hard he tried, because Cao was in everything.

Cao made up the entire universe.

Cao *was* the entire universe.

Cao was even inside Timmy.

Or maybe Cao only seemed to be all these things because Timmy always felt Cao's presence, and that was only because Cao was just a figment of the little boy's overactive imagination.

This possibility was soothing to him, and though he kept hearing that Cao was going to take him away, over and over again as he lay there in bed, he decided to ignore the vibrations. And in his exhaustion, the boy was finally beginning to nod off.

Drifting between wakefulness and sleep, he began feeling those vibrations more powerfully—not as threatening, though…as soothing. He remembered that Cao, just like his parents, could sometimes be good and sometimes bad. At this moment, Timmy was feeling the good side of Cao.

Cao is taking you to a better place, Timmy, a voice rang out in the boy's head as he was hovering on the brink of dreams. *A far, far better place. Trust in Cao.*

He wondered if there really could have been a better place than being with his often mean parents. Maybe there was. There were certainly better places than his school, with its bullies…only Ms. Cavanaugh was someone he'd miss from this world.

Those waves of energy that he felt all around him and through him…they were so comforting now! They felt like a massage all over and inside his body. After all that fear he'd been feeling just up until now, this feeling was just the calm he needed.

It was like getting the hugs he needed from his mom and dad…but far too rarely got. It was better than Ms. Cavanaugh's hugs.

The electric waves started feeling like liquid ones, now. His eyes were totally shut. He smelled dirt.

He opened his eyes. Instead of his brown sheets covering his body up to his neck, he saw mud. It was making waves as he struggled in it.

The firm, grassy land outside the quicksand was too far away for him to reach it, as it had been for the two men in that old movie. Whining, he stretched and stretched his filthy, muddy arms, but couldn't get to the firm land.

Cao is taking you now, Timmy, the voice whispered in a reverberating echo. *Don't be afraid. Accept what is happening to you.*

He, of course, didn't want to accept it.

Up to his chin in the muck, he kept reaching out in all futility for something to grab onto. He also kept sinking, however slowly.

He remembered how, whenever Mom and Dad hit him or otherwise punished him, they said it was for his own good. Is that what Cao meant by how he was being taken to a better place? Was Cao punishing Timmy for his own good?

He remembered that scene from the movie: the two men who fell in the quicksand and died in it—they were carrying things that looked stolen. Was their death a punishment from God? God seemed like Mom and Dad to Timmy, in their punishing him and telling him he was doing wrong. Cao seemed like his parents in that way, too: in making Timmy die in this quicksand, was Cao punishing him for getting out of bed when he wasn't supposed to? It felt that way to him.

The mud was up to his mouth now. He was spitting the stuff out. It seemed no better than dog-dirt to him.

His heart was pounding. His breathing was fast and desperate, what would seem his last few breaths ever.

The mud was just under his nose now.

He didn't dare move a millimetre.

That dog-dirt-like smell was unbearable…yet he had to keep breathing.

Cao is taking you now, he heard.

Then his whole head went under.

Nothing but black surrounded him.

It was cold. He was shivering all over.

How long could he hold his breath?

One arm, from the elbow up, was above the surface. His hand reached frantically for something to grab onto and use to pull himself out.

There was nothing to grab.

His hand kept trying to find something as his arm sank down to the wrist.

Then his hand stopped moving.

Instead of just breathing the mud in, passing out, and dying, though, Timmy felt something strange and unexpected happening to his body. It didn't just sit there, a prisoner of the quicksand. It began transforming into quicksand, interacting with it, *becoming* it.

He felt the boundary between himself and the quicksand dissolving. There was an electric charge as this change was happening.

Instead of dying, he felt as though he was falling into a deeper and deeper sleep, slipping into a blacker and blacker void. *Is this all just a dream?* he wondered.

His fear was fading away. He felt calmer, increasingly at peace.

Soon, he sensed no difference at all between his body, what was left of it as such, and the quicksand. The electrical charge of Cao zapped in brief bursts from time to time.

Cao has taken you, Timmy, the voice said, *to a far better place, away from your pain.*

There was something strange about this voice now. Something unexpected. Something new.

It was no longer a voice separate from him.

It was his own voice.

Timmy had melted into nothing.

And yet, he had also become everything.

Timmy *was* Cao.

***

The next morning, his parents were shouting from the living room to his bedroom to wake him up and get him ready for school.

"Come on, you lazy brat!" his mom yelled. "Get up, get over here, and eat your breakfast!"

No response.

"Do I have to go in there and smack you around again?" his dad yelled.

Silence.

Both parents cussed and stomped over to his bedroom. His dad threw the door open so hard that it smashed against the wall beside it.

"Hey," Timmy's mom said to his dad. "You'll make a mark on the wall." Then she looked in the bedroom. "Timmy, what are you…?" she began, but both of them froze when they saw his bed.

The two of them just stood there, their eyes and mouths wide open.

A hole in the middle of the bed, the size of Timmy's body, replaced where he once slept.

His mom and dad came up to it and looked down the oval hole.

The black down there seemed bottomless.

The two of them just stood there, frozen in shock, for another few minutes.

"Timmy's gone," his mom said. "We're free of him."

"Yeah," his dad said. "He won't…be troubling us…anymore."

Neither of them could smile, though.

"Ungh!" both of them grunted all of a sudden. "What was that?" she asked.

"Static electricity?" he said.

"We're not touching anything to give us that," she said.

Then they both started feeling waves flow in and out of themselves.

Waves everywhere.

THE STORM

BY J.T. LOZANO

The storm was predicted to be here late last night, but it never showed. I can't say that I'm surprised, though; the meteorologists usually get things wrong around here. He was right about a storm coming, though, just not the one he predicted.

I stood outside my house as I looked to the east and saw the massive clouds rolling towards me. To me, it was a beautiful and welcome sight. I felt safe and comfortable in the middle of a thunderstorm, always have. I watched in great anticipation as the clouds crept closer. My anticipation grew with every passing second, and I grew more anxious. I was tempted to run out and meet the storm halfway. I looked at the houses in the distance and thought how lucky they were to be in the middle of the storm. I wished I were there with them, soaking in the rain. I always laughed at people when they ran screaming from the rain, acting like it was hurting them when water hit their skin.

With each passing second, the clouds got closer as they teased me. It started to get darker, and my anticipation grew. The wind picked up, and the sweet aroma of wet dirt trickled into my nose. I loved that smell, the early sign of a good storm. The sky above me darkened, and I grew happier. In the distance, I could see the signs of the storm that was making its way to me. My smile widened at the thought of running out under the clouds and allowing the rain to wash my body from head to toe. The thunder rolled in, and as it passed over me, I could feel my body shake. Chills ran up and down my spine, and goosebumps covered my skin. My gaze fixated on the coming storm, and in the distance, I saw a pair of lights.

They got closer and closer, and my curiosity grew. I wondered who was driving in the rain and for what reason. They were moving fast, too, as if they were trying to stay in front of the storm. As they got closer, I could hear the car's horn blaring through the night. The car got closer, and the driver sped up and leaned on the horn. The car flew down the dirt road and skidded to a stop in my front yard.

The driver was an older gentleman who was clearly spooked about something. He practically jumped out of his car and ran up to me, waving his arms in the air. "Get in the house!" he cried out. "The storm is coming; get in the house."

I just looked at him as he made his way to my porch. He tried to push me into the house, but I refused to give in and spun away from him.

"Why would I miss this storm?" I asked him. "I love storms; they are relaxing."

The poor man just looked at me with fear in his eyes. "Not this storm, I have seen it. This storm is not one that you want to be outside for. Get inside the house, and if you have a basement, I suggest you get down there."

I could hear the quiver in his voice as he blurted out the words. I watched him for a moment and just laughed at the silliness of his words. I had been through plenty of storms, and they were all the same. The only ones that were dangerous were the ones that had lightning riding along with them. I looked over at the storm and studied it for a few seconds. "Look, old man, I am going to enjoy this storm. There isn't any lightning mixed in, which tells me there isn't any danger associated with it. You can go inside the house if you'd like, but I am going to enjoy the storm."

The old man gave a worried look and then began to make his way into the house. He reached the door, then turned and pleaded with me once more, but again I refused to pass up the storm. I watched him disappear into the house seconds before the first drop fell to the ground. I waited for a few moments, then stepped out into the yard. I held my hands outstretched and waited for the rain to fall on me. A drop hit my skin, and I felt a light burn. I pulled my hand back and looked at my skin. Where the water drop hit, now stood a red welt. Another drop hit, and another red welt appeared.

The rain increased. The water drops sizzled as they hit my body, and I saw smoke rise. The rain speed increased, and as it pelted my skin, I could feel it burn. I looked down at my skin, and holes formed in it. The water was burning through my skin. I turned and ran to the sanctity of my porch as I tried to cover up my arms. The water continued to fall on me, eating away at my clothes first, then it went after my skin. By the time I made it to the porch, my clothes were mostly gone, and parts of my body were burned. I stood there in shock, trying to make sense of things, but I couldn't stop thinking about the pain coursing through my body. I watched the rain pelt the car that the man drove. Before my eyes, I saw the car disappear a little at a time.

The rain began to hit the roof above me, and within seconds, it broke through and started hitting the floor around me. One drop hit what was left of my shoes, and it sizzled as it made contact. I moved my foot back and watched as the water burned through the floor. I didn't stay to see anymore and ran into the house and straight into the basement, where I found the old man cowering in the corner. I joined him, and together we listened to the storm as it rolled past us. When everything was quiet once more, we made our way back out of the basement. Miraculously, the walls and door were still standing. I slowly opened the door and stepped out. When I was outside, my jaw dropped, and I was left speechless. Everything around me was completely gone, and the only evidence that a house once stood in the area was the door that led to the basement.

HAZE

It all happened so quickly. I wasn't prepared for it to go by so fast. I had heard stories about it, but I never believed those stories. Perhaps I should start at the beginning of this whole mess. My name, well, that isn't important, but I guess if you need one to get the story moving along, you can call me Ex. I grew up in this sleepy little town and moved away the first chance I got. I felt bad when I left, though. I didn't feel bad because of my parents; I felt bad because I abandoned my younger brother. I was eighteen when I left, and he was only eleven.

Needless to say, he looked up to me as was usually the case between siblings. I remember he used to follow me all over town. I would tell him that he was annoying, but secretly I enjoyed having him follow me around. The day I put this town behind me was the day that I laid to rest all the stories that my parents had spoon-fed me all my life; unfortunately for my kid brother, Tommy, it was now his burden to carry.

It has been six years since I left, and I had managed to forget all the stories, or so I thought. All it took was one phone call to prove me wrong, though. I was coming home from work when my phone began to ring. I looked down and saw it was my mom calling, and I winced at the thought of answering. I know it sounds bad, but it was always the same thing; when are you coming home? Why did you leave? Your brother keeps asking for you. I had a rough day at work and wasn't in the mood to find ways to dodge the questions. I placed my finger on the screen and was about to swipe left to ignore the call, but something told me to answer it. Against my better judgment, I answered the call, and a hysterical voice came through.

"You have to come home, it's starting." I recognized the frantic ranting of my mom right away.

"Calm down mom, what are you talking about?"

"Tommy, he's been marked. You need to come home now." That was the last thing she said before she hung up.

I tried calling her back a few times, but she never answered. I wondered if it was all a ruse to get me to come home, but the panic in her voice seemed real. I slid the key into the lock and stood there for a moment before I removed the key and headed back home.

I drove through the night and reached home in the early hours of the morning. As I drove into the town, I noticed that nothing had changed; it was as if I had stepped back in time. Boys were playing football in the park while the girls were off to the side, jumping rope and playing hopscotch. The parents sat nearby, talking to each other and not paying much attention to the children. Everything seemed like it was when I was a child here, but I could feel something in the air. There was a heavy feeling, as if something was happening.

I kept going and soon found myself pulling into the driveway of my old childhood home. I sat in my car as the memories of my childhood flooded my mind, along with the old stories. My mother came out of the house in a rush and met me as I stepped out of my car.

"Hurry, we don't have time." She blurted out as she grabbed my arm. I was rushed into the house and up the stairs. We didn't stop until we stood in front of the door to Tommy's room. "He's in there," my mom whispered. "He won't come out. I've heard him talking to someone, but he is alone. He's been marked."

I put my ear to the door and listened carefully but heard nothing. "Mom, I think you are overreacting. I don't hear him."

My mom begged me to go in and talk to him. Normally, I would have ignored her and found a way to move on, but I figured going in there would be better than staying out in the hallway. I slowly opened the door and peeked in. The lights were turned off, and the windows had been closed. The only light in the room was a small red dot on the ceiling, marking the smoke detector's position. I stepped into the room and closed the door behind me. I flipped the light switch, but nothing happened; the darkness still encompassed the room.

"Tommy," I called out. "Tommy, it's me, Ex." I walked over to the window and slowly opened the blinds to allow some light in. I turned away from the window and saw Tommy sitting in his bed facing the closet. He was perfectly still, and his eyes were glued to the top of the closet. I sat next to him and looked up in the same spot he was staring at, but saw nothing. "What are we looking at?" I asked him as I nudged him a bit.

Tommy's eyes stayed focused on the closet as he spoke to me. "The man is in there, waiting."

I looked in the closet but saw nothing. I walked over to the closet, turned on the light, and again saw nothing in there. I stood there for a moment and watched Tommy. His eyes stayed glued to the top of the closet; he never acknowledged me. It was as if I wasn't there. I left the closet light on and made my way to the door. I grabbed the doorknob and turned back to see Tommy get off the bed, only to turn off the closet light, then return to where he had sat before. As he sat back in his bed, he began saying something. I stood there and listened to him for a while before I stepped out of the room and left him to sit alone as he recited the same words over and over.

I made my way downstairs and into the kitchen, where I found my mom pacing. She saw me enter the room and stopped. Her eyes locked on me as I grabbed a soda from the fridge and sat down to drink it.

"Well," she asked.

"Well, nothing," I answered. "He's probably spooked. It might be because of those stories you have been putting in his head. I'm surprised I didn't end up that way, to be honest."

"Those weren't stories, they were precautionary tales."

I just looked at my mom and took a sip of my soda. "I see that you upped the ante with Tommy. Why did you go and teach him that dreadful poem?" I asked as I made my way to the door that led to the backyard.

My mom stopped what she was doing and stared at me. "What poem?"

I just chuckled a bit. "Come on, Mom. The poem he was repeating, the one about the man and the haze." My mom just looked at me as if she didn't know what I was talking about. "Beware the man who leaves his mark; he lives in the shadows and the dark. He stalks his prey for days, then takes them with the haze. Tommy was repeating it over and over." My mom stood there motionless as I repeated the words I heard my brother utter.

"I didn't teach him that poem," she insisted.

As I looked at her with a smile, I realized that she was telling me the truth. If she didn't teach him that poem, then who did? I looked out the door, and a haze rolled in. My mom got more hysterical. She ran out of the kitchen and up the stairs while I followed close behind. As we made our way up the stairs, we heard some rustling coming from Tommy's room. It sounded as if something was being dragged across the floor. The sound stopped, then it was followed by a loud scream and the sound of glass breaking. My mom frantically tried to open the door, but it was locked, or so it seemed. I moved her out of the way and kicked in the door to gain entry to the room.

As we stepped in, we came across a sight that stopped us in our tracks. Everything had been thrown out of the closet, and the bed had been overturned, as if there had been a struggle. I walked over to the window, and as I looked out, I could see the haze disappear as quickly as it had appeared. Once the skies became clear once more, I looked down the street and saw other parents standing in their children's rooms staring at the sky.

Still to this day, I don't know what happened to my brother, but that poem Tommy was repeating on the last day I saw him still plays in my head.

SARAH

It was the middle of summer, and the heat was in full force in the southeastern states. The dog days of summer were right around the corner, the worst time for a newbie to the region. A newbie such as Rycco, his wife Star, and his teenage daughter Cris. Rycco and Star walked in the front door of their new two-story home, arm in arm, filled with joy. Soon afterward, Cris sauntered in with a look of disdain on her face. She made her way to the living room and plopped down on the sofa. The voices of her parents carried throughout the house, and Cris could hear them giggling as they meandered from room to room. Soon her dad walked into the living room, and his smile disappeared when he saw her sitting there without a smile.

"Look, Cris, I know you didn't want to move from New York, but we had to." Cris just rolled her eyes at her father as he spoke. "It's for a new job, which will be better for us in the long run. At least here we have our own house with a yard, and if you want, we can finally get that dog you've always wanted. Can you at least go upstairs and pick out your room?"

Cris stared at her dad, then grunted as she got up and stomped up the stairs. Cris reached the top of the stairs and was greeted by a hallway that ran the length of the house. There was a total of four doors, two on each side, and a fifth door was flush against the wall behind the landing on the other side of the stairs. Cris made her way around the stairs, opened the lone door first, and stepped through. The door led to a balcony that faced the front of the house. From her position, Cris could see beyond the front lawn. In the distance, there was a lone tree that seemed so old that it could fall apart with only a slight breeze. The tree had no leaves, just branches and twigs that darted out in all directions. The thickest branch curved, and it looked like a finger that pointed to the right. Cris stared at the odd formation, which to her looked like a backward "c".

After a few moments, she went back inside, and as she closed the door behind her, a faint scratching noise could be heard. Cris listened closely, and it sounded as if someone or something was scratching the glass on the door behind her. Cris opened the door once more but found nothing on the balcony. The next door she opened led to a bathroom with an old-style tub and a porcelain white sink with gold faucets. The mirror seemed old but was in surprisingly good shape. The floor was made of hardwood, or so it seemed. Cris thought that it was charming to say the least as she walked out and headed to the next door. The next two doors led into bedrooms that were clearly meant for young children. The walls were in good shape, but Cris wasn't exactly thrilled with them. If she were going to be forced into one of those rooms, she'd have to make some changes.

The final room was the one that had the best potential in Cris' mind. The room was bigger than the others, and the walls were a pale white color, perfect for decorating anyway she deemed fit. The floors were cleaner than the others, and the hardwood in this room felt different. Cris could see herself in this room, and she continued to explore. As she grabbed the door to what she hoped would be a closet, a noise came from above her. She stopped and looked up, and as she did, the noise moved away from her. Cris listened intently, and she heard sounds coming through the ceiling, as if something was being dragged across the floor. The noise started in the far wall and moved across the length of the bedroom Cris was in, then out into the hallway. Cris followed the noise, and as she stepped out into the hallway once more, she saw a ladder that she swore wasn't there before.

The ladder led up into the attic, and Cris looked at it with a puzzled expression. She walked over to the stairs that led back down and called for her parents. She got no answer and then made her way to the ladder that led into the attic. As she stood at the foot of the ladder, a giggle could be heard upstairs. She called out for her mom and again got no answer. Cris thought about it for a while before proceeding up the ladder. At the top of the ladder was a huge room that ran the whole length of the house with no walls. It had one giant window towards the front, which caught Cris' attention. She opened it up and met with the image of the tree once more. She stared at it again as it grasped her attention. There was something about the tree that was mesmerizing to her, but she didn't know what it was.

Her gaze was broken when she heard something scurry behind her. She turned and caught a glimpse of a shadow darting into a dark corner of the attic. Cris cautiously made her way towards the corner, not knowing what she had just seen. For all she knew, it could have been any number of things. Cris knew it was probably a bad idea to go looking for whatever was scurrying around up there, but at the moment, she had nothing better to do. She came within feet of the dark corner, and as she squinted her eyes to try to get a better look into the darkness, something grabbed her shoulder. Cris let out a loud scream and turned around to find her father standing behind her.

"Shit, Dad! You nearly gave me a heart attack."

Her dad just laughed at her and apologized. "I'm sorry, Cris, I was just wondering if you found our room yet."

Cris looked at the dark corner, then looked around the attic. "I think I want this one." She answered as she looked around.

"The attic?" Her dad asked. "You want the attic to be your room?"

"Yeah, why not?" Cris answered.

Her dad looked around and then looked at his daughter. "Why not?" he asked again.

Cris and her dad went downstairs, and she spent the rest of the day hauling her items into her new place and making the room her own getaway. She only stopped when she was called down to eat dinner. After dinner, Cris excused herself and headed back into her room. As soon as she got to the top of the stairs, something caught her eye. The stuffed animal that she had left on her bed was now on the floor, along with one of her pillows. Cris thought it was weird, but just picked them up and placed them back on her bed. She lay down and closed her eyes to get some rest as the day came to an end. Her eyes got heavier and within minutes she dozed off.

Cris' eyes shot open, and she sat up in her bed. She looked around and saw that the clock by her bed announced that it was a little after three in the morning. Cris lay back down, and the second her head hit the pillow, she heard a soft whisper. She sat up and looked around, seeing nothing.

"It's just your nerves, Cris," she told herself as she lay back down.

She closed her eyes, and then she heard someone hiss her name in her ear. Her eyes shot open, and she saw the face of a young girl around her age staring at her. Cris let out a scream, and she jumped out of bed. Within seconds, she heard footsteps running up the stairs and into her room.

Her dad flipped the lights on and gave her a worried look. "What happened? Are you ok?" he asked as he ran to her.

"I saw a girl standing next to my bed. She was looking at me." Cried out Cris.

Rycco looked around the room as he held his daughter. He looked for signs of anyone being there but saw nothing out of the ordinary. He knew his daughter wasn't one to make up stories, but there was no proof of anyone being there. Rycco even checked the window to ensure that it was closed and locked. "There is nobody here, Cris. If you want to, your mother or I can stay here with you. Or you can sleep in one of the other rooms for tonight. We can check things out further in the morning."

Cris looked around and nodded her head. "It's ok dad. It was probably just my imagination since I'm in a new house. I'll be ok."

"Are you sure?" Rycco asked before he left. Cris simply smiled and waved him off. Rycco smiled back and descended the ladder, but left the light on.

Once he was gone, Cris looked around and laughed at herself for letting her imagination get the best of her. She sat in her bed for a while to let her mind calm down. She grabbed her MP3 player and began to listen to her music as she walked across the floor and turned off the lights again. She went back to bed and lay down in hopes of getting some rest. She lay back and closed her eyes, her hands waving in the air as if she were conducting an orchestra. She began to sing along quietly to her music as she lay in bed. Halfway through the song, she felt something cover her mouth, and a weight pressed down on her chest. She opened her eyes, and the girl she saw earlier was staring at her with a menacing sneer.

Cris tried to scream, but no sound came out of her mouth. Cris was picked up and thrown violently across the room. She tried to get up but was quickly grabbed again, and her body flew back once more, slamming against the wall. She fell to the floor and looked up to see the young girl walking towards her. She had a look that shook Cris to her core. Cris felt her hair get grabbed as she was being dragged around the attic. Cris was dragged the whole length of the attic from one wall to the other. After what seemed like an eternity, Cris was dropped. When she thought the ordeal was over, she was once again tossed back, and her head bounced off the wall. Her body fell to the ground once more. As she looked up, her vision became blurred. The last thing she was able to make out before she passed out was the young girl crawling on the floor towards her.

The following morning, a knock came on the front door. Rycco went to answer the door as his wife made breakfast. "Michael," called out Rycco in a gleeful tone. "It sure is nice to see you. Could have used you yesterday when we were moving everything in, though. By the way, thanks for letting us use your house."

Michael simply smiled at Rycco as he walked into the house. "I had all intentions of being here yesterday, but I got caught up at work."

"Yeah, sure you did. It's ok though. We managed. Come and join us for some breakfast."

"Thank you," Michael responded as he followed Rycco to the kitchen. "I hope you are all liking the place and are settling in well."

Rycco grabbed a plate and placed it in front of Michael. "We are all liking the place, although Cris took a while longer than us to get there. She wasn't crazy about the place until she found her room."

"Which room did she settle on?" Michael asked as he took a bite of his breakfast. "Let me guess, she got the big room upstairs?"

"Actually," Rycco began as he took a sip of his orange juice. "She moved into the attic."

Michael stopped eating and looked up at Rycco when he said that. "The attic? That's not possible."

"Why do you say that?" asked Rycco.

"Well, the attic has been boarded up as far back as I can remember. Nobody has been allowed to go up there."

Rycco looked at his wife, then back to Michael. "It wasn't boarded up yesterday. Cris and I both went up there. I helped her carry her things up there. I even ran up there in the morning because she was having a nightmare. Said she saw a girl in her room, but we didn't see anyone. She thought it was her nerves and decided to stay up there." Michael jumped out of his chair and ran to the stairs with Rycco close behind him. "What's the problem?" Rycco asked as Michael kept going until he stopped at the top of the stairs.

He pointed toward the ladder leading to the attic. "That's the problem." He said as he pointed up.

Rycco looked up and noticed that the entrance to the attic had been boarded up. The wood looked old, as if it had been there for decades. "No, that can't be. It wasn't boarded up yesterday."

Michael ran down the stairs and into the backyard as Rycco stood there looking at the boarded-up entrance. He returned a short while later with a ladder and a hammer in hand. Michael climbed up the ladder and removed the board so he could open the attic door. Once it was open, Michael climbed in, followed by Rycco. The attic stored all of Cris' belongings just like Rycco had stated, but there was no sign of Cris. They searched the room and found locks of hair scattered throughout the room. There was some evidence of something being dragged all around the room, and they ended up by the big window. Rycco frantically opened the window but didn't see any sign of Cris.

"Sarah," whispered Michael as he scanned the room.

Rycco overheard him and questioned Michael. "Sarah? Who is Sarah?" Michael ignored Rycco and went to the window. As he looked out the window, he saw the oddly shaped tree that had caught Cris' attention. "Who the hell is Sarah?" demanded Rycco.

Michael hung his head for a moment and then looked at Rycco. "Sarah was a young girl who lived in this house many years ago, long before my family acquired it. What I am about to tell you is a legend I was told while I was growing up, or at least I believed it to be a legend.

A long time ago, a family lived here in this house, back in the early sixties or so. The only daughter of the gentleman who owned this place was a sixteen-year-old girl named Sarah, and this was her room. All the boys wanted to date her, and all the girls wanted to be her. One fateful summer night, while the family slept, some of the kids from town made their way in through that window and grabbed Sarah. They carried her out the window and across the yard to that oddly shaped tree. Once they got to that tree, they tied a noose around the thickest branch they could find, and they hanged her. They left her there for her parents to find the following morning. Nobody ever knew the reason behind the brutal attack, and nobody was ever arrested for the crime.

The family tried to cut down the tree many times, but something always prevented the tree from being cut down. They even tried burning it, but the tree wouldn't burn. The family left and sold the place shortly after her death because they couldn't live with the reminder of what transpired in here.

Many families have tried living here ever since, but each time they were scared off by noises coming from this very room. Anyone who dared to stay in this room vanished overnight and, in most cases, they were never seen again."

Rycco looked out the window once more and stared at the tree across the front yard. "Are you telling me that I'm never going to see my daughter again?"

Michael simply kept his gaze on the floor. Rycco hurried past Michael, and he headed down the ladder. He went to the shed in the back and came back out with an axe as he headed to the tree with Michael close behind.

"What are you doing, Rycco?" Asked Michael.

Rycco made his way to the tree and stared at it for a moment before he brought the axe to his shoulder. "I'm going to chop this thing down."

"It can't be done. People have been trying to do it for many years." Exclaimed Michael.

His words fell on deaf ears, and Rycco began to swing the axe at the tree. The first few hits just glanced off the tree, and Michael watched as his friend attempted the impossible. After a few more hits, the axe finally hit a spot on the tree, and it cut into it. Rycco noticed it and continued to hit the same spot. After a few more hits, a red liquid began to ooze out of the tree's trunk. Rycco kept swinging the axe, and the small chip grew into a small hole. The small hole kept getting bigger and bigger. Rycco kept swinging away until he heard a loud crack.

Rycco threw the axe to the ground and stepped back as a chunk of the trunk fell off and liquid poured out as if a dam had been broken. The ground around the tree turned red, and Rycco and Michael watched as the liquid flowed out along with some other items. When the liquid stopped flowing, Rycco began sifting through the items that rolled out and found that they were human skulls. As he handed one of the skulls to Michael, a body fell out of the trunk of the tree and landed face down between Rycco and Michael. Rycco turned the body over and let out a loud, blood-curdling scream, and he held the body close to his chest. Michael just watched in horror as Rycco held the lifeless body of his daughter.

THE OTHER SIDE OF THE ISLAND

BY CHARIS NEGLEY

Finch was fading fast.

Leif had never been so desperate in his life, if the existence he was living could even be called that. He and his younger brother had been in their current undead state for almost two years now. But existing was existing; Leif had come to terms with that. The problem was that Finch was about to no longer exist.

His cheeks, once round with youth, were now hollow with starvation. He moved with more and more lethargy. Leif had to act quickly if he didn't want to spend the rest of his existence alone and grieving.

They were two of the few dozen residents who remained in Thorne Bay, Alaska, since the outbreak. From what Leif had seen, not a single human remained.

When it all started over five years ago, Leif thought they were safe. Prince of Whales Island was isolated, and its town had fewer than five hundred residents. Tourism, however, was what kept them alive. The outbreak had stopped all of that. Leif and his father had lost their jobs. But there wasn't much need for jobs at that point. What counted was staying alive. Nearly everyone in Thorne Bay who didn't leave had become fishermen.

But even a zombie outbreak that started thousands of miles away eventually reached the isolated.

Leif and his father had been bitten by a pair of zombies as they pulled their catch to shore one evening. On their horrified, stumbling walk home, his father took a bullet to the head.

Leif couldn't blame the man who'd shot him as much as he wanted to. For a living person, guns were the best defense against a zombie. The virus infused the zombies with inhuman strength, giving them the power to break open a skull with their bare hands.

But what happened to Finch was all his fault. When he came home and saw his little living brother, his undead body had been struck with the desire to eat Finch's brain.

But he fought it. No matter what he was, no matter what he'd become, he would not kill that boy. He *loved* that boy.

So instead of tearing his skull open, Leif bit Finch's arm, turning him, too. There was nothing to crave about a zombie's brain. No nutrients there anymore.

But he still felt guilty whenever he saw his little brother's mottled skin, knowing he'd stolen Finch's chance to grow up. To truly live.

But he wouldn't have lived another day in a world like ours, he told himself. He had to keep believing that.

After their father had been killed, Leif and Finch had rarely left the house until the living people of Thorne Bay were few and far between. Leif had gone out to hunt each month. An entire brain could sustain him and his brother for that long. A few ounces could sustain them both for a week, and the remains could be preserved as long as they were kept cold.

Every time he braved leaving the house, he dreaded dying. He wasn't afraid of the pain or even of what came after. He was terrified of leaving Finch alone. Alone to starve to death, wondering how exactly his big brother died.

But each time, Leif came home alive and with food.

Two weeks ago was the first day he returned empty-handed. He had been out all day, and though he saw a few zombies from after, looking as ravenous as he, there had been no sign of living people.

Growing desperate, he had broken windows, forcing his way into homes. But he never smelled the scent of warm human blood. Most homes were as empty as his stomach. The ones that weren't housed territorial zombies that Leif was lucky to get away from unscathed.

He was near tears that night returning to his brother. The disappointment on Finch's face had been more gut-wrenching than the hunger pains that wracked his stomach.

Leif had gone out a few more times since then, to no avail. He only had scratches and bruises to show for the skirmishes he'd gotten into with other nervous, feverishly hungry zombies. Since food had been running low, there was little kinship among even his neighbors anymore.

Finch had grown frighteningly thin since they had last eaten two weeks ago. Some days, he cried from the pain—low, moaning sounds that Leif had to cover his ears to block out, lest he cry, too. Other days, Finch paced around the house, gargling and grunting as he seemed to see things that weren't really there. These past few days, he'd hardly moved at all. What kind of big brother was he that he couldn't even feed this child?

Leif made up his mind at last. They had to leave.

A few months ago, back when there was still food enough to go around, a neighbor had told Leif of a rumored farm of humans in Craig, Alaska, which was forty miles away and on the other side of the island. At the time, Leif had scoffed at the idea. A human farm? It couldn't be any more than wishful dreaming by hungry zombies.

But what if it was real? It didn't matter anymore. It was the only hope they had left.

Leif packed a satchel with a knife, a can of bear spray, and a handgun, despairing over the few bullets he had left.

Where are we going? Finch asked through a yawn as Leif lifted him onto his back.

Craig, Alaska. The other side of the island, remember? I think someone drove us there sometimes when you were little. Ever since becoming a zombie, his memories of life before had become hazy. *There's a human farm there. All the brains you can eat.*

A pain hit his always-aching gut. He bit back a groan. His mouth salivated at the thought of the supposed farm. When he had been eating enough brain, the cravings were manageable. But now that there was nothing to eat, no living people in sight, the need was agonizing.

He didn't care how many people he hurt. How many skulls did he split open? Finch was dying. A second time. Leif wouldn't let it be his fault again.

It would be a forty-mile walk to reach Craig. With it being the edge of winter, snow would pick up, making for a more strenuous trip. There was less sunlight in December, letting the days hold only seven hours of daylight. Leif didn't want to risk traveling in the dark. While his strength and sense of smell had heightened as a zombie, his sight hadn't.

With Finch on his back and Leif being in terrible shape to make the journey with how hungry he was, too, he didn't think he could make it in less than four days. Did Finch have four days? Probably not. Leif was banking on finding someone along the way, as unlikely as it seemed.

Against his shoulder, Finch made a series of grunts and gurgles. When Leif heard full-grown zombies make such noises, it was unsettling, frightening, even though he was a zombie himself. But when someone like Finch tried to make himself heard, it was almost cute. He had been five years old when he'd been turned, and his voice still remained in the soft, high-pitched (albeit raspy) cadence of a young child.

Leif looked over his shoulder at his brother. *Okay, buddy?*

Finch looked at him with that glazed-over stare that the undead all seemed to have. *Hungry.*

I know, kid. Soon. I'll find a way to feed you soon.

Leif lifted his head, hoping that if there was still some higher power up there after this devastation their world had fallen into, they were still listening. *Help me save him. I'll do anything.*

***

Upon leaving the safety of the house, Leif found himself always looking over his shoulder for danger. Zombies and wolves were the biggest concerns this time of year. Dread pooled in his stomach as snow began to flake from the sky, then fall steadily, masking the scents of the forest. He felt like he was being watched from every angle, blind to whatever could be hunting him. All he could do was pick up his pace, his legs trembling.

But there was one scent even the snow couldn't hide from him. Through the faint notes of torn flesh and fresh blood, it was as clear as crystal: human brain.

His feet were moving on their own, saliva pooling in his mouth. *Leave Finch, leave Finch,* the remains of his consciousness chanted in the back of his head, but he didn't comprehend the thoughts. He needed to eat.

It's never this easy, came another thought. *Something is wrong. Not safe.*

But safe didn't matter. Eating did. Existing another day did.

He was almost upon the corpse before he saw the haggard zombie hovering over it, blood streaked down his mottled face.

Leif instinctively lurched back as the zombie lashed out with his sharp nails, grunting and gurgling and hissing in a way that made Leif shrink in terror. Finch still clung to his back, making almost as much noise as their opponent.

Leif looked into the zombie's eyes, desperately trying to communicate. *Sorry. I didn't know you were here. We just need to pass through.*

But Leif had never successfully communicated with anyone other than his brother or the neighbors who had since left. This zombie clearly couldn't understand him. Nor did he seem to care to. The zombie growled again, snapping his teeth as he jumped at Leif.

Leif let Finch slip off his back, tackling the zombie in the air. He had gotten in brawls like this before. Over food, mostly. And when food was involved, fights were almost always to the death. At such a primal state of existence, being fed mattered more than anything else.

For Leif, it was the second most important thing on earth. But if he had to kill this zombie to make sure his brother ate today, he would do so without hesitation.

Leif jammed his fingers into the eyes of the other zombie. His nails found purchase, eliciting a guttural howl from his attacker. He hoped Finch had had both mind and energy enough to hide or get to a safer distance.

Narrowly avoiding the zombie's teeth as it made for his neck, Leif thrashed his fist against the zombie's skull, eliciting a sickening *crack.* The zombie collapsed without another sound, unmoving. Leif slammed the body's head with his fist once more, making sure he was dead, then stood and scoured frantically for his brother.

Only a few yards away squatted Finch, his hands over his head. Wide-eyed, he looked at Leif, then the other zombie, lying broken on the ground.

Dead? asked Finch.

Dead, Leif agreed, jerking his head toward the human and her mostly-eaten brain.

With all the self-control in his body, Leif sat back on his heels as his brother stumbled to the corpse and ravenously dug into the brain, his little fingers tearing it into pieces with a *squish.* He shoved handfuls into his mouth, blood dribbling from his lips.

Leif lifted his brother's chin to make eye contact. *Slowly,* he instructed. *Pace yourself.* While their zombie bodies were a little more resilient than their living ones, eating too quickly or too much after nothing at all, or consuming anything other than brains would make them sick. All of this would be for nothing if Finch just threw everything back up.

The undead boy nodded, returning his hands to the bloody mess of the brain. After several more swallows, he held out a piece for his older brother. Leif smiled, accepting the morsel, savoring it as long as he could in his mouth before swallowing. More. He needed more. Leif gritted his teeth and looked away, wrapping his arms around his aching stomach. Finch first. Finch would die if he didn't eat now. For himself, Leif thought he could last another few days without the nutrients, maybe a week.

Finch grunted, drawing Leif's attention back. *Eat?*

You've eaten most of it? Leif inquired.

Finch looked down at the woman's cracked-open skull, now almost empty but for the back of the brain. He nodded, his lips pulled tight in guilt.

Leif waved, drawing his brother's attention back up to him. *No, that's good. That's exactly what I wanted you to do. Good boy, Finch.* Leif crawled forward, digging his hands in for what was left of the brain. Every muscle relaxed as he chewed. After a few small bites of bliss, there was nothing left.

Feeling rejuvenated from even the bit of food, Leif hefted Finch's light frame onto his back again. The boy wrapped his thin, cold arms around Leif's neck. *Good,* Leif thought. *He's much more alert and awake than he was earlier.*

Though he didn't think he'd traveled as many miles as he would have liked to—maybe four or five—by the time his body was ready to give up for the night, Leif was pleased with the distance they'd gone, especially since they both had something in their stomachs. More days to live.

Seeing no other shelter for the night, Leif got to work making a lean-to to guard him and his brother from the snowfall while they slept. One good thing about being a zombie, though, was not being bothered by temperatures anymore. Propping soggy branches against a tree and layering armfuls of decaying, wet leaves atop them for a makeshift roof, Leif was proud of his quick work. Finch looked pleased, too, beaming as he crawled inside like it was an adventure.

As he watched his brother smile, something that hadn't happened in weeks, Leif felt more alive than he had in a long time. Finch was always his reason for getting up another morning. And if Finch was happy in this awful world, then Leif could be overjoyed.

Finch yawned wide, looking at his older brother as he lay down on the snowy forest floor. *Leif, what is the human farm like?*

Leif lay down beside him. He vaguely remembered being human and going camping with his family, roasting food over a fire after fishing or hiking. If he closed his eyes, he could almost believe he was alive and there again, nothing more to worry about than getting bitten by mosquitoes in the night. *I don't know, Finny. But there will be food to eat. I* will *get you food to eat, no matter what. I don't want you to worry about that.*

Finch's eyelids were beginning to droop. *What if the other zombies don't want us there? What if we're not able to talk to them?*

I'll take care of it. That's not something you need to worry about, little one.

Finch wrinkled his nose and yawned again. *Not… little.*

Leif reached out to ruffle his brother's hair. *Good night, buddy. I love you.*

Love you, too.

Leif watched Finch drift off to sleep, rubbing the boy's shoulder. He feared what the next days might have in store for them. This trip would take twice as long as he'd first assumed, if they kept up this pace. And though they'd eaten, it hadn't been enough of a serving to sustain them for a week, let alone make up for the past two. Finch's happiness and energy would soon go out like a candle.

No, he told himself, feeling his own consciousness ebbing. *I won't let that happen.*

***

The next day brought more light snowfall. It slowed their pace but, at the very least, seemed to be keeping the wildlife away. Leif didn't know how much longer they'd have that luck, though. He knew an inopportune encounter with a ravenous or territorial animal could take their lives as easily as hunger or another zombie could.

Finch walked on his own for the first hour but drooped with exhaustion, reaching his arms up for Leif to hoist him onto his back again. Another hour into their journey, Leif froze at the sound of crunching snow ahead. Gently, he lowered Finch from his back, gesturing for Finch to stay behind him. On careful feet, he crept forward.

Through the trees, right off the edge of the road, stood a family of three gaunt zombies. Leif didn't recognize the boy and his parents, but even if they had come from Thorne Bay, that wasn't surprising. With their distorted faces, zombies were hard to recognize, and it wasn't like he had interacted much with anyone in the past few years. Even if Leif had known them before they were in a zombified state, there was no way to tell. Other than his father, he didn't remember anyone from his life before.

These three stared back at Leif, looking as surprised and wary as he felt. For a moment that stretched out forever, none of them moved.

Can you hear me? Leif tried to direct his thoughts toward them.

No response. Of course.

But after several more moments of tense silence, the female zombie raised her hand in a gesture of peace, taking a tentative step forward. The others with her made gargling protests, none of which deterred her. To Leif's confusion, she bent and picked up a stick from the ground, beginning to draw in the snow.

As the lines came together, Leif's stomach clenched in dread. He looked back at his brother, making sure he was still safe, then directed his gaze to the depiction again.

She had drawn a wolf.

***

A few haphazard gestures from the female zombie soon made it clear that there was a pack up ahead, and she and her family weren't traveling any further for the day.

Frustration and unease battled inside Leif as he sat at a distance from the other zombies, Finch tucked protectively in his arms. He didn't quite trust them yet, but he would feel more comfortable traveling in a group. He felt too exposed walking alone with Finch. Traveling companions might be good for all of them.

Eventually, the small boy from the other family started drawing in the snow, as his mother had done. Finch wriggled out of Leif's arms, stepping forward to see.

Leif growled, grabbing Finch's wrist. *Stop. They're not safe.*

Finch shook his head and pointed at the boy. *He's drawing a map.*

What? Leif peered over. Sure enough, the boy had drawn Prince of Whales Island. With caution, Leif moved his grip to Finch's hand and walked over together. The parents shot wary glances but stayed put as the brothers crouched beside the boy.

He had marked a dot for Thorne Bay, then a dot on the other side of the island for Craig. Leif pointed at that dot, tracing a line between the two of them along where the road should be. The boy nodded. Leif smiled. Maybe they could be civil, now that they knew they all had the same goal.

When the long hours of sunset began, the male zombie stood, pointing down the road, making a few grunts, and looking at his family members as they communicated through their thoughts. The boy walked back over to his drawing, motioning for the brothers to join him. With his finger, he drew a pictogram that looked like a house, a short way down a fork in the road.

Finch looked up at his brother, grinning ear to ear. *They know of a cabin!*

Leif nodded, keeping his next thought to himself. *Hopefully, the wolves have moved on or won't care to bother so many of us.*

Sure enough, what could only have been a mile or two down the fork, a tiny cabin sat tucked just beyond the trees. No lights glowed from inside. No smoke rose from a chimney. Weeds crept around the base and the door.

The male zombie approached the cabin, rattled the locked doorknob, then smashed his shoulder against the door. His sheer strength forced it open with a clatter.

The inside smelled of mildew. Stacks of firewood sat piled, and a small cot lay in the corner, but there was little else in the humble abode. Leif guessed it had been a hunting retreat for those wanting to get away from town years ago.

The male zombie led the female and the boy to the bed, where there was just enough room for the two of them. He took a seat on the floor, motioning for Leif to shut the door.

As he did so, Leif felt like collapsing in relief. *They're letting us stay.*

He still kept his distance, taking his rest on the other side of the cabin. He kept his back to the wall as he lay down, eager to stay alert and as safe as possible alongside these strangers. He curled himself around Finch, keeping him as unexposed as he could.

Darkness descended, and Leif drifted into uneasy sleep.

***

The next day brought slower travel as they trudged through the inches of snow. Leif longed for the days he had been fully living and entirely full. Unsatisfied with his last eating and with

Finch on his back for most of the time, Leif ached with the strain of what should have been an easy walk.

Halfway through the day, as Leif led the five of them down the road, Finch prodded him, making a raspy, high-pitched whine. He pointed at a hill through the trees, and when Leif's gaze followed, his stomach turned in horror.

Two gray wolves watched them, fluffy tails swishing in anticipation. Finch whined again, and *I see them* is what Leif would have said if he still could speak. Instead, a series of growls and grunts issued from his throat, but Finch seemed to get the gist, going quiet.

The other zombies had seen them, too, going stiff. The male took a step forward, keeping his family behind him. Leif took Finch off his back, setting him beside the other boy. He made eye contact with his brother, who had gone tense with fear, his lower lip quivering. *We're going to be fine. Stay behind me.*

He drew the knife from his satchel, wishing he had more than three bullets in his gun. Was now the right time for them? What if he needed them later?

One wolf let loose a howl, and both began to circle the zombies. A dismayed sound from Finch turned Leif's head to a third wolf on the other side of the road. Leif would have cursed if he could. Surrounded. Were there more?

Gaining courage, the wolves made their way to the road. The zombies shouted and growled, but the animals didn't back off. Panic clawed its way up his throat as he realized there was no safe place for his brother with two wolves in front of them and one behind.

One wolf drew the boldness to leap forward, snapping at Leif's leg. He shouted as loud as he could muster—broken, guttural noises—and sliced his knife across the wolf's flank as its teeth clipped his pants. It yelped and jumped back, baring its teeth and snarling. Leif bared his right back, matching its growl.

The second wolf jumped at the male zombie with its jaw open. Without a weapon, he had nothing to defend himself but his own hands. He shouted and grappled the wild dog, grunting as its teeth found purchase on his arm. The female zombie ran to help him, swiping her sharp nails at the wolf and fastening her teeth in its shoulder.

A young zombie's cry sounded behind Leif, and a strangled noise of fear leapt from Leif's throat. But it wasn't Finch in trouble. No, the third wolf had its jaws around the other boy's calf, pulling him off his feet. The zombie child made raspy yelps, reaching in terror for his parents.

Acting on instinct alone, because this boy reminded him so much of Finch, Leif ran for him, slashing his knife across the wolf's snout. Yelping, the wolf turned tail and ran. Leif pulled the boy to his side, holding him close. The poor thing was shaking, tears rolling down his cheeks as dank blood dripped from his leg.

His mother made a choked, horrified sound, grunting with effort as she tried to get away from now the two wolves she and her partner were fighting.

But if the first wolf had been scared away, Leif believed the other two could be, as well.

Ushering the other boy next to Finch, Leif positioned himself between them and the wolves, praying the third wouldn't return. He waved his arms and made all the noise he could, loud gargles and groans and growls. Behind him, the boys started to do the same, although their young pitches were some of the most unfrightening sounds Leif had ever heard. The other zombies took up the call, regaining their fight. Leif lunged forward, stabbing the wolf that had been gunning for the male zombie. It yipped, jumping away.

The other wolf dove for Leif, sinking its teeth into his leg. He made a low sound in pain, but the wolf's preoccupation with his shin gave Leif the time to drive his knife into the top of the wolf's head.

The animal collapsed, and the one with it ran, limping as it retreated into the trees, kicking up snow in its wake.

At once, the female zombie ran to her son, falling to her knees to wrap him in her arms. Her partner was close behind, crouching to check his son's wound. When the female looked up at Leif, her posture was full of gratitude.

Leif nodded, accepting her thanks. Perhaps this could mean the tension between them all could lessen.

He looked down as Finch pulled at his pant leg. Leif knelt, taking his brother's face in his hands. *Are you hurt?*

Although he was shaking, Finch replied, *No. Are you okay?*

Leif kissed his head and embraced him, nodding against his shoulder. For now, that security was enough.

***

That security didn't last long. The remaining hours of the day were spent in tense trudging, each zombie on high alert as they scanned the trees for spying wolves.

But hunger was another predator that gnawed at them. Unsure how far they were traveling, Leif grew frustrated and worried. The wounds in his leg weren't helping, making him limp.

They stopped again for the night when the sun was almost down, creating lean-tos to shield them from the weather and wildlife.

On winter nights like these, there were too many hours of darkness for sleeping. So, Leif spent many of them talking with Finch. He was growing scared again, watching Finch's energy deplete. At least when they talked, Leif knew his brother was alert.

Do you remember anything about Craig? Leif asked.

Finch screwed his eyes shut, thinking. He opened them back up. *It was pretty much the same as Thorne Bay, right? But more people.* He tilted his head. *Hey, Leif? What happens on a human farm? How do they make sure the people don't escape? Or… do they eat many of the people?*

Leif sensed the discomfort in his brother's tone. He never liked killing people, either. The concept of eating their brains was just as repulsive. But they needed it. It was just the way the world was now. Kill or be killed. Eat or be eaten. It was horrible, he knew that. But morals had gone out the window five years ago.

Maybe things would be different for Leif if he didn't have Finch. Maybe he would have let himself starve to death ages ago. But he had a little boy to feed. That was ethical enough for him.

I don't know what it will be like, he answered honestly. *It might be pretty scary. I can't promise it won't be. But we're both going to survive. That, I can guarantee.*

He *couldn't,* really, but he felt better thinking so.

***

The next day was more of the same, only slower. At least the pain in Finch's leg had diminished since scabbing. Neither was there any sign of infection.

But exhaustion weighed down their steps more than injury. Everyone dropped their pace, looking more and more ill as time passed and the snowfall grew harsher. As the snow piled up, their energy waned, and they had to stop moving an hour before sunset near a ravine, where the trees thinned out.

Leif felt like his stomach was chewing itself from the inside out. He sometimes found himself groaning without meaning to, feet dragging in the snow.

The five of them went to gather branches for shelters again, digging through the powdery snow underneath trees. Leif was looking forward to resting his feet for the long hours of darkness when he heard a high-pitched, panicked cry.

Whipping his head in the direction of what Leif immediately recognized to be his brother, his stomach dropped to his feet.

An outcropping of snow crumbled beneath Finch, sending the kid falling back over the edge of the ravine.

Quicker than Leif could scream, the zombie man was there in just three strides, lashing out to grab Finch's arm, pulling him back, and throwing him away from the ravine's edge. Finch gasped and skidded on his hands and knees in the snow.

Leif ran to him as fast as his weakened body would allow. He fell in the snow beside his brother, gathering him into his arms. Just a few feet beyond, the ground dropped off into a steep cliff, a frozen river far below. The snow had hidden the true drop off. No wonder Finch had almost fallen.

Leif was shaking harder than Finch was. He cupped the back of the boy's head with his hand, needing to feel the tangibility of him being safe. *I almost lost him,* he thought in terror. His entire reason for existing, for living another day, and it had almost been torn from his arms.

Leif had imagined a few times what he would do if Finch ever died. At this point in his miserable existence, he could think of no feasible option but taking his own life over that grief.

He didn't realize he was crying until Finch brushed the tears from his face. *It's okay,* he said. *I'm okay.*

Leif nodded, swallowing back the sob in his throat. Finch was okay. Leif may not have been able to save his dad, but he did have this family left. He would do absolutely anything to protect him. *Thank God for that man we're traveling with.*

He looked up at the zombie, wishing he could speak to express his thanks. The man gave a simple smile; he understood.

***

Day five felt like an eternity. Thankfully, no more snow had fallen in the night. Leif didn't know how they could travel more than a few miles each day if the snow piled much higher.

They had to be getting close. If they had gone as far as he thought they had, they should reach Craig by the next day, if not that very evening.

But even a day felt ages away. Leif felt like he was going to die if he didn't get food in his stomach fast. Finch often made pitiful moans against his shoulder, needing the same thing.

As they searched for branches that night for what would hopefully be their last shelters, Finch made gibberish noises, drawing Leif's attention. He almost slumped to his knees in relief.

Finch stumbled through the snow, kneeling beside the corpse of a human, its skin blue and frozen. How had it gotten there? Perhaps Craig was close. Maybe this person had gone out hunting. Or sometimes, people just died. It didn't matter. They had found food.

The other three zombies raced to the body. But instead of going for the person's head, like Finch was trying to crack open, to Leif's horror, they dove at his brother, growling and snarling. The man wrapped his hands around Finch's neck and squeezed.

Leif let loose a guttural shout, throwing himself at the man. Gone were the zombies of just days ago. Lack of food had made them unpredictable and feral. Leif and Finch were now nothing more than competition to them. Creatures who needed to die.

Leif snapped his teeth, roaring as the zombie dug his own into Leif's shoulder, drawing blood. At least he had let go of Finch. Leif rolled, pinning the man underneath him. As the zombie struggled, Leif realized he wouldn't be able to keep him down. He locked eyes with his startled brother. *Run. Now!*

Finch obeyed. But as he started to stumble through the snow, the female zombie and the boy pursued. *No.*

Leif pressed his elbow into the man's chest to keep him down, wincing as he used his injured arm to pull the knife from his satchel. With a surge of strength and control that could have only come from desperate fear for his brother, Leif drove the knife into the zombie's chest. A strangled groan issued from the man before he went still.

Leif reached back into his bag for the handgun and cocked it, aiming for the female zombie, who had pushed his brother into the snow.

BANG!

The bullet lodged in her head. She collapsed at Finch's side.

The other boy let out a screech, stumbling back from the fight. With a frantic glance at Leif, he tried to run, but his legs only carried him a few steps before he fainted.

Leif ran to Finch, checking him for injuries. Trembling, Finch brought his hands to his neck.

Did he hurt you? Leif asked frantically, his hands hovering around his brother. He didn't know what to do or if he could fix anything if Finch were really injured.

Leif's eyes shone with pain as he rubbed his neck. Bruises were beginning to form. A few scratches from fingernails dripped blood. *It hurts.*

How badly? Finny, I need you to focus right now. Is it really hurt? Or do you think the pain may stop soon?

Finch sat still for a few moments, swallowing back tears, but he brought his hands back down to his sides. *It hurts. But it's okay. Better now.*

Leif's shoulders sank in relief. He directed his attention to the other boy in the snow. He rolled the little body over, shaking him gently. He didn't know if he actually wanted him to wake or not. But he was a child. Just hungry. Just following his parents. He didn't deserve to die any more than Finch did.

But the child didn't stir. Perhaps the hunger had finally gotten to him. Leif sighed. There wasn't anything he could do for him anymore. Maybe it was for the best. He and his parents could go to the afterlife together instead of remaining in this awful world any longer.

He and Finch dragged themselves to the human corpse. Leif cracked the skull open to get to the succulent brain inside.

As they ate, he forgot the pain in his shoulder as the ache in his stomach subsided. They ate their fill, and Leif collected the remains of the brain to bury in the snow and preserve wherever they made their shelter.

When they camped for the night, he held Finch closer than he had the subsequent nights. He didn't need the warmth. His chest, however, felt like it was going to cave in on itself with guilt. But a guilty conscience was nothing compared to a dead brother.

He had done what he had to. But that didn't negate the fact that there were three more bodies outside than there had been the night before. He was a monster, and it felt awful.

But there were more awful things to feel.

***

In the morning, Leif and Finch emerged from the dense forest, the town of Craig stretching before them. Most of the town lay on a peninsula, frozen water surrounding it on all sides save for the one facing the road.

It was quiet. Leif hadn't meant to get his hope up, but he'd hoped for immediate evidence of a human farm. The leftover brain in his satchel, if kept properly preserved, would only last them a month. They *needed* the hope of something more. Or else, Leif was going to watch his little brother die, if he didn't die first.

The quiet unsettled him as they walked through the streets, stopping to peer around every corner before moving on. Every few turns, he swore he heard voices. *Human* voices. Being caught unaware by an armed human would mean death. Leif gripped Finch's hand and looked down at him. Even against his discolored zombie skin, dark bruises in the shape of the male zombie's hands were stark against Finch's neck. Scratches from his nails remained, too, just starting to scab. A desperate sense to protect welled in Leif's throat. He wouldn't let anything happen to Finch again. *Don't let go, buddy. Or, if you have to, stay close unless I tell you to run.*

As they moved through the town, it became increasingly obvious that they were not going to find a farm. There was no evidence of any organized captivity. Leif felt sick. Had their journey been in vain? Should he just have left himself and his brother to starve in their home? At least that would have been a peaceful death. But they had come so far. Been through so much. He had *killed* to get here. It couldn't be for nothing.

He kept looking around, swearing he saw movement in the corner of his eye. But each time, whatever it was evaded him. Or maybe he was paranoid, and there was nothing there at all.

Finch tugged on his pant leg. *Do you hear that?* He pointed toward a building up ahead. The windows were boarded up, but the door was open, swinging on its hinges in the wind. Leif sniffed, catching the scent of humans in the air. Thrill and fear stirred together in his chest.

He looked down at his brother. *I'm going to investigate. Maybe some people are being kept over there. Or maybe just survivors. Dangerous. Don't follow until I come back.* He pointed to a small house nearby. *Hide.* Finch nodded, obeying.

Gun in hand, Leif made his way toward the building, the human scent growing stronger. He hesitated in the street. This wasn't a good idea.

He didn't have time to make any decisions regarding that thought before something smashed into the back of his head, and his vision went dark.

***

Leif's eyelids fluttered open, a low, guttural groan coming from his throat. The smell of rust and dampness filled his nostrils.

He sat up abruptly, realizing his surroundings. A cage. He was in a *cage*. Not even large enough to stand in. As panic set in, he looked around in the dim light filtering in through the boarded-up windows, trying to make sense of his surroundings. Tables and chairs littered with random supplies filled the space. His satchel was gone.

Leif reached out, his fingers brushing against the cold metal bars. Gripping them, he pulled, then pushed, trying to force them apart, but while human bone cracked easily under his strength, these did not.

Finch. Where was his brother?

Leif looked around the room, spotting Finch in a similar cage a few feet away, still unconscious. Leif made a soft growl, trying to wake him. There was no response. He grunted, more urgently, a mix of fear and desperation in the sound. Finch stirred but didn't wake up.

"You're awake. Good."

Leif's attention snapped to an approaching woman. Her skin was clear and dark, not mottled like a zombie's. Lines framed her mouth and crinkled at the corners of her eyes, which shone with curiosity and caution as she studied Leif. Behind her stood a younger man and woman, both with pale skin and curly blond hair. They were closer to Leif's age, about twenty, and were holding a crowbar and a baseball bat, respectively.

Leif narrowed his eyes, a growl rumbling deep in his throat. The woman held up her hands.

"Can you understand me? I'm not here to hurt you. As long as you stay calm and cooperate."

Leif looked back at his brother, willing him to wake. Had they hurt him to get him here, too? Was he okay?

"Is he with you?" the woman asked.

Leif nodded, a low, pleading sound escaping him.

She looked at his brother more closely. "His neck is hurt." She turned her attention back to Leif. "Tell me, if we opened his cage to help him, would he be aggressive? Would he bite?"

Leif shook his head. Finch didn't have a fighting bone in his body. And if Finch woke up, he could tell him to remain calm.

The woman signaled to the other humans. They approached Finch's cage, their movements deliberate and careful.

"Kamani, are you sure?" the young woman asked.

The older woman nodded. "We wanted to understand their kind." She nodded toward Leif. "This one isn't so mindlessly aggressive, Georgia. We may be able to learn something from him."

"Maybe he's just not hungry," the man said, fear swimming in his eyes. "What if he gets hungry? Or the little one?"

"He cares about the little one, Milo," Kamani said. "He'll be able to keep him calm. And he won't do anything to us while the kid's vulnerable." Kamani shot Leif an apologetic smile that he was almost ready to believe. "Sorry to put it in terms like that. I'd like to trust you. But it's going to take a little time, I'm sure you can understand." She nodded at Finch. "We'll help him. But we need you to stay calm. Can you do that?"

Leif hesitated, his mind a whirlwind of fear and hope. He didn't have another choice. He nodded, his growl softening, becoming close to a whimper.

As Milo and Georgia set to unlock the cage, Leif watched every movement, his body tense, ready to react if they harmed his brother. Finch rubbed his eyes, sitting up. He spotted the humans first, a snarl springing from his lips as he pressed himself against the back of the cage, looking around frantically until he spotted Leif. The humans paused, waiting to reach for Finch.

Finch, Finch, Leif communicated as calmly as he could manage.

Leif! Finch's eyes sparked with terror. *What's happening? Help me!*

Little one, you have to trust me right now.

Finch's lower lip wobbled. He shuddered, too frightened to even protest the nickname. *Humans kill. They* kill, *Leif.*

I know, kid. I know. But we woke up here. They had the chance to kill us, but they didn't. If they wanted us dead, we'd be dead already. They're different. I think they want to understand us, too. Can you please be calm for me? They're going to let you out and treat your neck.

Finch hesitated, then nodded. *But you'll help me if they hurt me?*

Leif felt the threat of tears in the back of his throat. This boy had such trust in him. How did Finch expect him to help when he was still locked in a cage? But he nodded. *Always. They will not hurt you as long as I'm here.*

Finch's shoulders slackened. He crawled out of the cage, letting Milo and Georgia lead him to one of the chairs. They sorted through a mess of bandages and medicines on the table, beginning to treat Finch. Their movements were gentle and deliberate, though their hands trembled whenever they got close to the little zombie.

"Thank you," Kamani said to them, her expression softening. She looked back at Leif. "You're not like the others we've come across. The rest are frenzied. But you have a sense of awareness. Even compassion."

Leif nodded, then pointed at Finch and growled softly, conveying his concern. Kamani tilted her head, likely trying to piece together his meaning.

"Is he…your family?"

Leif nodded again with more emphasis. Kamani's eyes softened with understanding.

"Ah. I see. You'd do anything to protect him, I'm sure." She gestured to her companions. "I'm Kamani. And these are Milo and Georgia. Brother and sister, if you couldn't tell."

Leif nodded, pointing between himself and his brother.

"Ah, you're brothers? Well, Milo and Georgia are like my family, too. I'd do anything for them." She looked pointedly at Leif. "Including understanding your kind to keep them safe. We may even be able to help each other, young man."

The turn of phrase took Leif aback. For just a moment, his chest swelled with pride to be referred to as a person. By a human, no less. Did she see in him what he'd been before?

"So, you can understand if I have some questions for you," she continued. "Please, bear with me. Have you eaten recently?"

Leif nodded. Kamani pulled a pad of paper from her jacket pocket and jotted something down.

"Have you experienced extreme hunger before?"

Nod.

"Have you been near a human or a human brain before and practiced restraint? Even when extremely hungry?"

Leif thought back to a few days before when he'd practiced as much self-control as he had in his life, letting his brother eat before him without knowing if he'd get to eat at all. He nodded.

"Have you been around other zombies before?"

Nod.

"From what you've seen, do they tend to practice the same restraint?"

Leif shook his head.

"If there's no food or territory to fight over, do zombies usually attack each other?"

Head shake.

"Do you eat each other's brains? Could you even?"

Shake again.

Kamani gestured to Finch. "When he woke up, you were looking at each other for quite a while. Were you…" She laughed and shook her head. "Forgive me if this sounds foolish, but were you somehow communicating?"

Leif nodded, tapping his head.

Kamani's eyes lit up. "Telepathically?"

He nodded, then pointed between himself and Finch.

Kamani's brow furrowed. "Just…between the two of you? Can you communicate with any other zombies?"

Shake.

"Is that normal?"

Nod.

Kamani smiled, continuing to write. "You've already been an incredible amount of insight, young man. And I have hundreds of other things I'd love to ask you, but there's more pressing business." She looked over at Milo and Georgia. "Is the boy all right?"

Milo nodded. "A few scratches and bruises. Looks like someone tried to strangle him. But he should be just fine."

"Good. Now, my friend," she addressed Leif, "we have a lot of people still in Craig. Maybe…"

"Nine hundred," supplied Georgia, administering a cold compress to Finch's neck.

"Yes, that's it. We've stayed relatively safe ever since the outbreak. But we still come across the occasional threat. Our own people have been turned or killed when we haven't been careful." Regret filled her eyes. "That guilt has fallen on me. Around here, I'm in charge. So, I've been trying to figure out a solution. What I would love are scouts to help us spot or scent when another zombie or group of zombies is close. From what you've told us, it would be much safer for someone like you to—"

"Nngh!"

Leif whipped his head in Finch's direction. Finch's teeth were gritted as he held the side of his neck. Milo stepped back with his hands held up, his panicked gaze darting toward Leif. "I'm sorry!" he cried. "I was just sterilizing his open cut, I swear!"

Finch breathed heavily, locking eyes with Leif.

You're safe, Leif assured him, willing himself to relax. *I'm sorry it hurts, but I promise they're helping you. Please, just—*

Can you hold my hand?

Leif sighed. That wasn't as easy as he made it sound. But for Finch, he would try anything.

He motioned to Kamani, pointing to himself, then Finch, clasping his hands together.

Georgia tilted her head. "What's he saying?"

Finch reached out his hand for Leif. Kamani smiled, understanding. She looked at Leif. "I will let you hold his hand. But be aware, all of us are armed, with more weapons than one. I trust you, but at the same time, we have to be wise. Can you assure me if I let you out, you won't attack?"

Leif nodded. Once free, he pulled up a chair next to Finch, careful not to make any sudden movements that might startle the humans or spur them to violence.

Finch's eyes glittered with nervousness. *I'm scared.*

It's okay. You know what? We'll do it together. Leif grunted to get the people's attention, pulling the collar of his shirt down to expose his shoulder. An array of teeth marks marred it in a crescent, some of the punctures still seeping.

"Ooh." Georgia winced. "Yeah, we'll have to sterilize that, too." Hands shaking, she looked to her friend. "Kamaniiiii?"

Kamani sighed, walking over and taking the alcohol and rag. Her tone held a ring of apology as she said to Leif, "You can understand their caution. We'd like to build trust with you, though." She wet her rag as Leif took Finch's hand. He winced as she began cleaning his shoulder. "Goodness, you two got into quite the scuffle."

When finished, Finch climbed into Leif's lap, resting his head against his brother's chest. Leif lay his chin atop Finch's head.

Kamani moved her chair close to the brothers. Leif was shocked at her amount of trust in them.

"As I was saying," she continued, "many of us have been desperate to know more about zombies. Craig has survived so far, but we don't have any idea if there's any other place on earth like ours. As in, sustainable cities that are still populated with humans. But there's so much we don't know about our present world. We don't know if what's happened to people like you can be reversed. Or if cohabitation between our kinds could work. At least on a larger scale.

"But those are things for us to study over time. One of the most practical ways you can help us right now is scouting, as I said. While staying safer in the presence of zombies than we can, you could alert us of any who are close." Her gaze dropped to her lap. "Now, as it is now, we can't do anything for them, but," she looked back up, "in exchange for your help, with the amount of people we have still living here, we tend to have a death about once a month—from old age, sickness, or otherwise. Around that often, you could have the brain of the recently deceased. Would that be enough to feed two of you? I would do everything I can to ensure your safety and your little one's."

Finch grunted, frowning in disapproval at how he was addressed. Leif would have laughed if he were able.

What she was proposing sounded insane. Never would Leif have imagined a living person to be so open to working with a couple of young zombies. The thought scared him. And excited him. What she was saying made a lot of sense. Clearly, she had been pondering the possibilities for a long time. He and Finch just happened to be the right zombies at the right time.

Leif realized Finch's presence had literally kept him alive as much as the other way around. If he didn't have Finch to worry about, he'd probably be as mindless as the rest of his kind. Attacking at any possibility of food. No care in the world but to keep himself alive.

And what about that other family? he wondered. What made him any different from them? They loved each other, but they'd resorted to violence anyway when their food was threatened. Leif would also fight tooth and nail for his brother to eat.

But what if there were no uncertainty about the next meal, like Kamani was saying? What if there were no guilt associated with eating anymore? What if he and his brother could thrive instead of only surviving?

Natural death wasn't always consistent. Was he prepared to go a week or so without in order to wait for the next meal? Did he have the self-control to let his brother be hungry again, even when there were hundreds of humans around them?

He could. He had to do this. And if scouting could save more people, their town would eventually build its numbers. With human life and death continuing as they used to, he and his brother would always have enough to eat, just as Kamani was saying.

Leif stretched out his hand, causing Kamani's eyes to go wide. Her lips parted, then broke into a smile as she took hold of his hand, shaking it. Leif marveled at the warmth of the contact. He wondered if there had ever been such a civil, safe interaction between a zombie and a human.

"Wonderful," she gushed, taken aback. "Now, you must understand, this can't happen all at once. You'll be under strict surveillance for the foreseeable future, especially as we speak with the rest of Craig about who you are and how we'd like to coexist. But first things first. What should we call you?"

Leif stood, hefting his brother up and supporting him on his hip with his good arm. He jerked his head to the door.

Kamani's brow furrowed, but she nodded. "All right, we can go out. Stay close to me, though. Milo, Georgia, follow behind. Make sure no one tries to hurt them."

Leif stepped out into the open air right after Kamani. The crisp winter air was a welcome reprieve from the musty building. He set Finch down, then pointed to the trees, barren in their December state.

"Tree?" Kamani guessed. "Your name is tree?"

Leif pressed his lips together and shook his head. He crouched down in the snow, brushing it away to get to the ground. Sure enough, a layer of decaying, soggy leaves remained. He picked one up, holding it out.

"Leaf?"

He nodded, pleased.

Milo laughed. "Well, that made it easy for us. Let's hope your brother is named Rock instead of Andrew or something."

Leif smiled, shaking his head. He began to trace a rough pictogram in the snow. The people leaned over to inspect it.

"Oh! It's a bird," Georgia exclaimed. "Bird?"

Leif nodded, raising his eyebrows and waving his hand, urging her to go on.

"Robin?" Milo guessed.

"Wren," Kamani said.

"Lark?" Georgia went on.

"Duck!" Milo burst out.

Georgia pushed his shoulder. "That's not a name, idiot."

"Hey, it could be!" Milo sniffed. "Okay, then… Raven, Jay… um, Dove? Wait, that's a girl one, right? Uh, Finch?"

The boy sprang up at the sound of his name, nodding.

Milo beamed, looking down his nose at Georgia. "First try." She shoved him again.

Leif watched these people, remembering for the first time in years what it was like to joke around, to be with people his age, to live instead of fighting not to die. He wished so badly that he could speak with these people. That he could have friends again. That his new normal didn't have to be so awful anymore.

Maybe, over time, they would figure it out. Maybe, someday down the line, he could live without looking over his shoulder. What would it be like to live without the constant danger of death?

Leif took Finch's hand again. He was willing to try trusting these people. The possibility of a new, safer life, and maybe even a fulfilling one, too, was worth the risk.

Kamani nodded her head. "This way, Leaf, Finch. Let's get started."

***

Their first week in Craig had been nerve-wracking, but it solidified Leif's trust in Kamani, Georgia, and Milo. Their surveillance over him and his brother had been just as much for his and Finch's safety as it was for the humans'.

Understandably, not everyone was on board with Kamani's plan at first. Finch and Leif had been gawked at, cowered away from, and, once, even spat upon.

But others had been kind. Kamani's household was warm in every sense of the word. She held an aura of peace around herself. Leif had many opportunities to observe her, since she always accompanied him when he left the house. With the people she met, her presence lowered the tensions that Leif's presence caused. No wonder she was their leader.

Her attentiveness to him and Finch made Leif feel safer than he had since his father died. He'd had to be a parent to Finch for so long. Now, someone who was actually suited for that role had stepped up. Leif didn't remember having a mother in his living life, but he imagined if he had, this must have been what that relationship felt like.

When the week was up, Leif and Finch ate more of the leftover brain from the frozen man, which Kamani helped them preserve. Georgia and Milo saw this and seemed to abandon any final doubts they'd held onto about their new zombie companions. Hunger, then the eating that followed, hadn't made Leif or Finch aggressive or uncontrollable in any way.

One or both of them accompanied Leif scouting at first, more to ensure his safety from the people of Craig. But eventually, Leif felt comfortable enough going out on his own. Even the few people he'd met that still had their concerns about him and his brother weren't likely to hurt them, which would put them in the way of Kamani's displeasure and lawful punishment. Kamani had made her guardianship of the boys clear. So far, that claim had been respected.

The young people of Craig had been quicker to warm up to them than the older population, coming to meals at Kamani's house to interact with the zombies. At first, Leif believed they were doing so on dares, but then, they genuinely seemed to enjoy being around him and his brother.

The first night he truly felt at home, though, was returning from a solo scouting trip. A fire crackled and popped in the fireplace, Georgia was helping Kamani cook stew in the kitchen, and Milo sat in front of the fire, reading a book aloud to Finch and a few other children who had stopped by for dinner and games.

Tranquility surrounded the household. Leif hadn't thought that possible in their frightening, broken world. Finch was thriving, giggling with others his age. Leif had a safe home to come back to every night. Able to act as a brother again instead of a parent, he felt the weight of the world lifted from his shoulders.

Uncertainties still loomed ahead. The earth was still forever different. But he wasn't so daunted by it anymore. That fear was fading fast.

SOCIAL MADNESS

BY K.R. MOORE

1

Early. Morning in the bedroom of a Miami residence. There lived a boy named Cecil who, if asked, would probably get his home mixed up with his social media accounts. The 10th grader cried out. "You gotta be kidding me!"

Hunched up on his laptop, he read the scores of mocking comments with his blood boiling. It wouldn't be long before sweat threatened to mat his long emo shag hairstyle to his head.

"But it's not-"

"Braindead morons...that's all I see all day!"

He stayed, fighting the good fight for hours. From before he ate breakfast on his desktop, through school on his phone when the teacher wasn't looking, all the way to his walk home after getting off the bus. His eyes were glued to a screen.

Finally, he was snapped to reality with a harsh shove from his close friend Clarissa. A dark-skinned, glasses-bearing girl with a passion for Irish fashion, "Cecil dude...you've been glued to that phone all day...I'm surprised the teacher didn't catch you." She pouted.

"You don't understand, Clarissa. I'm not the one to take crap lying down." He gripped his phone hard with vein-popping strength, "If people try to strip me down online, I'm pulling my pants right back up and hitting them with my belt."

"That...sounded nowhere near as cool as you thought it was going to be."

"Whatever..." He muttered and sank his hands into his pockets.

Clarissa pushed her glasses up and thought for a moment, "Hm... Hey, how about we hit the court after chilling at your place! You look like you have a lot of stress to blow off."

Cecil pushed back his long hair and pursed his lips, "Aight, fine. We can go after we get this homework out of the way; it's easy tonight." He smirked as he grabbed her hand and gently led the way to his house.

***

Barely over an hour later in Cecil's room, Clarissa shut her binder and tucked away her papers with a victorious smile, "Wow, you weren't kidding, that was quick!" She lay back in one of his beanbag chairs and checked her watch, "It's not even five, let's go!"

She looked up, and her wide smile reversed upon seeing Cecil angrily scrolling away on his computer, "Hey, I thought you were...doing your homework."

Her tapping on his shoulder jolted him out of his trance, and he pulled his headphones off. Her glare immediately told him to fess up, "Sorry, I was trying to find some music to do it with, but then I spotted this!"

She glanced at the screen and saw a massive essay of a comment replying to the video, "What's this?"

"A braindead hate video on the CCU!" Clarissa just sighed, knowing he wasn't going to miss a chance to defend his favorite movie franchise.

Cecil tapped the screen, "Look at these comments, look at how many likes there are in general! I've been listening, it's cherry picking the smallest bits of criticism and making them into this whole big thing!"

She took the mouse and scrolled through the comments, "Ugh...yeah. These are really weak, but honestly, they're nothing new." She minimized the window before walking over to his drawer and digging into it.

"W-Whoa, hey! That's my private place!" Cecil protested before a pair of workout clothes got tossed into his face.

"Take a break from the screen for once in your life and ignore the idiots. Put those on, I had P.E. today, so I'll be changing back into my fit in your bathroom."

She playfully waved goodbye, "Meet me on the court when you're done."

Once Clarissa had left, Cecil sighed and lay back in his swivel chair. He popped the desktop back on and continued with his dissertation against the poster and his supporters.

"So stupid..."

He would've fallen into another trance had it not been for his phone going off. Cecil checked to find another one of his friends from a few states up, calling, "Huh? What does he want?"

He clicked it on and spoke while still writing, "Sup, dude."

As soon as he was asked how everything was going, Cecil didn't miss a beat, unloading everything. "And so basically, I'm going crazy over everyone attacking me. Seriously, when did people online become so toxic?"

He sighed and looked at the sheer number of negative hate videos, some of which were regarding his favorite things, clogging up his recommended sections, "You're a big internet star? How do you deal with it?"

He listened before viciously shaking his head unsatisfied, "No, I can't just ignore them! Half of the day, my phone is blown up with notifications of people responding to me or picking fights!"

"You have another idea? Well, let me hear it."

"Okay, I'm looking it up."

He typed the name as he spelled it out, eventually ending up on an obscure but not too sketchy-looking website. "Well, geez, here it is. I could barely find it. The ModNote is it?" He studied the webpage. It was just a black screen with a bar holding the aforementioned title and a brief tagline right above the order button.

ASSERT CONTROL

"So what does it do?" His friend's explanation was less than satisfactory.

"In other words, you just read the tagline...okay, fine, I'll check it out." He clicked the button hesitantly. However, any and all resistance went out the window as soon as he saw the wondrous price of zero dollars.

Not seeing the problem in trying out a free product, he sat back after finishing his order before catching the time in the corner of the screen, "Shoot, I'd better get changed before Clarissa calls. I'll chat with you later, this better workout unlike your last few ideas."

With that, Cecil hung up and threw on his clothes to get changed before heading out. Unaware of the green sparks surrounding his computer as it briefly shorted out upon processing the receipt.

***

About a week later, Cecil was doing his usual phone browsing in the basement, spending the last few hours of his peaceful Sunday reading through discourse, "Hey there, how was Merritt Island?"

"Oh, it was fine, the Kennedy Space Station was nice! At first, I thought I'd be stuck working another boring weekend at the family restaurant, but they surprised me.

"Man, I'm jealous, I wish my parents would just up and decide to take the family to see rockets because we're all bored." Cecil rolled over and looked at his laptop, "I've just been waiting on that thing to show up in the mail already."

He could hear her grumble over the line, "Oh, don't tell me you're actually still listening to that guy again? Seriously, when was the last time any of his ideas ever turned out good?"

"Well, I mean, I'm sure he's had some hits."

"Like?"

A vast void of silence filled the line for a moment, "Anyway, Clarry, you almost home?"

Clarissa gave a cocky scoff, "We'll be back tomorrow. Sucks to have school the next day, now it'll be extra boring after seeing the inside of a real rocket."

They chatted for a while longer before she got back, "Oh, we're pulling up to the house. Call you back later!"

He bid her goodbye and hung up before rolling onto his back and staring up at the ceiling, "I wonder if I posted about being in space. Would people still find a way to ruin that for me as well?"

"Cecil, go water the plants, please!" His dad's voice called out from above.

"Sure thing dad."

He sloppily threw himself onto his feet before shoving on some sandals and opening the door, only to nearly trip on a box that had been waiting for him by the curb, "What the...a package? Nobody knocked on the door." Cecil leaned out and checked the neighborhood. Nothing but kids playing, dog walkers, joggers, and more. Not a single sign of a delivery person, however.

With suspicions still lingering, he set the box inside before going on with his task of watering the flowers and roses in the backyard. After that was done, he set the box onto his desk and began investigating, "Well, it's addressed to me..."

"Wait, did that thing I ordered finally come in?" With excitement, he swiped a butter knife from the kitchen and practically tore the package apart soon afterward. What resided inside was not what he expected. It was a green and silver tablet, slick but bizarre.

"What is this thing?" He investigated the technology and flipped it over, reading the name on the back.

"The...ModNote? So it really is that thing."

He powered it on and soon, like many normal tablets, the steps for configuration soon came on. He read them out loud with intrigue, "Instructions...this tablet is meant to Shepard online toxicity. Should a person online be spreading trouble, simply type their username into the prompt this tablet displays when turned on. Then rate their actions on a scale of 1 to 10. The ensuing punishment will be reflective of their rating and will, more often than not, result in their removal from the internet one way or another."

"Wha...what does all that even mean?" He scratched his head before slamming it down onto the desk with an aggressive sigh, "Dangit... That dude seriously should've looked into this more. I've never seen a more obvious gag toy."

He sat back in his chair for a moment, looking at the time, "Welp, I got some time to spare, I guess."

Thinking of a target, he scrolled through his reply section and found a particularly troublesome bully online who wasted no time calling people highly offensive names that would hurt the souls of certain groups.

"That punk. Think you can just spout ableist slurs like a comedy routine? Well, I think that's a fine rating of...7." He filled out the user's name and description of his actions before hitting submit.

As the buffer bar spun, he thought back to how the actual mods of the blog he was on failed to do their job, "I even reported that guy after he went as far as to call me the hard R days ago. But as far as I can see, his account is still up." Cecil groaned and waited before a confirmation message popped up.

"This thing is pretty realistic, I'll give it that." He smirked before tossing it aside, deciding not to waste any more time with it.

***

A couple of hours later, Cecil found himself struggling to pull a pie out of the oven on time, nearly failing to help his mom prepare dessert on time. As the smoke from the oven covered him, he heard his dad call out for him again, "Hey Cecil, could you come in here?"

Eager to get away from the scene of the crime, he bolted into the living room, "Hey dad, what's up? By the way, could you tell Mom we might have to go out and buy a pie for tonight?"

His dad just sighed, not questioning the comment, "Your cousin Jeremy...he attends Lawkid University in New Orleans, correct?" He asked fearfully.

"Yeah, why?" His father just gestured to the TV with a sullen and worried face. Cecil followed his intent and looked over at the screen. Despair quickly grew across his face.

It was the six o'clock news, and the events depicted looked urgent with an entire university caught on a helicopter aerial cam. The headline on the screen said it all.

LAWKID UNIVERSITY ON LOCKDOWN AFTER BOMB THREAT.

PERPATRATOR APPREHENDED.

"Unreal. Did they say who made the threat?"

"It's on now. Look at the bottom screen."

THREAT WAS INITIATED IN A FLUTTER POST BY ONIKI674.

"That's the guy's username!"

As if he were being listened to, the reporter on TV gave a brief overview of the situation, "About two hours ago, a Flutter user going by the name of ONIK674 tweeted that he would blow up the University of Lawkid for its Disabled Equality program. The post was immediately reported to special authorities, and the user was taken into custody the following hour for questioning. His post and overall account have been removed from the internet."

The once skeptical boy was speechless, "The ModNote is real!"

"Hm, did you say something, Cecil?"

He covered his mouth and scurried away as fast as he could, "I have to go back to my room!" Without giving his father a chance to inquire further, he bolted back and shut the door.

"What's going on? Threatening to attack special needs people?" Cecil collapsed into his chair, sweat pouring down his face. "I know the dude was a waste of space, but would he really do that?"

"The ModNote. This can't be real, can it?" With a swallow, Cecil opened his conversation history and found another online user who had given him a really hard time lately. He rated his comment the same score as the one before.

While waiting for another event to trigger to confirm his suspicions, Cecil toggled the options in the corner. He found an array of settings from restrictions, to a cam to follow all the actions as they happened, "A live feed? Yes, display."

He watched with chills as the ModNote posted a fake video online of the user in question doing unspeakable things on his account. Given that the user had over 500k followers, the video quickly exploded and was removed, with the account itself quickly vanishing for breaking the rules.

"Unreal."

He gripped the tablet with wide eyes, "This ModNote punishes people socially on account of their actions and ruins their reputation. Whether they actually did what the tablet says they did or not doesn't matter."

Soon, he found himself writing down a slew of usernames.

***

The following morning, Clarissa was doing her best to stay focused on class after her adventurous weekend. A futile effort, however, as she kept finding herself doodling rockets instead of listening to Civil War lectures.

She was brought back to her senses with the snapping of her pencil, "Zeke, mind lending me an extra? I promise I won't bite it again; I'm not stressed today."

Her spiky green-haired friend simply crossed his arms with a pout, "Yeah, right, I'm not taking any chances." He grumbled and handed her a tough and durable utensil made of steel, "Here, take this bite-proof pen."

"Thanks." She sighed before overhearing Zeke's phone vibrate. With haste, he whipped it out and scrolled the news.

"Dang, you're on your phone too?" She looked around to see tons of heads down and scrolling as the teacher at the front of the room was too busy on her computer to notice, "Come to think of it, everyone looks distracted."

Zeke raised an eyebrow, "Wait, you mean you haven't been keeping up?"

"I was out of town over the weekend, remember?" She yawned with a tinge of annoyance, "Don't expect me to spend my desperately needed sleeping hours following whatever stupid drama online."

Zeke challenged the comment, quickly did a search, which turned up over 20 stories of chaos regarding online sites and certain users, "Well, you might want to check out this one. And this. Don't forget this one as well."

"W-Wait, this all started last night?" She grabbed his phone and started reading the headlines individually. "Those are multiple people getting caught up in crimes out of nowhere!"

Zeke sighed and lay his head down, "Yeah, and some fairly big names too. I mean, FutoKing? I often listened to his podcasts while cooking. Never thought he would get taken in for mass data theft."

Another kid behind them tapped onto both of their shoulders, "Oh, that's nothing, I heard that."

One by one, more students joined the conversation with Clarissa, informing her of all the scandals as she slowly became overwhelmed. Soon enough, she popped up from her group's desk and walked over to Cecil's, where he was standing with papers. "The assignment can wait, Cecil. Did you know anything about—"

Her urgency came to a halt as Cecil turned around with a loud yawn. His usually slender, straight hair was wild and ragged, his clothes were wrinkled and stained with syrup of a no doubt rushed breakfast, and lastly, his eyes kept nodding off to the side. Clarissa took a step back, surprised to see him so exhausted, "Whoa... you don't look so good! Do you want me to help you to the nurse?"

Cecil shook himself awake and threw on a smile, "Uh, don't be ridiculous, Clarry. I just didn't get much sleep over the weekend. I was busy with one of my AP classes; they had a big project over the weekend. Sleep be damned."

The nerdy girl raised an eyebrow, "But I thought you said the weekend was boring. You never mentioned anything about a project." Her eyes veered down to the papers to see what he was working on. Cecil turned and blocked her sight with his shoulder.

"Well, the assignment itself was really boring. Plus, I just didn't want to talk about it. That's all."

"But..."

"Oh, you know what, I'm thirsty!" He bolted to the door, not even bothering to ask the distracted teacher for permission, "You want anything?"

"Uh, not really?" Without giving her a chance to continue, he was out the door in a flash, leaving a confused Clarissa to simply stand there in her own rumination...

***

A few hours later, lunchtime had hit, and Clarissa and Cecil found themselves sitting with their chaotic group as they laughed, joked, and debated. Oftentimes, with their mouths still full, "Ya'll can't eat any quieter?" She groaned.

One of their burly friends, Keith, just shook his head with a hyped smile, "How can we? With all these stories coming out, it's like skeletons are just dancing out of closets across the world!"

A slender pink-haired girl named Trish announced her favorite story thus far, "Look at this, UzyMack a.k.a. Jeremy Simane was just brought in for questioning after supposed leaked footage got sent to the NSA about him abusing his wife!"

"That's the guy who often bashes the CCU super hard, right? I'll bet Cecil is happy about that." Trish and everyone else in the group looked over to check the chronically online boy, who apparently had no reaction and just sat there gobbling up his spaghetti leftovers from home.

Clarissa scoffed and came to his defense, "That's ridiculous, guys! Cecil may not have been a fan of his claims, but everyone knows this situation sucks overall if it's real!"

"I mean, they got footage, so it must be legit," Cecil said with a shrug, barely even looking up.

"Dude." Clarissa's face almost fell at the nonchalant response. Her eyes wandered again and spotted something in Cecil's sloppily half-zipped backpack. A green and white tablet with the title of ModNote barely visible from the side.

"What's that?"

***

Later that evening, Cecil and Clarissa walked together along the roads that led to their neighborhood, same as always. Though there was a tangible tone shift, "You look mad." Cecil muttered as he caught his friend giving him the side-eye.

"You could call it that. What *is* wrong with you lately? We stayed after school to cheer Keith on at his football game like everyone else, but you were on your phone browsing through replies for most of it!"

"I wasn't on it that much, it's just...I find football a bit predictable. Personally, it never interested me."

"First of all, I had to literally smack you on the shoulder to look up whenever our team scored a touchdown." She pouted, "Second, that's a blatant lie. Does this look like someone who isn't interested in football?"

Just then, Cecil went red in the face as Clarissa whipped out her phone and pulled up a mere month-old picture of him and Zeke together, shirtless, with the school team's initials painted on their chests and screaming to the heavens as Keith scored a touchdown.

She chuckled as Cecil just grumbled, "One of my favorite picks, never getting rid of it." She fake-kissed the photo before her eyes caught someone just barely out of sight, "Hey, who's that?" Just ahead of them, they spotted a man in a black suit sitting slumped across a park bench with his hands clasping his head.

He mumbled: "If this keeps up, I'm ruined."

Against her better judgment, Clarissa approached the man, not having it in her heart to ignore someone so obviously in despair, "Hey, uh, you good?"

He looked up at the two and shushed them, "Leave me alone, kids, I need to think."

***

Cecil looked up from his phone long enough to register the man's face and immediately stepped in between him and Clarissa, "Wait a second... You're Demayo!" He exclaimed with fiery rage.

The man looks up, a little confused, "You know me?"

Though caught off guard by his sudden hostility, Clarissa eventually realized what was going on and joined Cecil in being equally upset, "Now I see it. Roberto Demayo! You're the scum who gave my family restaurant a bad review online! It really put them in a bad spotlight for months."

"Clarissa? Who's-"

"That would be me." She seethed before taking a deep breath and cooling herself, "Well, now that I know who you are. I guess you can at least tell me what's wrong."

"There's no point, I can tell you're still mad at me for giving my honest opinion on things. The fact of the matter is that your mother couldn't make an omelet to save her life."

Clarissa's fists clenched at the chiding remark, even after she was willing to hash out his problems with him. Even though her rage was nothing compared to Cecil's, who stared at the pompous man with near bloodshot eyes. Wasting no time, he whipped out his phone and typed in the critic's name into the search before showing it to his friend's face. Revealing what his career went down the drain for.

Her face went pale. "Abusing animals?"

The critic leaped up to his feet and approached the two angrily, "That's not true! I mean, I'm not the fondest of dogs, but those pictures of me aren't real!"

His pleas fell on deaf ears as Clarissa backed away, "You truly are just a sick man, aren't you. No good food-sense, and now this? Come on, Cecil, I'm not wasting any more time here!"

They quickly left, continuing their walk home as the harsh critic went back into despair on the bench, "I hope the cops get him." She muttered, looking at him one last time.

"Hard agree." Clarisse looked back to say something else but was instead caught off guard by the sight of Cecil looking back at the despaired critic with a smile. A dark grin that Clarissa would struggle to get out of her mind for a long time to come.

Two Weeks Later

Okay, settle down, everyone." The teacher sighed as the students could barely stay still, "Now. I know there have been a lot of scandals and confessions popping up online, but I don't want you to get too caught up in the drama. Some of the stuff depicted is really intense."

"A letter from the principal about online safety will be mailed to all of your homes later this week for your parents' perusal. In addition, I'm sending out an extra copy early for you all to read yourselves throughout the day. Don't even think about trying to toss it away the second you leave the classroom. Every teacher is sending these out, we'll be watching." She stacked the papers accordingly before walking over to Clarissa with them, "Be a dear and pass these out, please? I need to get supplies for today's lesson."

"Sure, Mrs. Nijimura." She nodded and started delivering them one by one.

"Man, is Cecil still gone?" Zeke asked as he took a page.

"Afraid so, I haven't even seen him send anything in group chat for the last few days now." Trish added, "Maybe we should check up on him?"

"Nah, if he's really got the flu like he claims, then he won't want too many people there." Clarissa thought for a moment, "I'll go."

"I've been to his house the most, I know what and what not to touch." She turned back and continued handing out papers to other students as they walked and mingled about, "Even when he was sick, he'd nearly fight to come into school after a few days... what's going on?"

***

After school, she made good on her word and wasted no time pulling up to Cecil's house, "Ah, good afternoon, Clarissa. How has class been? I know Cecil sure has been missing it." His dad asked after popping open the door and letting her in.

He took her backpack and set it on the couch, "Truly odd. A severe case of stomach flu right out of the bat. He's barely been able to leave his room as of late. Well, the doctors said that what his body needed was rest and less stress, so I guess that's a good thing."

"Mr. Silworthy, may I step in and see him for a sec?"

"No need to be so formal here, Clarissa." He chuckled before reaching into a desk and pulling out a bag full of face wear, "Sure, but only for a few minutes, and you'll need to wear this face mask. I don't want you getting sick either."

"Thanks..."

"Cecil?" She knocked on the door before opening, "How are you doing, bud? You haven't been responding to my texts much...I just wanted to check in with-"

She stopped dead in her sentence upon finding the usually neat room littered head to toe with junk and clutter. There on his bed, Cecil sat with multiple screens on and was busy. From his desktop and pad, to his phone and laptop, "Oh, hello there, Clarissa." Cecil greeted, "Welcome to my domain!"

"D-Domain? This place is a pigsty! And look at you, should someone with the flu really be stuck on a bunch of screens like that?"

"It's what helps the time pass as I recover. Come on, sit." He patted a spot on the bed next to her that was riddled with used tissues, which made Clarissa go green in the face. Cecil noticed her discomfort and laughed, "Don't worry, I'll throw those out later. He swatted them off onto the already busy floor.

"That does not help."

"I've been having a lot of fun online lately. My social media accounts have never been livelier! Anyone who tries to start something with me suddenly never says anything after I call them out. Uploaders of those hate-and-vitriol videos are being turned on by their audiences after their actions came out." He kicked back on his bed, "And so much more. It's great!"

The concerned friend just sighed and laid a hand on his shoulder as he typed away, "Cecil, you should focus on getting better over anything else. You missed a science quiz last week and some of our Programming Club meets. Keep that up, and I'll have to draw out the app design without you."

Cecil snickered as he continued typing out a lost post on a forum before softly veering over towards her with bloodshot eyes, "H-Huh, what? Oh, right, well, you've got good art skills. Just do the sketch, and I'll help with whatever when I come back." He then opened another tab and got back to typing.

"Are you even listening?" She grabbed his hand, "Cut that out!"

"Now, how could I do that after having been hit with these two idiots?" He motioned for her to lean over. Completely frustrated and losing patience, she eased her way closer to see the screen properly. Still tense from being in the gross room.

"These two sickos get this hate group to massively downvote me just because I called them out for their complaints being in the minority."

"Are y'all talking about another movie franchise? Dude, just give it a rest! If they want to hate, then they're the ones missing out. You, on the other hand, look like you're missing out on your mental health!"

Cecil shrugs and continues typing away, "I can't just let this slide, Clarry. You remember when that critic destroyed your family's restaurant online? Well, that's the type of pain I feel every day while fighting for my senses on the internet."

"That's not the same, man..." Clarissa sighed before seeing something shiny out of the corner of her eye on his desk, "Hey, what's that?" She leaned over, angling herself above the piles of trash to snatch the ModNote, "I've never seen a pad designed like this."

Cecil ceased his typing and froze as his eyes caught Clarissa's fingers just barely touching the screen of the tablet. That's when he sprang up like a released mattress coil. His bones ached and popped loudly, as it was the first case of sudden action they saw in over a week.

His hand clutched her arm fiercely in a vice grip, "DON'T TOUCH THAT!" He bellowed, staring her down right in the eyes. His own eyes were bloodshot and full of palpable mania that made Clarissa shiver inside.

His grip got tighter and soon Clarissa began to shake outwardly as well, "Cecil... You're hurting me!"

He glowered at her like a feral predator before his senses snapped back. He eased his grip, "S-Sorry..."

Clarissa quickly reeled in her arm and caressed it, praying for it not to bruise. The two stood in silence for a bit before the door popped open and Cecil's father looked in with a concerned expression, "Everything alright in here?"

"Yeah, we're fine." She sighed. " I was just."

"Clarissa was just leaving. It's getting late, and you know how these Miami thunderstorms are." The disheveled boy interrupted while giving her a side-eye.

"Oh yeah, Clarissa, I can give you a ride home before the storm sets in."

She shook her head with an awkward laugh, "O-Oh, that's okay! My brother is actually the one who dropped me off. He'll drive me back."

"Oh, okay, you two stay safe and tell him I said hello!"

He smirked and left.

Clarissa grew saddened as she watched his father walk away. Normally, Cecil is nearly indistinguishable from his positivity. However, the boy before her was nothing like that.

"Well. I'll talk to you later, Cecil."

He didn't even bother to look back and simply waved half-heartedly as he kept typing. Clarissa just sighed and closed the door behind her as Cecil stayed in that position, typing and scrolling away on all of the devices surrounding him until his body gave out a few hours later.

***

The house was dark with nearly no lights on, a clear indicator for Clarissa to sneak in. Using a secret window-picking technique Cecil taught her when they were kids, she slipped right through the slim opening and fell right onto the living room couch. Wasting no time, she eased over to Cecil's door and cracked it open.

She spotted the unkempt boy snoring loudly on his bed with the covers over just half of his body. He was out cold. "Good, he's finally asleep." She eased in and found the tablet right where it was the first time.

"Are you really the cause of all the weird stuff going on lately on ModNote?" she whispered to herself before nabbing it. She powered it on and scrolled through its user interface, not knowing what exactly to look for until stumbling upon the instructions and settings.

"All the restrictions are turned off, but then what?"

She found a section called *Submission History* and clicked on it, revealing a long list of names. Many of which she remembered.

"These are the usernames of people who have been appearing on the news!" She covered her mouth hastily and leaned over to see Cecil still out cold and slumped off the bed. Clarissa sighed gently before continuing to read through the history. Deducing that all who were accused were also subjected to falsely generated stories.

"Wait, does this mean even the footage shown on the news was made by this thing? Who sent him this?" Suddenly, it all clicked, especially with the instructions taken into account. It took everything in her not to curse Cecil's sketchy friend with everything she had.

"This is all his fault!" She whispered angrily, "I knew his dumb ideas would lead to trouble again." She then spotted a roughed-up notebook under Cecil's bed and crouched carefully to snatch it. At first, it was a mess of internet usernames all crossed out for multiple pages. Some, however, were real names of those who happened to share them online, regardless.

Clarissa continued to flip through the crossed-out names before eventually getting to a new page. One full of fresh names with no lines drawn through it. She flipped to find more and more before eventually speeding through constant pages of names. Eventually, the names stopped, but she lost count of how many were written over after the 200th mark.

"Good god. I've got to get this away from Cecil as soon as possible." She gulped as his strange behavior over the past two weeks finally began making sense. The shut-in boy began tossing and turning more fiercely. Clarissa looked over and thought about taking the ModNote and throwing it into the Miami Beach ocean but ultimately decided it was too dangerous to take it from him without a proper plan.

With quick thinking, she returned the tablet and notebook back to where they were and left the room. Bolting out of the house and down the street, terrified at the thought of being tailed by a vengeful psycho hiding within the body of her best friend.

***

The next evening, Cecil was still going strong on his arguments against the two haters, "These absolute slums are really pushing my buttons...what's worse, they've got their whole group of contrarians attacking me!"

His back cracked under the strain of being hunched all day, "If this keeps up, I wouldn't be surprised if they tried to pull a false report to one of the mods and get me banned. All so they can stay in their precious little bubble. The morons!"

He then read a particularly brutal reply that took all the strength he had not to bite his already sore tongue clean off, "They...ow. They didn't need to say that."

He whipped out the ModNote, officially having had enough, "Useless trash." The tablet wasted no time analyzing their usernames and generated a prompt along with some deeply revealing information.

"Interesting, their IP addresses are within this town. They're not too far away." He smirked. With a rugged laugh, he began entering their usernames and rating them. His ability to tell right from wrong and handle decisions in a healthy manner was effectively slipping from his mind.

He smirked and clacked away on his keyboard, "You both get a full ten out of ten on the toxicity ratings...you both are truly disgusting." He chuckled.

He read through the proposed generated justice and read through it quickly, "Oh my. These prompts certainly are interesting!"

He read on, "Wait. This actually looks pretty serious. M-Maybe I shouldn't..." The description of what the two trolls would go through was a disaster. Truly monstrous. So much so that for the first time in days, Cecil began to take some agency.

Suddenly, he felt a strong sting in his eyes and began to rub them, "Ow. Dang, did something get in there?"

"What was I thinking about?" Like a candle being blown out, the few thoughts of his own had been snuffed out in a flash. He shrugged and tapped the submission button, "Oh well, send."

His father called out. "Cecil, time for dinner! I made fries and fish. You're feeling well enough to have that at least, right?"

"Coming, Dad!" His voice was hoarse. Despite his throat having begun to hurt earlier that morning, he couldn't pass up one of his favorite dishes. He arose and reached for the door. Or at least he tried to, as something held his hands back.

He looked down to find long plant-like stems wrapped around his wrists with thorns scraping his skin. Though the pain was fierce, Cecil couldn't find the energy to express it and simply looked at them with a blank face, "What are these?" He tugged at them for a bit before spotting that they originated from the ModNote itself.

Despite his tugging and pulling, it was clear there was no chance of being free. Ultimately, he decided to leave them be and take the tablet along like a lifeline, "Hm... Fine then, guess I'll eat while working."

As he kept the ModNote close, the thorns' pull eased, "That feels better." At that moment, the only thing crossing his mind was how thankful he was that his parents often ate in their room.

***

The next day in school was more of the same for Clarissa, "He's missed another day." She mumbled while looking back at his yet again empty seat.

The thunder of an early morning storm rumbled outside, mixed with the sirens of several police cars gathering not too far from the school. The two combined nearly drowned out the teacher, "Okay, class, today we will." The commotion outdoors intensified.

"What on earth is going on out there?" As she was listening in on the commotion outside, the school PA resounded throughout the entire building

"ATTENTION, MAY ALL FACULTY PLEASE REPORT TO THE MAIN OFFICE FOR A MANDATORY MEETING. PLEASE COME RIGHT AWAY."

"That's a little unorthodox." Mrs. Nijimura turned to her students and put on a reassuring smile, "Well, I'm sure they're just going to discuss some big student prank like earlier this year, no worries. Please review, stay seated, and review pages 46 - 58 until I get back."

The moment the door closed behind her, everyone immediately jumped from their seats. Sprinting towards the window in a crowd to see what the commotion was.

"What's going on?!"

"Move over, I can't see!"

"Hold on, there are ambulances too!"

People pushed and pulled as they tried to get a front row seat.

The commotion was overwhelming. Clarissa just stayed in her seat along with Zeke, who had no interest in rushing past the crowd, "Wow, sounds like some serious stuff is going down." He snickered.

"Yeah." Clarissa gulped, thinking about what she had learned the other night, "I hope it's nothing too big."

After a few minutes, the teacher returned. Everyone bolted back to their seats. "Alright, class, now don't blow my eardrums out over this, but..." Clarissa tensed hard upon hearing her voice that clearly carried a heavy tone. "Due to an incident only a couple of blocks away from here, school will be letting out early."

What followed was an earth-shattering roar of excitement from every single student in the class, along with the same being heard throughout the halls and across the entire school. Every teacher had the same news.

"I said, don't blow my eardrums out!" she growled, "Anyway, the buses have been notified and are on their way. If your parents drive you, please notify them immediately. If you walk, please hurry home as soon as possible."

The teacher went over the safety protocols used in times of emergencies.

Zeke and the nervous girl shared a perplexed glance, "Hold on. School is over at like 10:30 AM? Now that's a new one?"

"Yeah, it is." Clarissa felt the surge of anxiety course through her as her mind took Cecil, the ModNote, and came up with the worst scenarios.

"Come on, let's meet up with the others and try to figure out what's up."

Clarissa sighed and walked off on her own, needing to settle the butterflies in her stomach. "You go on, I'll get a drink from the vending machine and catch up."

***

Clarissa hastily downed half a bottle of grape soda before hearing her name called across the hallway, "Hey there you are!" It was Keith bundled up with her other friends, with their phones out and on the news.

"Keith, what's the matter, you guys?" she asked hesitantly.

"Well, uh...we found out some details on what's happening."

That was when Zeke rushed down the steps, phone in hand and screaming, "THEY'RE DEAD!"

The principal rushed out into the hallway and tried to apprehend him, "Mr. Mackerel! Do not just shout anything out!"

He struggled to get the news out from deep breaths, "The people held up in the apartment down the street...they got gunned down by the cops!"

"What are you talking about?" Clarissa stammered before yanking Zeke away from the principal's clutches and into their group.

"There were two guys held up at a shootout down the road. Apparently, some secrets about them got leaked online to the cops. Really sick stuff!" He showed them the details of the accusations on his phone, and the fearful girl nearly lost her breakfast.

"How do we know it was real?" She asked with a green face.

Zeke shrugged, "We never will. Whatever happened, both were chased into a corner together, and when finally backed up against the wall by the cops, one of them idiotically pulled out a knife and...you can guess what happened."

"More online people? Let me guess, and their usernames were even leaked to the cops as well, huh?"

"Yeah, here they are." He scrolled down the news site that showed the victims' usernames. Clarissa's heart nearly stopped upon reading the familiar IDs.

"Th-those are..."

The principal broke the group apart and called for all attention, "Everyone, when the instructions are to head home. It doesn't mean crowd the halls and gossip!" He then spotted someone scurrying off and turned the corner at sonic speed.

"Look at Clarissa as an example; she's already out of here." Zeke and the others looked back to see nothing more than a half-empty bottle of soda dropped, spilling onto the floor.

***

As fast as her legs could carry her, Clarissa sprinted throughout town. Running through the shopping districts, parks, and even alongside the beach in a desperate hurry to save her best friend. The rain and lightning were in full swing with the dark clouds above casting a shadow almost as dark as the worries she held within, "Cecil, Cecil, please pick up!" His phone failed to reach him. It was as if nature and luck were part of a conspiracy to stop her efforts, but it didn't matter. Her willpower saw to it to save him from the hellish tablet.

"Why? Why did that thing have to end up finding him?" she cried out and, while charging faster throughout the rain, "I knew I should've taken that thing while I had the chance!"

***

The window creaked open as Clarissa used the trick from earlier to slip through, "Cecil?" She whispered before tumbling back, just barely seeing him in the living room with the lights off. With the darkness outside, it was nearly pitch-black inside.

"Good morning, Clare Jones." His voice was dreadfully hoarse, and he remained facing away from her. "Wait, isn't it a little early to be out of school?" He chuckled sinisterly, "My, don't tell me you ditched."

Clarissa did a double-take. Not only was his body language bizarre, but he did something nobody had done in years by using her full name. "Dude, you aren't even talking like yourself. I mean, seriously, if anything, I should be the one asking you questions."

He ruffled his hair, which was already a train wreck of its former style, "Why are you here? If you want to visit, do it after school."

"Well, you see, it already is."

Cecil crouched down, grasping his head as if a horrific migraine suddenly took him over. "What are you talking about?"

The nervous girl slowly inched her way towards him, "There was an incident near the school involving two guys, and they closed early because of it. "Have any idea what that could've been about?"

"Why're you asking me?" His fists clenched with visible veins popping harshly.

"Well." Clarissa gulped hard, wanting to test all her options before going further. "Wait, where are your parents?"

"At work, of course, where else?"

"Well, I guess that was a dumb question." There was no backing out, so she just jumped right in. "Across town, two people got chased into a corner by police, where they fumbled the interaction and got gunned down. These people had the same usernames as the ones you showed me yesterday."

Two green lights instantly shone from his face, illuminating where he was facing, "Oh really, what a coincidence."

"There is no coincidence, Cecil!" she yelled, "Did...did you kill them?"

Though he was still facing away, Clarissa could see the gentle curve of his smile peel upwards, "I don't know what you're talking about."

"Stop lying!" Just barely through the darkness, she was able to spot the ModNote gripped tightly in one of his hands, "People are dead because of that freaky tablet, right?"

"Those guys died?" He rose back to his feet as Clarissa finally mustered up the courage to go all the way.

"I'm taking that tablet from you!" She declared before stomping towards him.

"No, you won't," he warned with a less hoarse, deeper voice.

"Just give it to me, man. This is for the best." She reached out for the tablet and was met with a clutch around her arm.

"You're not going anywhere." He turned towards her, his voice now deep and unrecognizable.

"H-Hey! Let me go, or I'll kick you in the—"

All courage was zapped out of Clarissa when she finally saw Cecil's face. The lightning illuminating the room was enough. What stood before her was a boy with dark black veins popping up on his face, throat, and arms. The iris of his eyes had changed to a deep gray, with his pupils having been warped into a glowing green. His skin was chapped and pale, and his body overall was dreadfully skinny.

Despite looking like a demonic bag of bones and veins that could fall apart any minute, his strength was horrific.

"If you don't stop struggling, I'll break your arm." His voice stretched out in a self-harmonizing double-pitch. His smile widened to a gum-bearing monstrosity, "It wouldn't be hard at all. Right now, your bone feels about as sturdy as a twin in my palm."

It took everything in Clarissa's power not to tear up over the situation, "Who are you? You're not my Cecil!"

"Leave now, girl. If you don't," a thorny vine popped from the ModNote and wrapped around her leg, "I'll break more than just your arm. We wouldn't want Cecil to see you punished, now would we?" He taunted.

"Okay. Let's all be cool here." She slowly eased herself away from the ModNote and eyed Cecil's possessed body with a pleading look. As soon as the grip on her limbs loosened, however, she instantly rushed in with a counterblow, head-butting him in the nose and dazing the boy. Thorny vines exploded from his body and went wild, slicing up everywhere in an attempt to cut

Clarissa. When he came to some modicum of his senses, he saw the room lit up with the light of the open door and no ModNote in sight.

"Get back here, you whelp!" He roared as the blood from his nose and body went flying.

Outside, Clarissa ran as fast as she could. She had only one plan, and if it didn't work, she knew she was as good as dead.

In a reality that seemed closer by the second, Cecil's body was dangling over her as the vines ran like the legs of a giant spider. "You're just as bad as the names online! Always fighting, always hating, spreading nothing but misery and despair everywhere they go!"

She went into full sprint mode, only getting a bit further before a full-strength blow sent her flying through a pair of gates and dazed her onto concrete. Before her vision could even clear, she saw the monstrosity of thorns, blood, and glowing green towering over her, "They're just faceless names. Why do you care? They'd all be better off dead for our sakes!"

She coughed as the rain pelted her face, "If you've let those faceless names infuriate you this much, then they've already won!"

"Shut up!" He eyed the ModNote in her grasp with pure mania, "Those scumbags that died were subjected to my very first 10 out of 10 rating. I wonder...if I were to give more people a 10, would they be tricked into peril as well?" He smirked with deep desire."

He attempted to grab it, but she refused to let go, "Cecil, don't!" Clarissa pleaded.

"Cecil isn't here anymore, you ignorant girl!" He raised his hand, commanding a bundle of vines to latch around her neck. Clarissa clutched at them, fighting off the attack, "And maybe it's time you leave as well, for good."

She kicked and turned, slowly losing the fight before the tablet was finally ripped from her hands. He laughed in victory before preparing to type down one of the thousands of names he had spent the last 36 hours committing to memory.

He typed in the first name and prepared to hit submit when something crashed into his face. The boy fell back onto the concrete, his head now even more of a red and black mess. "What was that?" He looked around to find a basketball bouncing near one of Clarissa's hands, which had stopped struggling against the vines.

The boy's anger swelled, infuriated that she would use the last few seconds of her life for a cheap shot like that. However, as the rhythm of the bouncing continued, something reawakened within his mind. In a short moment, for just an instant, Cecil's eyes returned to their original color, and his voice reverted ever so slightly, "A basketball. H-How long has it been?"

"Huh?" Clarissa asked hoarsely as the vines held their ground.

"That basketball. The court." In that moment, just there and then, humanity appeared to return to Cecil."

"Clarry?" He dropped the tablet as he studied the basketball courtyard where they had spent so many of their precious days together.

The vines weakened, and the girl took her chance, leaping from death's doorstep, "Sorry , man, but I have to do this." She grabbed the tablet and smashed his already messed-up face for the third time that morning, knocking him out completely.

***

A rhythmic beeping solely brought Cecil into consciousness, "Where am I...?" He spoke up before grabbing his still terribly sore throat.

Half his face was bandaged up. He was barely able to see Clarissa walk into his view. "Miami Central Hospital. Your parents are on their way." She also had a few bandages around her leg and arm. Though what really caught Cecil off guard were all the dirt stains on her outfit.

"Clarrisa. What happened to me? What day is it? I just remember staying at home more often because I wasn't feeling well." He recalled the past couple of weeks with as much detail as he could, "I was trying out the device I found online, you remember when I told you about that, right? It was interesting at first, but I can't remember much after that."

Clarissa just nodded and handed him a phone, "Check the date."

"I think your phone is busted. Ain't no way I was sick for weeks!"

Clarissa's expression fell with pain as she described everything that happened.

"I... I see." Cecil bit his lip, confusion and guilt wracking him for the crime of threatening his close friend.

"I'm sorry for all of that. "The last thing I remember was Keith's football game and writing names down then. After that, things start to get hazy. Almost as if I was blacking out." He thought long and hard, "I think that was the case. I wouldn't even believe myself had I not just seen it, but it looks like the ModNote possessed you somehow."

Clarissa just grumbled and sat on the edge of the bed next to his foot and lightly smacked it, "Why did you order that thing anyway?"

"My buddy said..."

She slapped his other foot, "Oh, I am absolutely adding this to his track record. Would it have killed him to at least look up a review before he recommends something?"

"I thought it would make social media more bearable...sometimes it feels like I can't enjoy anything because there's always someone fighting me." He slumped back and groaned in frustration, "No matter what, it's like I'm being cyberbullied from every direction."

"Cecil, you probably weren't able to hear me earlier, so I'll say it again."

"If you're letting people online get to you to the point of all...THIS!" She gestured to all of him, "Then they have already won."

"What if someone else found out about the ModNote and connected you to those two deaths before me , huh? Then you'd probably get caught in hot water, all because of that damn thing taking advantage of you."

Cecil nodded somberly, "Where is it anyway?"

"Well, after I called an ambulance to come and get you, I dug a massive ditch out in a place I won't disclose and buried that thing." She gently caressed his cheek, which slowly saw the dark marks fade, "It looks like the farther away it is from you, the faster you can heal from it."

She chuckled and eyed her dirty fit, "So you can now see why I look like I just hugged a pig."

"Well, I guess that makes sense." Cecil smiled before noticing Clarissa thinking more and more.

"But honestly, I've been thinking about it while on the bus here, and I'm not so sure it was the best idea."

"What do you mean? We need to get rid of that thing! It took me over."

"Yeah, because you let it feed off your emotions." She thought to herself more, "I've got a confession to make. I snuck into your room the other night. I also noticed you removed all the restrictions. That was an intentional trap, and you fell for it!"

Cecil fell silent and let his head droop down.

"By letting you take the restrictions down yourself instead of never having them, it was like willfully submitting to the ModNote's desires. If we just get rid of it, what changes?"

Cecil grumbled as Clarissa went on with her epiphany, "What are you saying? That I go and use the same thing that almost killed you? The thing that almost ruined my life?"

"How do I know you won't just order another once everything has calmed down?"

The paranoid teen quickly froze and went quiet yet again.

"You need to face this head-on, Cecil. Or else there will always be people taking control of you in some way."

He sucked his teeth and turned away from her under, "What do you even suggest I do then?"

"Nothing now, but when your body is all healed up, I've got a plan."

A knock on the door caught their attention before a nurse came in, "Cecil, your parents just arrived and are on their way to see you."

After she left, Clarissa leaned in and whispered, "If anyone asks, say you sneezed so hard from your flu that you fell out a window. That's what I told the doctors."

"Okay." He nodded before seeing her one last time as she walked away, "Oh, and Clarry?"

She looked back with a raised eyebrow, "Thanks for everything. I'm glad you're here with me in the real world."

She simply smiled warmly with a faint blush and nodded before leaving.

***

ONE MONTH LATER

Cecil was now back to his fully healthy and normal self, checked out a particularly nasty comment ranting about a post he made," So what do you think, buddy, should we act?"

Clarissa stared down the comment intensely from her spot on a bean bag chair, "Hm...it might not be worth dealing with. Maybe just check the replies to see what else he said."

Cecil did just that and nearly spat out his soda, "Whoa uh...I think everyone here might need a little reporting." He read the replies to the original comment and could barely keep from laughing at how needlessly awful it all got.

"What makes you say that?" The first thing her eyes landed on was a racist word that somehow didn't result in an instant filter.

She sighed and checked the user's own blog page, "Seriously? How has this guy's account been gaining followers? He's spreading hate!"

"Shall we?" Cecil asked again.

"Do it."

From across the desk, Cecil grabbed a slick red, white, and blue tablet. Similar to the ModNote but with safer options and possession-free.

"Very well, I give him a tough but fair 3 out of 5." He typed the name of the offending user in and submitted.

"Excellent, glad we were able to remove the second half of the options."

Cecil smirked, "I gotta admit, when you recommended we use our resources to rework the ModNote into something actually healthy, I was a little shocked. But hey," He held out the beautiful and reconstructed tablet, "The thing that took me over still hasn't come back, so I guess it's finally gone."

Well, since this just hacks the offending user's personal emails with warnings until they take down their bad content, I doubt it's something a demon or whatever that thing was would be interested in." Clarissa crossed her arms, proud of their work, "Good thing we were able to rent out the Programming club in private for a while. Our prototype is almost perfect!"

"Who knew spaghetti code could be so effective in preventing possessions?" He chuckled, embarrassed, "Anyway, I guess it needs a name."

He held it closely and thought, "I think I'll call it... C.L.A.R.R.Y."

Clarissa just busted out laughing, "Why that name? What's it even stand for?"

"I don't know. I just wanted to name it off of something reliable." He smirked, "Someone who brings joy to me."

The nerdy girl's face went red with a fierce blush, "S-Stop it! Don't say stuff like that..." She tried to hold back a smile.

"Why? W-What are you thinking?" Cecil added, now his turn to hide a smile and deep blush.

The two laughed together for a moment before Cecil's dad threw open the door with a suspicious look, "Hm...that sounds like you two should no longer be left in a room alone, giggling."

"Hey- Dad!" Cecil groaned, "Get out of here!"

He made an 'I'm watching you gesture to Clarissa' before the two cleared their throats and tried to change the subject. Still, however, unable to get rid of their blushes.

"I guess next we should work on a backup plan, should people still not listen after getting warning messages from us."

Cecil thought for a bit before snapping his fingers victoriously, "Just spam the mods of the website until they take action, then. Why should we do all the work?"

She jotted down the idea on her To-Do List before hopping up and stretching her back, "Sweet, let's go play ball now. I've spent enough time on the internet."

He grinned, "You don't know how happy I am to hear those words."

Cecil set the tablet aside and shut off most of his screens. He quickly switched into his sweats and headed where he met up with Clarissa again at the court. Happily playing ball till sunset.

Free from the thorny cyber-binds of online toxicity.

THE LITTLE PEOPLE

BY MICHAEL ERROL SWAIM

If you think there isn't anything to worry about in the woods, think again. Especially at night when it gets super dark, and you can really hear all the noises of the forest. Do you know what those noises are? Most of them are harmless creatures, but do you know what it means when the noises stop? When the insects, birds, and frogs stop singing and chirping? No? Well, I do. It means that something more dangerous than you is out there. Probably bigger too, and with lots of sharp teeth. So, if you are out in the woods, day or night, and it gets super quiet, run. As fast as you can.

DO NOT stop running either. Go back the way you came. Scream and yell, anything to try and scare whatever is chasing you away. Hopefully, an adult will hear you and come to help, but if you are alone, just don't stop. Don't even look back. That will just slow you down and give the creature or whatever it is a chance to catch up. Hopefully, you can run fast and far enough that you will make it out of the woods safely. If not, well…I'm sorry.

I know, I know. What a dumb story, right? Let me fill you in on something that happened to my best friend and me recently. I doubt you will believe it, but it might save your life someday. Believe me, there are more than just bugs and squirrels and cute little rabbits out there. There are things in the dark that people see but don't live long enough to tell the tale. Myths, legends, fairy tales, urban legends, or whatever you want to call them. I wasn't a believer at first, either, until I was nearly killed by a race of creatures that most people haven't even heard of. I'll tell you all about it, of course, but first, a little background information about my family and me is necessary for you to understand the story I'm about to tell you.

This all started not long after my grandpa passed away under mysterious circumstances when I was young, and it was a challenging time for the whole family, especially Grandma. Let me tell you, it was rough. Everyone was really sad for a long time after. Especially considering the shape he was in when it happened. He was located in the forest at the bottom of a cliff, on a pile of rocks near Lake Eucha (pronounced oo-chee), close to Jay, Oklahoma, the small town I live in. He was really banged up, like something had mauled him, like a bear. The thing about that is, there aren't normally bears around here. It's exceedingly rare. We don't have a lot of big animals that can do that.

Lake Eucha is usually a beautiful place, until that day they found Grandpa. Now I know it holds a dark secret that needs to be told, and I will never look at it the same. The lake is surrounded by hills full of trees with an abundance of deer and other wildlife, and plenty of fishing and camping areas. The good spots are harder to get to, and if someone doesn't show you where they are, you'll never find them. So, people keep their fishing spots to themselves and hope that no one ever finds them. Which is why those guys were upset when they found Grandpa. They had to give away the location of their secret fishing spot, and of course, the news was all over it. People from town kept coming around, too, trying to see where the old man got killed. It was sad. It was depressing for me, and for all my family, I would imagine.

The sad part is, Grandpa isn't the only one who was found out there like that. They find bodies out there by the lake all the time, now it seems like. The police chalked grandpa's death up to him being drunk and falling off the cliff. For them, it was an open-and-shut case, but not my Nani. She never would accept it. Grandpa hardly ever drank beer and went to the lake as much as

Grandma would let him. He would have known his way around. In fact, he knew the whole area around the lake. He grew up in Jay and lived in the area his whole life. Our ancestors made the journey a long time ago on the Trail of Tears, and I guess our family just loved it here and stayed.

Grandpa knew every nook and cranny of Lake Eucha and the surrounding area. He knew the water, the forests, all the good fishing spots. Nani knew that. She swore it wasn't an accident and assumed something or someone had killed him. Every day, she went out to the spot where he was found. As a kid, I thought she was trying to be closer to him, trying to commune with his spirit or something. I was wrong.

Turns out she was doing her own investigation. We all thought she was nuts at the time. Oops. Anyway, she would scour the surrounding area where they found grandpa, looking for clues or any hint that would point her in the direction of some kind of explanation for his death. Day after day, she went out there. He was found next to his fishing gear and his favorite camp chair, close to the water. A spot he usually went to fish in solitude. It was his favorite place. I liked it too. He took me there a few times. It's a peaceful place. At least he died in a place he loved doing his favorite thing. I thought Nani would never stop going there. We missed her. She was gone all day, it seemed like. For more than a year, she went out there and looked around, looking for anything that could have been overlooked. She never found anything. I would have been surprised if she did.

Then one day everything changed. Grandma came home early, and from then on, she was different, more like she used to be. She had come home white as a sheet, and my mom could never get her to tell what frightened her so. Grandma only went out there one more time about a week later. Something had happened that day, or she saw something, but would never talk about it. We all speculated, of course, but we never realized that we already knew the truth, in a way. I was glad she stopped going out there, though. We certainly ate better when she was home. The only thing we kids knew how to make was pancakes and grilled cheese. My mom was a terrible cook. She was hardly ever home anyway, and Dad was working all the time back then, so we had to rely on ourselves while Grandma was gone.

Not long after the day she came home scared and white as a sheet, she started spending more time with us kids and teaching us stuff. She would often have us go out and collect blackberries and huckleberries, and she would show us how to make pies and cobblers and other sweet stuff like that. She made sure to tell us not to go near the lake, though. Every time. Grandma was extra firm on that rule. We learned how to cook all kinds of stuff, too. Not just desserts. She taught us how to make her famous frybread once, and then we wanted to make it all the time. Sometimes she would read to us at night, to help us fall asleep, I guess. I have some good memories of those times.

That's probably why I like to read so much these days. We heard all kinds of books. When we got older, we would sometimes read them to her. There were westerns, scary stuff, fantasy, and plenty about our Cherokee heritage. At the time, I thought those stories were so boring, but I listened anyway. It made her feel good. She told my cousins and me the same stories over and over. We learned about how the world was made, the Creator, Jistu (jeese-doo), the trickster rabbit, the Thunderers, the Stoneclads, and many others. I found out later that some of the stories were, in fact, lessons.

Storytelling was also her way of filling that hole in her heart that Grampa's death had caused. It's a Cherokee tradition, with stories passed down from generation to generation. She had heard everything she told us from Grandpa, who heard from his father, and so on. Stretching back into the old days. Now that I am older, I feel I must continue the tradition, only I'm not much of an orator; my preferred method is pen and paper, or finger and keyboard. It's the only way I can tell stories. I have too much anxiety when it comes to speaking in front of groups of people. It freaks me out.

The last time I saw Nani, just before she died at a ripe old age of ninety-two, she told me a new version of a story, about the Little People, or in Cherokee, Yunwi Tsusndi (yun-wee joon-stee). It was her favorite. I heard it so many times. This time it was different, though. I thought it was her being delirious as she was close to the end. First, she told me the same old story about the Little People, then she got real quiet and serious. She then told me that my grandpa was killed by them that day at the lake and warned me to be careful in the woods there. He had to have been, she said, because the last day she went out to the lake, she saw them herself. Grandma said to always respect them and leave offerings out at night for them, like she always did. It was the only way to keep them happy. There was a place on her mantle above the fireplace in her house where she left little treats and trinkets out at night. She left them on a small silver tray in front of a little wooden dollhouse.

She went to be with our ancestors the next day, and I had to go to another funeral. This one was a cheerier affair, as Grandma was old, and we knew it was her time to go. What happened to Grandpa was sudden and took everyone by surprise, so it was more of a shock. Lots of crying happened then. Not so much this time. It was more of a celebration of Nani's life than anything. It was about a week after that when I decided I wanted to go out there to grandpa's old fishing spot and look around, see for myself what it was like. I had never been out there in all my thirty-four years. I figured it was time. I didn't really believe in all that stuff about the Little People being responsible for grandpas' death. In fact, I didn't believe in them at all.

My friend Skipper and I made plans to go out there together. I really didn't want to go out there by myself. I mean, that place is kind of sacred to me, and it felt creepy going there myself, so Skipper came along. His real name is Byron, but I call him

Skipper because he was in the Navy. I think it's hilarious. He hates it. He used to tell me this story about how one time he was helping load the refrigerators with frozen ground beef, and he didn't turn around in time, and got knocked out. Knocked out by frozen hamburger. Hilarious. I wish I could have seen it.

So, we went out to the lake. I remember Skipper drove his old Jeep because my car was in the shop. It was a bumpy ride, but it was a nice summer day. Not too hot with a gentle breeze, and we parked at the campground nearest to grandpa's spot, got out, and started walking through the forest. It wasn't far, but there wasn't really a path, so we had to blaze our own trail up and down hills, through the underbrush and forest debris to get there.

Minutes later, we were making our way up a rocky hill when we encountered three tiny, hand-sized houses huddled together in a small rock alcove. In front of them were various treats on the ground: gummy worms, a Twinkie, and other sugary snacks. Everything looked new. Oh boy. I knew what it was. Skipper didn't. It made me slightly nervous.

"What is that?" he asked, pointing at the houses.

I remembered that one time, when grandma had come here a week after grandpa died, and I wondered if she had put the houses there. I got even more nervous at the thought, and the tracks on the ground meant that other people had been out here recently.

"Those are houses for the Little People, and other hikers or travelers have left offerings for them," I replied.

"The Little People?"

"It's a Cherokee legend my grandma used to tell me. Allegedly, they are small people who live in the woods near bodies of water. They can't be seen unless they want to be seen and are usually nice and sometimes help Cherokees in their time of need. They have magical powers and will violently punish those who disrespect them."

"You're kidding, right?"

"No, people really believe in them."

"Really? You don't believe it, do you? I mean, come on, it's like the Easter Bunny or Santa Claus, not real."

I didn't know what to say. Being out here, seeing this after all those years of Grandma telling me to make sure and leave something out for the Little People, all came back to me, and I started thinking. What if she was right? I didn't want Skipper to think I was a wuss, though, so I half lied about it.

"No, but I grew up hearing about it. I mean, it's just stories parents and grandparents tell to keep kids in line."

"Are they supposed to be that small?"

"The Little People are supposed to be knee-high. These little houses are just symbolic, I guess."

Before I could stop him, Skipper stomped on the houses, smashing them. He kicked the remains down the hill. In the back of my mind, I could hear my grandmother lecturing me, and I wondered if I should say something to him. That's when I noticed that all the sounds of the forest had gone silent. No birds, no bugs, no squirrels running around. Oh no.

I opened my mouth to say something when Skipper laughed and bent down to pick up the Twinkie and quickly opened it. Just as he began to take a bite, a small figure appeared in front of me, looking angrily at the damage Skipper had caused. He dropped the Twinkie. Oh, no. Oh, wow. It's them. The Little People. They really are real.

"Skipper," I said calmly.

"I know, man. I see it." He whispered.

I was shaking. I had never been more afraid. I couldn't believe it. It was one of them. It had to be. The creature before me resembled a knee-high man with long hair that cascaded down to the ground. Its clothes looked like they were woven from moss and adorned with small feathers and little stone arrowheads. I was closest to it, and it waved a tiny hand toward me in a weird motion, and my body went rigid. I quickly fell backward to the ground with a loud thump. I tried to cry out, but no sounds came out. I tried to move, but nothing worked. My mind was intact, but I couldn't move my muscles. I lay there and kept trying to move my arms and legs, but nothing worked. I was paralyzed. I began to panic. The creature turned its attention to Jared, who was slowly backing away. It jumped on his shoulder, shrunk down to the size of a dragonfly, and tried to crawl in his ear. It must be saving me for later. Skipper was wildly swiping his hands at it and made a connection. The creature cried out and fell to the ground, stunned.

Suddenly, I could move again. I stood up and began to run. Skipper followed suit, but he was much slower than me. I looked back to see him clawing his ear and screaming in pain as his left eye began to redden and swell, and it burst as the creature emerged from the socket. He fell to the ground. I screamed and kept running. It was coming for me now. I could hear its little wings flapping.

I ran like my life depended on it, which it did. I went back as fast as I could, the way we had come from toward the campground. There were tons of people there when we pulled up and parked earlier. As I ran, I tried to remember what Grandma told me about them. She said they only reveal themselves to one person at a time. Hopefully, with more people around, it would be safe if I made it to the car. Then hopefully the creature would slink back to wherever it came from. I looked back again, and it snarled and jumped at me just as I burst through the foliage and almost crashed into a tent.

A man standing nearby, putting a lure on a fishing rod, saw me explode through the trees. Must have been his tent. I stopped next to him and put my hands on my knees, panting from the exertion, trying to catch my breath. I made it. I was alive.

"Are you ok, man?" he asked.

"Is it still there?" I replied after I caught my breath.

"Is what there?"

"The Little People, one of them was chasing me. They killed my friend."

He laughed at me. Not just a little laugh, he put his hands on his hips, leaned his head back, and laughed heartily.

"Are you nuts? The Little People aren't real, dude. There is nothing back there. Weirdo." He said when he stopped laughing.

He went back to his fishing pole. When he looked away, I dared to glance back at the edge of the forest, and I saw a tiny pair of glowing eyes staring at me menacingly from the forest. The eyes grew as the creature went back to its normal size, and it slowly backed further into the woods until I could no longer see it. I sighed. I was safe.

Now listen, ever since that happened to me, I've never been back to that forest at Lake Eucha. I'm not saying you shouldn't ever go there. It's a beautiful place. Go check it out sometime. I will warn you, however, if you go there and you see signs of the Little People like me and Skipper did, have some respect. Leave them alone. Be nice. It may save your life.

EDGAR EVIL EYE

BY NEIL SANZARI

"Day of wrath and doom impending,
David's word with Sibyl's blending,
Heaven and earth in ashes ending."
–Dies Iraes

Ethiopia, Africa.

Almost seven weeks to the day since Pentecost.

"Sister Salammbô," says Magreth, a 7-year-old albino orphan girl, who just so happens to be under my sworn protection, "How is it that it's so dark outside? I can't even see my own hands in front of my face."

The initial part of an obscure biblical prophecy had been fulfilled when the great black cloud of cosmic proportions that you sent our way as a chastisement, composed solely of dark matter, enveloped the entire Solar System.

***

No moon, and no stars,
Not even a sliver
No moon, and no stars,
Not even a flicker,

***

"No worries, my dear," I tell the child, "You will see just fine when the lights get turned back on. Your eyes are okay, I assure you. It is just the long night come to stay with us for a while like an unwanted houseguest. But mind you, it'll just be for a while. Then everything should go back to normal, I promise you. Now let go of my hand just for a second, please, while I relight this candle, but stay very close to me. It was just the occasional breeze that put the candle out in the first place. I have plenty of matchsticks left in the tinderbox in my pocket for such an occasion. And then with the candle relit, I promise you, and your little brother too, that we will be on our way once again."

"I am not her little brother," says Godfrey, "I'm her big brother. Our dearly departed mother told me how I was born first, 'just before the cock crowed,' she said, 'and then Magreth was born sometime later, much later. After daybreak in fact.'"

It was then and only then that the seers knew for certain that the Three Days of Darkness had finally come to pass. But of course, by then, the whole world had been made witness to this horrific miracle of yours.

***

Nothing to illuminate
This long and terrible
Night with save for
The tiny flame that
Dances to the beat
Of a drum along
The wick of my
Beeswax candlestick,

***

I dig for a matchstick out of the tinderbox in my pocket and strike it against the flint on the side of the box, feeling my way in the dark, taking care not to burn the twins, who are huddling next to me as I do so. And even though I cannot see the tiny flame just yet, its sulphureous fumes immediately run up my nostrils and sting my sinuses, making me cough, and I wince at a slight headache beginning. And the matchstick falls out of my hand before I can bring it towards the candlewick in this still, as yet complete darkness.

***

Yes, a drum
Matching the beat

Of my thundering
Heart being played out
Just beyond the jungle's
Perimeter,

***

Time has become a strange thing under this heaviest of palls encapsulating the earth. A thing incalculable unless we have visual points of reference to go by. I can no longer tell one minute from the next in this terrifying condition unless I hold onto the finer details of what's going on around me. I want to scream, but I can't afford to lose my temper in front of the children. I have to let go and let God.

***

Mauvais Œil d'Edgar
Stares back at you all
Fishy-eyed from
The pervading darkness,
Yes, all invasive, he is,
Creeping around in
There with you
Within this vile
Claustrophobic
Dimension of
Crude matter in a
Formless embodiment
Of that most potent of
Evils–made real,

***

So, I dig for another match out of the tinderbox in my pocket and strike it against the flint on the side of the box. Again, taking care not to burn the children huddling next to me as I do so. And this time around, I also make sure to turn my head away in order to dodge the sulfurous fumes as best I can. And even though the lit matchhead stings my fingertips but good, with the flesh and fingernails beginning to get crispy like bacon on the grill, oh yes, I just caught a whiff of it still. OUCH! I dare not let go until the lit candlewick can suddenly come into view. Shocking the world around us by spreading its visibility to the farthest corners of this strangely silent enclosure of the jungle, finding its way up the side of a mountain, as if the toggle of a light switch has just been thrown.

***

Capable of
Cannibalizing your
Living soul with his
Dried-up tongue lashing
Out from within
The confines of his
Coffin-mouth,
Coughing up a dry
Heave, screaming
All broken-toothed
And diseased, the
Scream is a silent
Pale fart of a thing
With the commotion
Of baby spiders
Wearing dirty diapers,

***

And even now in the ultimate darkness just beyond the beeswax candle's circle of influence, I can see the dread hyena man peering at us as if from a gun-slit window in between the thick tangle of buffalo thorn and sycamore fig, and his crown is irregular in the eerie illumination of the candle.

***

Being loosed upon
The world from their

Freshly-hatched eggs
Looking like blind eyes
In their swollen orbits
With the extraocular muscles
Twitching, and the lacrimal
Glands weeping, bursting,
And then writhing,

***

It is just as I suspected. The hyena man has been shadowing our every move. I can see him now only with the piercing light cast by the candle.

Father Everest blessed the candle for us in its tarnished dish just before we fled the Port of Djibouti earlier today.

***

Yes, his mouth is a
Primeval cavity
Like the maw of a lamprey
Tattooed with
Lascaux paintings
From top to bottom
And loaded up with
Many a cobweb,
Giving shelter to
Myriads of fledgling
Parasites,

***

Oh, my dear sweet Jesus, where is your inexhaustible compassion now when we need it the most? Where is that living water of yours, we so crave?

***

The mother of this
Brood of thousands
Stands poised like
An esteemed conductor

Ready to launch
Her orchestra into
The blaze of a
Symphonic operetta
Corresponding
Directly with the
Threshold
Between spheres,

***

Now, I am being even more careful with my handheld to protect the flame lest the occasional breeze snuff the candle out once again. There is always one more trap door lying in wait for the unsuspecting soul, because this could turn into something even more catastrophic than it already is. I keep my eye on the children as they walk beside me. The grade is getting steeper as we begin to scale the mountainside. I do not wish to frighten them by telling them about the hyena man being so close at hand. Well, not just yet, as I begin to smell the rancid decay that is undeniably his. And he brings flies with him to taste of our flesh.

***

Where a serpent
Of vast girth does
Make the tunnels
Quake below with
Dust falling from
The rafters with
Its swift passage
This puff daddy adder
With the hide
Of Leviathan and
It's rumblings to
And from
Similar to that
Of a subway train

Making a racket
Upon its tracks going
Clackity clack,

***

"What's that smell?" says Magreth, while pinching her tiny nose, "And these flies! I'm getting bitten alive here!"

And Godfrey says, "Me too."

The hyena man's orange-yellow eyes reflect our honey-colored candlelight, and yet the orphans remain unaware of him. But for how long?

In the meantime, we are making poor time by foot following the railroad tracks up through this treacherous path carved into the mountainside to reach the Church of Our Lady, Mary of Zion's renowned Albino Asylum in Addis Ababa. We only have a few more hours to go.

Now, the hyena man is just one of many of Mauvais Œil d'Edgar's minions. I saw him earlier on the train, but only for a moment just before everything went dark.

Only the light of beeswax candles can penetrate the dark matter surrounding us, permeating the very air we breathe. Just the sheer claustrophobia alone of being trapped within this total pitch-black darkness is guaranteed to give a great percentage of folks across the globe heart failure.

***

Like a tapeworm
Strangling your
Ulcerated digestive
Tract, Swiss cheesed
With primordial
Black holes,
Speaking in tongues,
Looking down the barrel of
Smooth bore vs rifled
Consuming its own

Tail in the wake
Of your existential
Crisis, the oubliette's
Ouroboros,

***

The hyena man was sitting in the car behind ours. Unabashed by his dappled fur amid the telltale stripes from head to toe. None of the other passengers would sit in the same car with him. He had clearly made a spectacle of himself. And apparently, he didn't care one way or the other. Not even the wide-eyed conductor would dare tread foot in the car where the hyena man sat fidgeting. And the conductor went on and on about a tsetse fly having taken a sizeable chunk out of the back of his hand.

The folklore of this wasteland is steeped in so many rich tales of magical beasts and otherworldly happenings from shapeshifters to ufo's right alongside the harsh reality of nature's primeval savagery. And so, hyena men in general are a dime a dozen, as a certain laconic cousin of mine back in Chicago would say.

What makes this hyena man so unique is that he works for the witch-doctor, Mauvais Œil d'Edgar.

When the hyena man steps out of the thick cover of buffalo thorn and sycamore fig carpeting the mountainside, he takes his time walking towards us, tripping over exposed roots along the way as if in a dream, sleepwalking. And I ask God to lift the curse from the man in Jesus' mighty name, and he just falls down at my feet on the ground, writhing in agony. Bellowing like a hippopotamus in heat.

***

And you feel that
Awful ache in your
Gut, the same one
You have felt all
Your life watching

The clock ticks away
Those precious minutes,
Lost to time
Wasted like glittering
Bejeweled droplets
Of water
Resembling
Precious stones spilt,
Strewn carelessly upon
A Desert floor
Like tiny fragments
Of ground-up glass
Sparkling in the mix
Under the blaze
Of a white-hot Sun,

***

But then, finally, a calm comes over his curled-up form in the fever grasses swirling about in ominous spirals, wearing naught but a soiled loincloth and the unmistakable drapery and scarification of a Maasai warrior, and clutching a spear to boot. A spear that hadn't been there all the while, whilst he'd been dogging our trail as the hyena man. And this rogue warrior begins to snore away peacefully after such a long, arduous journey as the monster.

And before I can keep the children back at a safe distance, the ever-inquisitive Godfrey and Magreth approach the haunted man. They get too close to his face in such an endearing manner, with their shadows being made to play over the man's features and theirs as well, in the delicate firelight made by the candle that I'm still holding just to see his reaction at being healed by the Lord. Oh my God, how precious they are. If it is your will, I would love to raise them up myself with your help, of course.

***

And your dried-up tongue

Lashes out from
Within the confines
Of your coffin-mouth,
Coughing up a dry heave,

***

"Oh, my goodness, Sister Salammbô," says Magreth, "he is just like us."

"Yes," says Godfrey, "he is an albino just like us, but why does he only have one arm now instead of two?"

***

Screaming all broken-
Toothed and diseased,
The scream is a silent
Pale fart of a thing
With the commotion
Of baby spiders
Wearing dirty diapers,

***

Before the curse was lifted just now, the hyena man had both of his arms intact. But once he had been made to transform back to normal by the healing power of the Holy Spirit, his right arm had vanished suddenly, with only the dwindling vestiges of a limb left in its wake.

***

Being loosed upon
The world from their
Freshly-hatched eggs
Looking like blind eyes
In their swollen orbits
With the extraocular muscles
Twitching, and the lacrimal
Glands weeping, bursting,
And then writhing,

***

According to legend, there has only been one albino of distinction in all the world admitted into this select tribe of lionslayers. Could this be him? Can this really be my Othman, the sweet boy from my childhood, all grown up now?

***

No moon, and no stars,
Not even a sliver
No moon, and no stars,
Not even a quiver,

***

"Wake up, mister!" says Godfrey, "Hurry, we must reach the Church of Our Lady, Mary of Zion's Albino Asylum in Addis Ababa before the beeswax candle runs out on us for good. It is a good thing that we are almost there."

The sound of hot wax dripping onto my slippers from the candle dish and sizzling thereupon offers punctuation to what the little boy has just said.

"Please wake up, sir, before it's too late!" says Magreth.

***

Nothing to illuminate
This long and terrible
Night with save for
The tiny flame that
Dances to the beat
Of a drum along
The wick of my
Beeswax candlestick,

***

And with this chorus loud enough to wake up the dead, the man finally stirs, clutching his spear still, and looks straight up into my eyes with his one brown eye, and the other blue, unmistakably Othman's, and says with the faintest of smirks, "Is it true what they say about you, Sister? That you wield the Covenant of old as well as the new?"

"Don't be so dramatic," I say in return, "you already know the answer to that one."

***

Yes, a drum
Matching the beat
Of my thundering
Heart being played out
Just beyond the jungle's
Perimeter,

***

"What happened to your arm, sir?" says Magreth. "Why do you have just one instead of two like everyone else?"

***

Addis Ababa, Ethiopia,
The Church of Our Lady,
Mary of Zion, we were
Down in the cellar
Playing Hide and Seek,
While the monk said Mass
In the chapel upstairs
And I swear that I saw
When I first stepped inside
Of the Church of Our Lady,
Mary of Zion, I was peeking in
When I saw the Baby
Jesus being held down
By the monk on the altar
Breaking Him up into
Such tiny, little pieces,
So that the congregation
Could partake of his flesh
As He willingly surrendered
Himself up for those
In attendance,

***

"Oh," says Othman, "that is because Mauvais Œil d'Edgar stole it from me when I was just a little boy. He wants to live forever, and the only way he can do that is by eating little albino children like you and your brother. He cooks them up in a very special soup for himself. A very special soup indeed. But in my case, he did not consume my arm. He made a magic wand out of it instead. A powerful fetish to ward off his enemies with. It is one of his most potent weapons as a spiritual warrior from the dim past, because you see, he is very old. How old? I cannot say for certain, but he has hinted at having been a Vizier for the Pharaoh in the days of Moses, of whom he came into conflict a very long time ago.

"Meanwhile, this is a great honor for him to have taken my arm to protect himself with. You should see the hieroglyphics tattooed throughout the tiny limb's short length from elbow to fingertip. Mauvais Œil d'Edgar is such a great man. I am eternally grateful to him for having bestowed this most esteemed honor upon me."

***

Othman was "it"
And I pulled the curtains
To get away from him,
So, I could find a good
Hiding place, and that
Was when I found the Ark
Of the Covenant with its lid
Slightly ajar just enough
For a young teen like me
To hide herself inside of,
But the lid was far too heavy
For me to seal the Ark shut with,
And I started to feel like

I had butterflies in my stomach
When the Ark of the Covenant
Suddenly sealed itself
Shut,

***

"Ohh, Sister Salammbô!" says Magreth, "What are we going to do? Mr. Othman says the witch-doctor is going to eat us all up!"

"Yes," says Godfrey, chiming in, "Othman says Mauvais Œil d'Edgar is going to eat us all up!"

***

I screamed for Othman
To help me lift the lid of
The Ark of the Covenant,
And he was right there
For me but he told me
Through the lid I could
Barely hear him that it
Was far too heavy for
Him and I heard him
Struggling and then I also
Heard him weeping for God
To help him lift it up,
And that's when he
Told me that he loved me
At first, it was so dark inside
Of the Ark of the Covenant,
But then the interior started
To glow like the inside of
An oven and yet it was all cool
To the touch then the lid flew off
The Ark of the Covenant,
Shimmering whilst getting
Stuck in the ceiling and

Lightning lifted me up gently
Into the air above the Ark
Of the Covenant, crackling
All around me and Othman
Stood there below me,
Both of us transfixed
Within each other's gaze
Finding the world for
The most part at that
Moment in particular,
Bewildering,

***

"What is wrong with you, Othman?" I say, "Why would you tell the children such horrible things?"

***

I screamed for God
To put me down
But all that came
Out of my mouth
Was a lightning bolt
Riding my tongue
In the shape of a sword
Taller than I was
And still taller than I am
Today wearing this sober
Habit of my vocation
Like it was a hairshirt
And the Lord put the blade
To the boy's neck
And that's when the monk
Whisked him away
Just in time for to be
His willing substitute
And the head of the monk

Rolled under the Ark of
The Covenant with hardly
A drop of blood never to be seen
Nor heard from again,

***

"Well," he says, "because I've been aligned with evil for the better half of my life now, and I know no other way of living, my dearest Salammbô."

***

Addis Ababa, Ethiopia,
The Church of Our Lady,
Mary of Zion, we were
Down in the cellar
Playing Hide and Seek,
While the monk said Mass
In the chapel upstairs
And I swear that I saw
When I first stepped inside
Of the Church of Our Lady,
Mary of Zion, I was peeking in
When I saw the Baby
Jesus being held down
By the monk on the altar
Breaking Him up into
Such tiny, little pieces,
So that the congregation
Could partake of his flesh
As He willingly surrendered
Himself up for those
In attendance,

***

"That is a lie," I say to him, "you were an honorable child. And you were my friend. And if you hadn't been of good character, the Maasai wouldn't have let you enter their brotherhood. What? You think I didn't keep tabs on you? I was so thrilled for you when the lionslayers had accepted you into their fold, especially after the witch-doctor had stolen your arm. Such a winning stroke after the evil one's foul deed. You're the one who has the potential to be a great man, Othman, not this filthy monster ever plaguing us with his insatiable hunger."

***

How is it that I am
Suddenly standing amid
Gethsemane like the Lord
Our God did when he was
arrested?
And Othman delivers
The kiss that betrays me.
I am so rudely apprehended
With my wrists tied,
And the whips they are
Lashing me with
Like I'm a beast of burden.
I might as well be pulling
A wagon,

***

I wake up in the smothering darkness, bereft of my beeswax candle. I feel the evidence of its wax upon my fingers, as I search my pockets and the surrounding fever grasses frantically for even the remotest possibility of the candle being in my proximity. What happened to me? How did it get this dire so quickly? I call out for the children amidst the tears because my situation was dawning harder and harder upon me with each passing second. But no one is answering me.

Now I can feel the tangibility of time pressing down upon me, urging me in all the wrong ways like an uninvited lover striving to infect me with the enthusiasm of his diseased Bacchanalia. Consuming me, impaling me. And I scream with an unbridled fury, as I vomit up the lightning bolt of a sword from my childhood. The flash of its cosmic power exposing what the darkness had intended to conceal from me.

And I can see Othman and the children way off in the distance. With their backs to me, the children flanking him on either side. Walking away with him, hand-in-hand, just shy of a kilometer. And they are going the wrong way, as if heading back the way we just came, back to the Port of Djibouti. They continue to ignore my screams for them to stop. I know they can hear me even from this distance because the lightning bolt of a sword augments my voice with the most thunderous of volumes.

But then I hear something crashing through the jungle towards me, tossing trees aside effortlessly in its wake. What lumbering behemoth approaches me? I see the hint of a snake's psychedelic scales, writhing, gigantic in pattern. Racing towards me down the muddy slope of the mountainside through the vast range of buffalo thorn and sycamore fig. Undulating in locomotion like a runaway train threatening to derail itself. Clambering through the primeval forest just to get to me. Trying to frighten me in anticipation, this monster unseen so far, but I suspect it to be a colossal rainbow serpent, a seraph of some sort reflecting my worst fears within this chaotic Eden.

Meanwhile, the lightning bolt looping out of my mouth once more, like lariats spinning, places the crackling white-hot sword in my hand, encouraging me to enter into glorious combat. And I crouch in readiness with all the knowledge of a battleworn cherubim about to lay waste to whatever the devil has in store for me.

And there he is, my puff daddy adder, Mauvais Œil d'Edgar, boasting cyclopean proportions where it is impossible to see the serpent's entirety, as his length stretches off into seeming infinity.

"Our meeting is long overdue, Sister Salammbô," says the giant clown snake. His megalithic scales grinding against one another like the cracked surface of an eggshell, with the yoke bleeding through. And neon red hair flowing from his temples like ribbons blowing in the wind. Plus, a bulbous red growth on the tip of his reptilian nose, just about obscuring the rest of his blanched face, smacks of rosacea run amok.

"Let's put our pleasantries aside, shall we," I say, "and get this thing over with. I have children to save."

"Ha-ha, you must think you're some kind of a saint," he says, "but I know the truth–that Othman holds your lost virginity in the palm of his hand from all those many years ago when the two of you desecrated the Ark with yours and his fornicating in the dark, and he doesn't care a wit for your undying love. You are the most impertinent mistress of his Lord yet. How is it that your god allows you to go on disrespecting him like this? Your insubordination at these continued flights of fancy involving Othman arouses in me feelings of immense admiration for your talents as a lover. I am curious to see as to what pleasures you hold in store for me once I've subdued you."

And that is when the puff daddy adder lunges at me like a coil sprung. But before I can feint and hack off its monolithic head, Othman's spear shoots in from seemingly out of nowhere, finding its mark through one eye and out the other. And the monster is felled, frustrated by this interruption, flinging its titanic girth our way, hoping to smash us into pulp despite its being blinded. The clown snake's tail sweeps the countryside like an earthquake, wiping the jungle clean off the map.

Yet this does not bog me down one iota, and I lay in with the business at hand of beheading the great worm until the cut is final.

I am bathed in the blood of the serpent, and yet I am never to be turned from the Lord whatsoever.

***

In the aftermath, the lifeless body of the witch-doctor, looking rather homely, lies upon the smoldering ruins of the jungle aloft the uprooted buffalo thorn and sycamore fig stacked up high like a megalithic funeral bier spanning for untold leagues down the side of the forbidding mountain, with his head having been parted from his shoulders unceremoniously. Exhibiting the delicious evidence of hacking akin to putting a lumberjack's axe to task by whacking the base of a massive Sequoia sempervirens.

And in his hand, the dead wizard holds the magic wand that was once Othman's arm and hand. The mummified child's arm bears the absence of pigment like a gray ghost. And the glow of the once-fiery hieroglyphics tattooed upon the flesh long ago finally ebbs out like a dying cinder.

And the dark matter begins to dissipate from the earth, which allows me to sheath my God-sword by swallowing up the Ark's lightning bolt in one fell swoop.

And then Othman brings the children over to me, and I kneel down to hug them with all of my love and devotion.

MA'S ATTIC

BY KRISTA FARMER

Alex was tired of staring down at her knees. She'd been doing so ever since their sedan had turned off the interstate down that stretch of unpaved road her mother had warned her of. Keeping her head down, her eyes focused on a spot between her knees, was a trick her mother had taught her to keep the car sickness at bay. It usually worked, but just now her nerves were getting the better of her, jostled by the unnerving speed at which they were traveling.

Her mother seemed in a hurry, although Alex had only managed to absorb some of the reasons why. She rather wished she hadn't. That this was only one of those summer vacations all the girls at school had been talking about before school had let out. She tried to imagine herself—keeping her head down, her eyes focused on that spot between her knees—hiking in the mountains, swimming in the ocean, leaving the state as the sun settled in one long, orange line behind them.

Alex glanced over at her brother, Tom. He was still playing with his little red toy car, rolling it back and forth over the pitted upholstery beneath his window. Every time the car hit a pothole—their mother cursing, slowing, correcting herself, speeding up again—the toy car jumped in time. As if it too were experiencing rough roads.

By the time their car finally began to slow—along a wide and unpaved stretch of driveway—Alex really had to puke. The sour feeling in her belly had grown intolerable. Before the car had even rolled fully to a stop, white dust still settling in a cloud around them, Alex opened the door on her side and retched that morning's pancakes onto the dry ground.

"Oh my god, Alex," her mother said, coming around from the driver's side, "This is why I was telling you not to eat so fast this morning. I told you you were going to be sick."

Alex gazed up at her mother through a curtain of her own hair, now stringy with sourish chunks of pancake.

"You were the one hurrying me."

There'd been sounds coming from the house in front of them all the while—the light slam of a screen door, footsteps across a wooden porch—but Alex hadn't paid much attention to these until she suddenly heard a voice.

"Oh, stop yelling at that kid."

Alex swallowed some of the rawness down her throat before wiping her lips on the back of her hand. She slowly stepped out of the car, careful not to step in any of the mess she'd just made. An older woman—probably the grandmother Sal they'd driven all this way out to see, and whose existence they'd only learned of the night before—was just stepping off a rickety front porch.

"I had about the same reaction when I first saw this place," the old woman said, hobbling over to stand next to them. "I'd said to Libby at the time—this is the place you want us to live? I'd seen chicken coops more luxurious."

"Alex, do me a favor and get your brother out of the car," her mother said, turning her around in that direction before facing Sal again.

"That girl has always had a way with first impressions, Mom," Alex heard her mother saying as soon as her back was turned. "You should've seen her first day at school. Like a fire hose, that girl."

From inside the car, half-hidden behind smears of road dust and bug residue, Alex could just see Tom peering back at her. She watched him for a moment, considering what her next, best move would be. She knew that getting him out of the car would be no easy feat. Not with the way he'd been so quiet and glowering all the way over, shoving that little red toy car back and forth over the pitted upholstery as if he'd meant to bore a hole through it. There was a storm brewing in there, and she did not want to deal with it. Neither, she suspected, did her mother.

After a moment spent sizing up the situation, Alex decided the best thing for her to do would be to show a little force. To just get the whole thing over with, like ripping off a band-aid. She imagined walking up to his side of the car and wrenching the car door open with such force that he would have no other choice but to meekly follow along.

Instead, she found that the door handle on Tom's side of the car was stuck. She had to pry at it some to get it open. When it finally did, the door swung open only wide enough for her to cram herself inside the vehicle.

"Mom says to hurry up," she said, her confidence already mostly gone.

She noticed that Tom hadn't even removed his seatbelt.

"I'm not going," Tom said, running that little toy car back and forth over his reddened palm. "Tell Mom to take us home."

"She'll only make us stay longer. Say we're spoiled."

Alex reached over to undo his buckle, but Tom grabbed it before she could.

"I don't want to be here," he whined at her. "This place looks mean."

Alex sighed. The burning oil smell the car exuded as it stood idle had begun to make her stomach churn again. She half wished she had enough pancake left in her to spew, thinking a lapful of vomit might've been enough to propel Tom out of the car without further intervention.

"I don't want to be here either. But the sooner we go in, the sooner we can leave."

She was aware that this was the same logic their mother used to persuade Tom into the dentist's office and that it hardly ever worked then either.

"I'm not going," Tom said. "Tell Mom I'm not."

Alex sighed. She was beginning to lose patience. She'd just begun to catch snippets of her mother's conversation with Sal, although she'd been willing herself not to. To focus solely on the dilemma, which was Tom.

"—I know, but it's only for a little while. At least until they catch—"

Alex found herself staring down at the flaking bands of skin on Tom's forearm. They were leftovers from the splint he'd been forced to wear over the past few months. A greenstick fracture was what the doctor had called it, although that word—*greenstick*—still didn't quite make sense to her. She imagined bones, like decorative Halloween bones, glowing phosphorescent deep inside Tom's recently mended arm.

Seeing those flaky bands of skin, like the beginning molts on a lizard, made her think back to the day she'd first seen Tom in the hospital. That puffy look on his face; the stark white hospital gown he'd been forced to wear. That urgent, hushed way her mother had spoken to his doctor out in the hall, much like how she was speaking to Sal now. Alex had always had a knack for overhearing things she wasn't meant to. It was along these lines that she suddenly had an idea.

"Grandma Sal has a secret, you know," she said, leaning forward to whisper to Tom.

"I'm not going," Tom said, stubbornly.

"But you haven't even heard the secret yet."

"Tell Mom to take us home."

"But Grandma Sal has a pool back there. I heard her and Mom talking about it over the phone. It was meant to be a surprise for us."

This caught his attention, at least. He stopped staring down at his little toy car and looked hard into her face, scanning it for a lie.

"If you're good and come out of the car right now," she told him, "I can take you straight to the pool. I even saw where Mom packed your floaters."

Tom continued to simply stare at her, but she could tell he was thinking over what she'd just said. The idea of a pool was the exact right sort of lure to use on him; plausible enough to at least make him want to believe she was telling the truth.

"Will I have to put on sunscreen?"

"Nope, not since I'm here. I'm not Mom, remember? I don't care if you fry like a lobster. If you get all covered in big freckly moles—"

"Alex, Tom, come on! It's rude to keep your grandmother waiting," their mother called.

It was already beginning to heat up outside, despite it still being early morning. Dust hung in clouds around them, unstirred by even the slightest breeze. They stood staring at each other for a few additional moments before Tom finally, reluctantly relaxed his grip on the buckle. Alex helped him to slowly step down out of the car, through the narrow gap she'd just created.

"Can we step on the gas, kids? Please? I'm already late for work."

"We're coming," Alex shouted back.

Much to Tom's credit, Alex thought Sal's house did have a rather mean look to it. The place was built up instead of out, with a second floor as well as what appeared to be a small, sloping attic. From this distance, the house looked sort of like a leaning layer cake, somewhat deflated on one side, and perhaps the flavor of dirty vanilla; frosted with the occasional patched bit of paint, sprinkled here and there with the occasional cracked shingle. A porch wrapped around the front of the house. This porch also had a rather dramatic lean to it, which may have been caused by all the piles of stuff stacked upon it. There were so many things piled up here that it all became rather difficult for Alex to pick them out individually. There were some ancient pieces of furniture, some boxes of old, weather-beaten clothes, some heavily cracked flowerpots, the plants inside of which had long ago dried to faint mummy dust. Their mother—not wasting any more time now—quickly ushered her and Tom inside the house, behind Sal. Alex had just enough time to glimpse what might've been rows of dark, towering shapes before their mother swept both her and Tom into a tight, vision-obscuring embrace.

"This is only temporary," she whispered to Alex, "when you get home, things will be so much better. I promise."

"But things would be better if we were back home now," Alex protested. "Tom hates it already."

"Trust me," her mother said, suddenly pulling away, "This is for the best. And you'll like your grandma, Sal. Just try not to make it so hard on your brother, alright? Try not to make such a fuss."

Their mother left in a hurry. Alex and Tom, standing side-by-side, listened to the familiar grind and sputter of her sedan slowly pulling away, along with their last glimmer of hope. Alex felt her brother staring up at her but did not meet his gaze.

"Well, it's good to finally meet the both of you," Sal said, handing them each the backpacks their mother had packed for them the night before.

Tom refused to take his, so Alex grabbed it for him. She could tell he was being purposely difficult, the way he usually acted when he felt wary of strangers.

"I want to go home," he said, still staring up at Alex.

"Oh, honey, you are home," Sal said, smiling at him. "Home sweet home. Just be glad it hasn't been yours for quite as long as it's been mine."

Sal laughed. The laugh sounded not entirely unfriendly. Alex gazed around and saw that the towering shapes she'd noticed earlier covered most of the living room, extending into the rooms beyond it. These were more piles of boxes, some so swollen with age and the burden of their contents that they looked almost ready to burst. It was unlike any other house Alex had ever been in. She must've been making a face, for she gradually became aware of Sal staring at her.

"Where are we supposed to stay?" was the only thing she could think of to ask.

"Your room's upstairs, if you'd like to go up there now and explore. I'll have an early supper waiting for you both in the kitchen in a bit. I understand you might need a little refueling after this morning."

Sal winked at her. Alex glanced away, feeling slightly embarrassed.

Sal led them slowly up a dim stairway. The stairway itself, Alex noted, was relatively free of clutter, but the hallway made up for this by being almost doubly as crowded. Alex could discern a faint light glimmering around a row of stacks and thought that this was probably the entrance to the room their grandmother was leading them to. She was quickly proven correct.

"It's not much to look at," Sal said to them, as they all three stood staring in at it. "But your mother tells me you're both used to sharing."

Alex frowned. She'd not shared a room with her brother since she was practically a little baby. She didn't relish the idea of having to share one now. She looked dubiously around the room, which was also densely cluttered, but had at least a cleared pathway leading up to the decently sized bed.

"What about that closed door across the hall?" she asked, having noticed one on their way down the hall.

Sal shook her head briefly.

"Impassable," she said.

Or maybe *impossible*. Alex was not entirely sure. This place was so odd, and she was still a little unsure of how to respond to Sal. They both stood staring at each other for a moment before Sal abruptly turned away, calling back to them to holler if they needed anything.

Alex and Tom spent the next few hours halfheartedly attempting to explore their new environment; Alex with a sort of forced enthusiasm, Tom with a half-hearted reluctance. After a failed attempt to get that door across the hall to open for them, using one of Alex's slender bobby pins, they stuck mostly to the room they'd been assigned to. There was plenty enough in here to keep them preoccupied for at least the next couple of days, if not the next few years.

"Look at this one," Alex said as she walked up to a particularly stained-looking box by the doorway. "This must've been where they kept all the bodies."

She kicked at the box, afraid to touch it with her bare hands. One of its flaps sagged open. She found it was full of packets of old gardening seed, each packet being carefully sealed and labeled. Alex read a few of the names off the individual packets: *carrots, Nasturt…nasturtiums, forget-me-nots*. Her brother seemed not very interested in all this. He frowned down at another box, held tightly together with layers of old packing tape. Alex had to pry through these layers using only her fingernails, which left a thick, gummy residue pushed up underneath them.

There were some delicate-looking objects in this box, stored between bundles of tightly-wadded newspaper. In another box was a bunch of musty old sheets, on top of what appeared to be old-timey Halloween masks. She tried one of these on but could tell, by the look on her brother's face, that the effect was displeasing. The more interesting of these boxes contained what at first appeared to be long, dark, nylon ropes. These were actually old dog leashes, all tangled up with bits of pale fur still clinging to some of them. Had Sal owned a dog at some point? Had her mother? But Alex had always thought her mother hated dogs…

Tom, meanwhile, nonplussed by all the recent discoveries, began to make it clear he hadn't forgotten her promise of a pool. Desperate now to avoid the looming tantrum, Alex went even so far as to unpack his Lego set, which their mother had blessedly packed among the things in his little backpack. She offered to play with him, but he slapped the box out of her hand so forcefully that it sent Legos flying out all over the carpet, some of which were so gnawed out of shape they looked like tiny pieces of oddly colored bone rolling under furniture, between piles of nameless junk. Alex had to take a few deep breaths, like her mother was always telling her to, before speaking to him again.

"Fine," she said. "We'll go outside. But I don't want to hear any more complaining out of you after that."

She grabbed his wrist and began tugging him down the stairs, dreading every step. She was not even sure, at this point, whether Sal even had a backyard, let alone some miraculous pool. They made their way down into the living room, the air now heavy with foreign cooking smells, Alex thinking hard, all the while, on how she might avoid her brother's tantrum.

She saw that Sal was now seated upon a large red leather sofa, in front of an almost equally large television. She could just see the top of her grandmother's gray head, flickering with lights from the screen. Alex was not sure how to even begin to explain to her the lie she'd told her brother and was glad when the old woman showed no signs of having noticed them as they slunk by, toward the slits of lights they could just see spilling in through a row of slatted blinds.

Behind the blinds was a row of sliding glass doors, each smeared with dust and fingerprints. The light coming in from outside was glaring. Alex squinted as she fumbled with the latch.

She finally slid one of the doors open, just as Tom squeezed himself out beside her.

Sal's yard looked just about as she'd expected it to; strewn with more piles of junk. A shed stood in one corner, and Alex could see that its door was being held open by even more piles of junk. A flapping blue tarp hung over one of its walls, stirred by a slight breeze.

"There's no pool," Tom said, frowning up at her. "I don't see a pool."

Having expected just such an observation, Alex continued to scan her surroundings for a distraction. She suddenly spotted a huge doghouse standing over in one corner, nestled in the V of a rickety wooden fence. This doghouse's paint had faded over the years, and it looked as though it'd maybe withstood one too many blistering summers, but it seemed, at least, structurally sound.

"Oh, forget that stupid pool. This is way better. We could do so many things with this," Alex said, already attempting to drag him in that direction.

Tom resisted. He refused to even look in the direction she was pointing. He wanted a pool, or he wanted to go home. There seemed to be no other words left in his vocabulary. Alex could feel her patience slowly slipping. Especially when she turned to see his face all scrunched up, his eyes turning that even brighter shade of teary blue, his lips faintly quivering. She suddenly thought of her mother, and about how her mother was always accusing *her* of making such a fuss. Like she was the one who was always doing that.

"Oh, come on. Look over here," she said, still tugging at him. "We could set up all our things in here and never have to go back into Sal's house at all."

Tom still refused to budge. Alex finally dropped his hand, disgustedly, and moved off in that direction on her own. Up close, she found the doghouse to be in an even greater state of disrepair than she'd hoped. The interior was matted thick with cobwebs, all drooping from its interior like a darkened mass of silken curtains. Even worse, however, was the smell the doghouse exuded. It was as if something had, over the course of the doghouse having first been abandoned there, crawled inside of it to die.

Alex quickly pivoted, searching around for some other distraction. She was not, after all, keen on crawling around inside that thing. Pretending it was a fort, or whatever she'd been planning.

Alex suddenly spotted an old aluminum baseball bat, leaning up against a pile of rain-rotted magazines. There was a kind of blackened substance coating the bottom end of it, right where you might hit a ball with it. She didn't much care for whatever that blackened substance was, but the handle itself seemed at least relatively clean.

Alex glanced over her shoulder again. Tom was still standing where she'd left him, still on the verge of tears. She sauntered over and picked up the baseball bat, liking the light, quick feel of it in her hands. She swung it over her shoulder. A new idea was beginning to form in her mind, quickly gaining traction. She sauntered back over to Tom.

"Look over there," she said, suddenly pointing with the bat toward another part of the yard, wrapping her free arm around her brother's shoulders. "You see that over there?"

She was pointing to what appeared to be only more piles of junk, next to a pile of what appeared to be dry leaves. There seemed to be some objects glittering on the top of this pile of leaves. Beside it loomed that stuffed shed, with its faded tarp still slowly flapping. She could see, from this angle, that the tarp was being held in place by only a few angled bricks pinning it to the sloped roof.

"I don't see anything," Tom whined.

"But there are monsters over there, can't you see them?" Alex said, lowering her voice as she whispered to him.

"Monsters?"

"Yes," Alex said. "Sal's house is full of monsters. And only you and I can stop them."

Leaving him to stew over this new information, she went over to the pile of leaves, the aluminum bat still slung over her shoulder. She could see that they'd mostly fallen off the big maple tree in the neighbor's yard, the tree itself already flush with new summer growth. Up close, she could see that the things glittering on top of the pile were just as she'd hoped; bits of old crockery, jumbled with heavy plates and other brittle-looking things. Someone—this someone having undoubtedly been Sal—had attempted to weigh the pile down using clutter from around the house. As Alex drew closer, she homed in on a particularly delicate-looking plate.

She shot Tom a sneaky glance over her shoulder.

"There's one," she yelled.

She turned and swung. The bat connected with the edge of the plate. There was a hard *cracking* sound, although the plate seemed only to bounce off the tip of the bat before finally shattering against the wooden fence.

She snuck another glance over her shoulder. Tom's face was now caught somewhere between surprise and horror. She could tell her plan was working. She quickly searched for another target.

"And another," she yelled as she swung the bat again, this time shattering a large ceramic cup.

She was beginning to feel surprised by how good this all felt. She'd only meant it as a distraction for Tom, but was now beginning to feel a mysterious weight lifting from her. With each hard *swing* of the bat, she seemed to shed another pound of this newly registered mental baggage. She found herself hardly caring at all about all the things she'd just been so worried about.

Not sad about having to live in this hole with Sal, an old woman she scarcely knew, for maybe the whole summer. Not mad that she'd been tasked with looking after her brother again, as usual, although she felt not much older than him most days, and pretty much just as scared. Not frightened over what might be happening back home, between her parents, with a father whom she now nebulously presumed was on the run…

Tom was beginning to grow less apprehensive now and more interested in what she was doing. He began to cheer and cry out whenever she hit something that went particularly *smash.* Wanting something even grander to smash now, before Sal inevitably came out and put a stop to what they were doing, Alex spotted a heavy old T.V. lying on its back, its screen facing upward like a dying, blue-glazed cataract. She could see, with growing excitement, that its screen was already partially cracked. She immediately set to work on it, watching as the bluish screen webbed and fissured beneath the blunt end of her bat.

Alex was slowly growing aware—even through the loudness of what she was doing—of Tom crying out for a turn. Her head was beginning to swim, and she was almost out of breath. She wanted to finish what she'd started with the television, but was also wary of Tom's cries attracting Sal's attention. Hefting the bat over her shoulder, quickly glancing around, she noticed, for the first time really, all the shattered glass she'd left behind.

"Alright," she said, sobering a little as she approached him, "but you have to promise to chase monsters only on *that* side of the yard."

She pointed to the side of the yard, still relatively free of broken glass.

"I promise," Tom said, already attempting to yank the bat out of her hands.

She forced another promise out of him before handing it over. As soon as he was in control of it, he took off running in the exact wrong direction.

"Wait, Tom! No monsters that way."

In her haste to catch up with him, Alex tripped. She landed hard on her hands and knees, and almost immediately felt a sharp pain being driven up through one of her legs. The pain was so exquisite that it temporarily knocked the wind out of her. Her vision sparkled. Alex squeezed her eyes shut, hoping she hadn't done what she thought she just had, seeing ghost visions of jagged glass littering the ground. She suddenly began to hear her brother screaming.

Tom was now lying on his backside, staring up at something which loomed above him. Beside him lay that flapping blue tarp, now in a crinkly blue pile on the ground. She thought he must've accidentally torn it off while swinging wildly with the bat. She now saw that the tarp had been used to cover up something. This something was a large dog's head, spraypainted onto the side of the shed in messy, sprawling lines, which seemed in keeping with the dog's fixed and crazy expression.

"What's all this now?"

Alex had no idea Sal had come out into the yard until she heard her voice. Sal's shadow suddenly fell across her.

"Hurt yourself, did you?"

She'd been so caught up with what was happening with her brother, she hadn't even looked down to see what'd happened to her yet. Lying on her back now, her eyes caught on the silvery shard of glass sticking out of her knee. There was a surprisingly small amount of blood around the wound, although the skin had blanched pale, as if leached of color.

"Looks like your brother's been scaring himself silly over there," Sal said, turning in that direction. "Come over here, Tom!"

Tom glanced over at them. His mouth shut up comically, his face still glassy pale. To Alex's surprise, he got up and immediately ran over to Sal, clutching her hand now as if the world beneath him was steadily tilting. As soon as he spotted what'd happened to Alex's leg, his expression changed. It became even paler. Sal suddenly let out a shout of laughter as she gazed around the yard.

"Looks like you've both been busy out here. Cleaning up, I don't suppose?"

"Are they gonna have to cut it off?" Tom asked, referring to Alex's leg. "I saw that in a movie once. This guy got all caught up in a barbed-wire fence and—"

"That's enough out of you, Tom. Why don't you go inside and eat your dinner before it gets cold?" she asked, suddenly turning him bodily around toward the house. "Leave your sister be for now."

To Alex's further surprise, Tom obeyed her. With a final, terrified glance over his shoulder at Alex's knee, then at that thing on the side of the shed, Tom bolted as if whatever had gotten to Alex was currently chasing him.

"They're not going to have to cut it off," Alex shouted after him, "It doesn't even hurt that bad."

This was a lie. Alex had to hobble her way back inside the house, mostly supported by Sal. Her grandmother led her in through the kitchen, past the queasy smells of cooking, into a small bathroom at the end of a hall. Sal helped her to sit at the edge of a bathtub, propping her leg so that her now bloodied heel rested near the edge of a metal drain. Sal briefly disappeared, then came back holding a chipped brown mug. The mug contained a thick brown liquid steeping with a single tea bag. Alex knew what *booze* smelled like, and this was definitely the stuff. She shook her head and tried to push the mug away, but her grandmother insisted. The drink tasted awful. It burned its way down and made her feel slightly nauseous, but some of the pain immediately disappeared.

Sal took the empty mug from her and set it aside. She then turned to rummage in a little cabinet below the sink, spilling things out across the floor as she did so.

"I have a hell of a time keeping things organized around here," she said, chuckling a little to herself.

She eventually found what she was looking for—an old pair of metal pliers and a big, brown jug of hydrogen peroxide. Sal tested the pliers a few times in her hands to make sure they weren't rusted shut before turning to Alex.

"This might hurt a little. You ready?"

Alex nodded, still feeling the swift burn of the alcohol in her belly. Without much further ado, Sal set the tips of the pliers against the shard of glass in Alex's knee and yanked. There was a sharp pain, followed by almost immediate relief. Blood began to pour out of the wound, running all the way down her calf, puddling over the smooth surface of the tub. Sal leaned over and—probably anticipating Alex's refusal of this—sloshed some hydrogen peroxide over the wound. This was, by far, the most agonizing part of the whole experience. It felt like an army of steel wasps was now buzzing furiously down inside the flesh of her knee. The pain was slower to vanish this time. Alex watched as her blood, now mingling with pale stripes of hydrogen peroxide, sizzled in pink-and-white candy cane stripes down the drain. She turned again to watch Sal rummage through the cabinet below the sink. She pulled out a roll of gauze and a squished tube of antibiotic paste.

Sal sighed.

"I bet you're wondering, Alex, why it is you and I have never been formally introduced."

Alex did not immediately respond to this. She sat silent, waiting for her grandmother to continue. She'd honestly been dying with curiosity over this subject ever since they'd first learned of Sal's existence, only the night before.

"You remember me telling you about that woman I first bought this place with? Libby? She was an old high school friend of mine. We first bought this place back in, oh, I'd say '89, or '98. I've never been so good with numbers. When I decided to buy her out, only a few short years after we'd moved in, she was all too willing to agree. Not that we'd ever had a falling out, or anything. She was only all too eager to move back to the city, where mostly all of her social connections still were. The reason I wanted to buy her out was that I was getting ready to marry George, the grandfather you never met.

"Your mother came along not long after George and I were married. She was a stubborn and demanding one from the start, your mother. She always knew exactly what she wanted and wouldn't let anyone else convince her otherwise. One of the first things she ever wanted, more than anything else in the world, was a dog.

Alex's eyes widened. Alex's mother had always refused to even discuss the topic of owning a dog with them, or any other sort of pet. Her mind now flashed on those dog leashes she'd seen earlier. That terrible, cobwebby doghouse. That strange painting on the side of Sal's shed…

"I finally broke down around her tenth birthday. We all three went down to the shelter, and she picked out Callie. I always loved that dog—she was a good soul that dog—but she only ever had eyes for your mother. She was practically your mother's slave, that dog. She could've done anything to her, and that dog would've only sat there, politely, and batted her eyes, but your mother treated that dog like a queen. She was surprisingly responsible for her age. I never had to worry about who was going to clean up after her, or who was going to feed her, or make sure she had enough water in her bowl. Your mother was always on top of everything.

"It was around this time I started getting really into gardening. This might seem like an unrelated topic to you, but I promise, we're getting to the point. I'd never thought much about owning a garden before Irene came along. She put it into my head that I wanted to try growing some of our own food, mainly root vegetables and such. We were on a tight budget at the time, and

I figured it was a good way to offset some of our growing food costs. It was then that I noticed the first strange thing about this property. I should've brought it with George immediately, but it seemed such an odd thing that I could hardly find the words to describe it properly, even to myself. Although I guess I should've thought a lot more about it later on, when we had to bury that poor dog of your mother's."

Alex gasped. Here, she thought, was perhaps the heart of the mystery...

"Bury her? But what happened to her?"

"I'm getting to that, but I wanted to explain to you my garden first. I don't suppose you've ever seen a mandrake root?"

Alex thought about this for a moment. Her excitement was making it feel like her mind was splitting off in a dozen different directions at once. She hardly felt the pain in her leg now at all.

"Only from Harry Potter."

"Oh, well, I never read any of those books. I've never been much of a fiction reader myself. If I had been, maybe I'd have thought what I noticed later on was only a product of my own overactive imagination.

"The first thing that struck me as odd was the way things grew in that garden. They grew faster than I ever expected them to; faster than any of the instructions on the back of the seed packets I bought or the gardening catalogs I borrowed ever suggested. They seemed to grow with a strange, unnatural sort of vitality, too, as though they went through some kind of infernal engine on their way out of the ground. I pulled up one of the cabbages one day—nearly twice as big as my head, that one. Grown in less than a fortnight—and George asked me what sort of fertilizer I was using. I told him I'd forgotten to fertilize the garden at all, and he told me I ought to sign up for the county fair next year.

"The second thing I noticed, and perhaps worst of all, was the distorted way some of these things grew. Especially the ones that'd grown underground, the root vegetables and such. You remember that mandrake root I mentioned? I first learned about it in an old storybook I had as a kid. A little brown root with a tired, wrinkled face, that supposedly screamed whenever you tore it up out of the ground, causing whatever or whoever was nearby to go screaming, raving mad.

"It was this turnip I dug up that finally put an end to my gardening career for good. It didn't scream when I pulled it out of the ground, but it gave me an ugly thump anyway. I could've sworn it had a face. Like one of those faces kids used to carve into old turnips when there weren't any pumpkins around...or whatever. Two ugly little root holes for eyes, a little frowning crease for a mouth. I never told George about it, but I threw the thing away immediately. I knew I was done with gardening for good after that. George asked me why, of course, but I think he was also starting to become a little unnerved by the way things grew out there. None of us could bring ourselves to eat any of the stuff that the garden produced anyway—wrinkled and bloated as much of it was.

"I dug up the garden beds the very next day. Piled them up full of rocks, pebbles, and other odd bits of junk. I think it was around that time that my hoarding tendencies started to really come out. I'd always been a kind of hoarder, ever since I was a child, but the shock of that strange garden, not to mention other trying financial circumstances we were living through at the time, started me down a dark path."

Sal suddenly glanced down at all the mess still scattered on the bathroom floor. Alex forced herself not to follow her grandmother's gaze, not wanting to seem rude, or to have the story suddenly interrupted by her grandmother's suddenly deciding to tidy up.

"It was only a few years after the gardening incident that Callie died. She'd not been a young dog when we adopted her, and who knows what sort of life she'd led before us, but she probably would've made it at least a few more years had she not gotten out one night and probably eaten all our neighbor's chickens. We found her lying dead in the yard one morning, a bunch of feathers and blood still stuck around her mouth. She'd been shot, and whoever had killed her—probably out of meanness or spite or whatever horrible things go through people's heads sometimes—had decided to deposit her back in our backyard. I railed and screamed at all the neighbors. I threatened to call the cops, but animal cruelty wasn't as big a deal back then as it is now. A dead dog was just a dead dog in those days. I dreaded having to explain the whole incident to Irene. I managed to get her off to school early that morning on the bus, before she could discover what'd happened. George helped me bury Callie out in the yard. Your mother probably still thinks that poor dog died of natural causes, but there was nothing natural about what happened later.

"When Irene got home from school, I tried to explain to her what'd happened, leaving out the more gruesome details. I tried to distract her by having her go around with me to collect a bunch of pretty stones, rocks, flowers, and things to stack on Callie's grave. I was only really thinking about how to deal with my own and my daughter's grief. What I really should've been thinking about was what'd happened to all those things I'd so far buried out in that strange earth…

"I was sitting right there in the living room, right on that big leather couch, on the night Callie came back. It was probably very late by then. I'd had a lot of trouble sleeping back then, with all the stress I was under, and often only finally fell asleep toward early morning, watching whatever program happened to be on T.V.

"Something startled me awake. A soft scritch, scritching along the back sliding glass doors. I felt an immediate chill run along my spine. The sound reminded me of how Callie used to scratch at those doors to be let back in. I thought maybe someone out there was playing a cruel joke. Then I thought it must've only been a raccoon or a stray cat, that we'd probably get a lot of those coming around now that our only guard dog was permanently off-duty. I slid my slippers on and padded over there. In the yellow light from the back porch, I could see that whatever it was, it was much too big to be only a raccoon or a cat. It was Callie, Callie come back somehow."

Alex's eyes widened as she clutched at the edge of the tub now to stabilize herself.

"But how could—"

"I know, I know. I've tried asking myself all those same questions over the years. I've tried to think of every possible, rational explanation. It all comes down to a few simple facts. When I slid those doors open, Callie came trotting in to sit at my feet in that same way she'd always done—if a little more lopsided now—as if to say *here I am. I hope you've been expecting me*. She wore her familiar dog tags and collar, only now they were crusted with dirt. Her front nails, and probably her back ones as well, were broken off all the way up past the quicks. They left a few little dark spots of blood trailing behind her. We simply stood staring at each other for a few moments. Then she suddenly shook herself, scattering bits of clotted blood and earth all over the floor, and it was then that I think I started to scream. George and your mother came running down the stairs.

"We locked Callie outside that night. I thought maybe when I woke up the next morning, it would've all been just some terrible dream I'd had. I went outside, already steeling myself against what I might find, and saw your mother already out there, looking down at Callie with a mixture of horror and fear in her eyes. I'm afraid your mother never took to Callie again after that, although the dog never seemed to lose one ounce of the love she'd always had for her. Not that I ever blamed your mother for that. There were still some parts of Callie left—the deep love she still had for your mother, her rather slow and laidback nature—but the rest of her had been changed, just like those terrible root vegetables in my garden had. There was something grotesque about her now. The dog had lost that spark in her eyes that denoted a healthy spirit. Her teeth, which'd been deteriorating for some time before she died, were now waxy and yellow as old cheese. Her coat was stiffer, flatter, almost like taxidermy, and that large flat square of earth we'd buried her under, well, it wasn't so flat anymore…"

Sal stopped suddenly, looking hard at Alex.

"I'm sorry, Alex. I haven't meant to scare you."

"I'm not scared," Alex quickly lied. "Only, I don't think I can quite believe you."

Sal sighed.

"Well, I wish you'd believe at least some of what I'd just said. It would explain why your mother was in such a hurry to leave this place, as soon as she turned eighteen, and to have nothing more to do with it. Too many bad memories. Too many…bad associations."

Sal glanced down again at all the things scattered across the ground, looking sad.

Alex sat there, waiting to hear more. When Sal did not speak again, she judged they'd come to the end of the story. Sal abruptly stood up and helped Alex up from the bath.

As Alex passed through the kitchen, unaided now by Sal, who'd gone back to watching television, Tom strove to get her attention. She was not at all in the mood to deal with him again; his mouth was too crammed full of food for her to understand what he was trying to say to her anyway.

Alex herself felt not at all hungry. The day had been too exhausting, too full of new information for her to process. She'd learned so many new things about her mother, things she might never have known for years and years and years—if ever—had it not been for Sal. But could Sal really have been telling the truth? Her story seemed too incredible to believe. But if she'd lied…wouldn't that mean that Sal was secretly crazy? Had their mother left them in the care of a mad woman? Did that mean *she* was crazy, too? That she'd inherited something which would begin to make her hallucinate things like dead dogs coming back to life in the middle of the night?

Alex dragged herself wearily upstairs. In that big creaky bed now, she could hear her brother and Sal laughing downstairs. They were apparently getting on famously now that she'd been removed from the picture. She wondered briefly if they were maybe laughing at her—her and her stupid glass-breaking ideas—but quickly decided that she was too exhausted to care. She fell asleep and failed to wake up even when Tom slid noisily into bed beside her. She didn't wake up until she began to hear what sounded like a strange scratching noise above her.

The noise sounded like it was coming from the other side of the ceiling, directly above her head. Alex quickly sat up. She'd been having uneasy dreams, and the noise had simply been a part of them at first. It was dark in the room by then. As she listened, the scratching noises stopped, but when they started up again, seemingly out of nowhere, they sounded ever stronger. Alex felt as if her heart were about to leap out of her chest. Hadn't she noticed an attic up there earlier?

She felt a movement along the mattress, and a hand suddenly darted out to grasp hers. It was Tom. She could see the terrified gleam of the whites of his eyes, even in the dark.

"What is that?" he whispered.

"Shhh."

The scratching stopped, as if whatever had been making that sound up there had suddenly stopped to cock its head. They heard a low, unmistakable whine. Alex thought again of her grandmother's story. About the picture on the side of Sal's shed. About the doghouse, and the weird, furry dog leashes. Had Sal perhaps gotten another dog after Callie had died? But, according to her, Callie may've still been alive…

"What is—"

"Shhh," Alex whispered. "Just be quiet. Don't make any more noise."

Alex felt suddenly glad that Tom had closed the door behind him before crawling into bed. She hoped that whatever was up there was trapped up there for now, with no ability to open doors...

"Just try to go back to sleep," she whispered to Tom, lying back down herself. "And we'll ask Grandma about it in the morning. It might be just the rats."

But it wasn't just the rats—Alex knew this. She began to fall back into an uneasy sleep, still exhausted. Lumbering, unfriendly shapes moved throughout her dreams. They wove themselves into monstrous patterns. Just when Alex thought something was about to reach out to grab her, she heard a sudden voice.

"Irene! Irene! Hello? Are you in there? Are you in there, Irene?"

It was her father. His voice was coming from downstairs, just outside the house. She could hear him pounding on the door. Judging by the dim light in the room, it was almost morning. Alex could now hear someone moving around in the living room, the joints and springs of a wide leather couch groaning.

"Irene! Irene, for the love of—"

There was a pounding up the stairs, followed by her grandmother's face appearing in a crack in the doorway, mostly still in shadow.

"*Alex,*" Sal hissed.

Tom was wide awake now and gripping Alex's hand.

"You bolt this door, and don't you or your brother come out of that room until I call for you, you understand?"

Alex's throat clicked dryly. She felt too frightened to respond. Tom huddled closer to her.

"Do you understand?"

"Irene? Irene, open up!"

More pounding. Sal's face twisted, then quickly disappeared. She shut the door behind her. Alex heard another door (possibly a trap door?) creak open. Curiosity got the better of her, as it always had. She rushed across the room and opened the door a crack to peer out.

The murky darkness swam before her eyes. She heard a slight shuffling, followed by the long, pale swoop of a nightgown rushing past her, followed by something else…by a huge pale shape lumbering just behind…

"Irene! Irene, for the love of—"

Alex gasped, then slammed the door shut behind her. She bolted it, before running across the room to climb into bed beside Tom. Both were crying now, both desperately trying not to hear the commotion going on below. More cursing, more yells. Perhaps a heavy blow, followed by a long, blood-curdling snarl. A thought then occurred to Alex, through thick waves of her own fear. That she'd been right about her grandmother's house all along. That there were monsters in Sal's house. And they could bite and maim and rip and chew.

RECURRING THEME

BY FLOYD LARGENT

Eight-year-old Rory was sleeping *just fine* when someone booped his nose, causing his eyes to fly open. He reared up in bed and cried out, "Are you *crazy*?! It's like two o'clock in the mornin'!"

Then he looked at the faintly glowing kid standing beside his bed and demanded, "Who the heck are *you*? Do your parents know where you are right now?"

The dark-haired boy with a smudge of dirt on the bridge of his nose said, "No. No, they do not." His voice sounded distant and echoey, like it was coming from the bottom of a well. Or a really bad phone connection. "Could you help them find me?"

Rory settled on the side of his bed and said thoughtfully, "Huh. You're one of them ghosts, ain't you? Like in that old movie, *The Sixth Sense.* That was a good 'un."

"It was," said the glowing boy. "I am."

"So how come you're botherin' *me*?" Rory challenged.

"Dunno," the boy said in his weirdly resonant voice. "I've been wandering around for a while now, looking for someone who could help me, and I got pulled into you tonight." The boy looked around Rory's room. "I like your LEGO Millennium Falcon. Who's that guy with the armor on the poster?"

"That's the Mandalorian," Rory replied tartly. "Duh."

"Oh. I never heard of him. Guess he hadn't shown up before I... left." He blinked rapidly for a moment, then said, "My name is Sammy Cain. Can you help my folks find me?"

Rory looked at him for a long moment, then said, "I'm Rory Silver. And yes, I'll help, if you leave me alone till mornin'."

Sammy smiled and nodded, so Rory lay back down, yanked the covers over himself, and went back to sleep. Ghost or no ghost, he was getting his beauty rest.

***

It took a while for Rory to find Sammy's family and figure out how to get to their house without being hindered by "helpful" adults. The Cains had moved since Sammy had disappeared, which turned out to be *fifteen stinkin' years ago,* making it a little tough to track them down, but he did it. After four days of Internet searches, he discovered that they had relocated only a few miles away, ironically, less than a mile from Sammy's final resting place in the woods. As it happened, it was easy to get to their house: it was just off Rory's school bus route. All he had to do was get off the bus about ten stops early on the way back home from school. He managed to do that two days later.

Sammy's sister Mona Lou Cain, who had been born after Sammy disappeared, answered the door to Rory's polite knock. She was in one of those gum-popping Goth-chick phases, which came with a certain attitude. She had not, however, encountered Rory yet, who was the little prince of attitude, so their first meeting went like this:

Batting her eyes lazily at the diminutive figure standing on the front porch, Mona Lou chewed her gum a bit before she asked, "What's up, little girl?"

"Hey!" Outraged, Rory parked his fists on his hips in a classic Peter Pan pose (a posture his parents knew well) and barked, "What makes you think I'm a *girl*?!"

Mona Lou chuckled. "Could be your gorgeous hair, or your *cyooot* little face with that *adorable* button nose."

"Ha! Well, I'm a boy, Miss Vampire Lady! So there."

"Coulda fooled me. You *sure* you're a boy?"

Irritated, Rory tossed his head to shake back his long auburn hair in that way that only girls and pretty long-haired boys seem to master. "Well, I think I oughtta know! Am I gonna have to take off my britches to prove it?"

"Ha, no, I'll take your word for it."

"Well, good. I need to talk to your mama, it's important."

"She won't buy anything."

"I got nothin' for sale."

Moma Lou closed the screen door and called, "Moooom! There's a weird little boy on the front porch who wants to talk to you!"

Sammy's mama was really pretty and looked a lot like her daughter, without all the black, blue, and red trimmings. She came to the door, wiping her hands on a dish towel, with a questioning look on her face. "Hi there. Can I help you with something, kiddo?" She looked tired and a little lost.

Rory peered up at her, smiled brightly, and said, "Hi, my name is Rory. Do you have a little boy named Sammy?"

Mrs. Cain's eyes widened, she swallowed hard, and after a minute, she replied, "I did, but he disappeared a long time ago...what is this about?"

"He sent me to find you. So you can find *him*."

Mrs. Cain just stared at him for a while, then snapped, "What are you playing at, kid? Who put you up to this?"

"I ain't lyin', lady!" Rory insisted. "Sammy's been buggin' me for a week to find you and come take you to where he is! He's right here with me."

"I don't have time for this BS," Mrs. Cain snarled, turning to go back inside the house.

"Sailor Sam," Rory said quietly but firmly.

Mrs. Cain turned back to him abruptly, her eyes now wide as saucers. "What? What did you just say?"

"Sailor Sam," Rory said, looking mystified. He turned his head slightly to the side and muttered, "Yeah, yeah, I know, I get it," then looked at Mrs. Cain again. "Sammy says that when he was little, you used to sing a song called... "Band on the Run"?

Weird name for a song. Anyway, you sang it a lot. Sometimes you called him Sailor Sam after the guy in the song. And sometimes he called you jailer wo*man*, after the other guy in the song. Right?"

"Right," Mrs. Cain said vaguely, looking like she might faint. "How...how did you know about that? I don't think I ever mentioned it to anyone."

"I told you, he's right here with me." He glanced to the side again. "Yeah, so you said, *Sailor Sam*. Okay, lady, you want to come with me to where he is? It ain't too far."

Mrs. Cain lifted her hand to her mouth. Clearly, she desperately wanted to believe what Rory was saying. "Is...is my Sailor Sam alive?"

Rory sighed, his face falling. "You better sit down, lady," he said, pointing at the nearby porch swing. "This ain't gonna be easy for any of us."

Mrs. Cain practically fell into the seat, sending it swinging slightly. Rory sat himself down on the other end of the seat and said softly. "I'm sorry, but Sammy ain't still alive. He hasn't been for the past 15 years and 43 days, he says."

"He's — he's here? Right here?"

"Yes'm. Right now, he's sittin' between us on this swing."

Mrs. Cain turned to Rory, her face screwed up as she began to cry and passed her hands through the space between them. "You — you best not be lying, little girl."

"Boy! I'm a *boy*, okay? And my name's Rory. Rory Silver. I live over on Yankton Avenue."

"All right, then. So, what happened to my little boy back then, Rory Silver from Yankton Avenue?"

"I was gettin' to that. Do you know some loser named Junior Hickermon?"

She blinked slowly and eventually replied, "Yes. He used to be a neighbor. He was killed in a car accident about five years ago."

"Too bad," Rory said, scowling. "He deserved lots worse."

They fell silent for a long moment, swinging idly, before Rory said in a small voice, "That Junior guy, he grabbed Sammy from your backyard while he was playin' with his cat. He says it was a Siamese named Gravy Train, by the way...anyway, that guy dragged him right over the fence and way deep into the woods, while he held a hand over Sammy's mouth so no one could hear him screamin'. Kept going until they were so deep in the woods that no one could hear his screams at all. Then Junior, he..." Rory took a deep breath, freaked out by what Sammy was telling him. He looked into the dark eyes of the ghost boy with the smudge across the bridge of his nose, which he now saw wasn't dirt but blood, and continued. "Well, he did nasty things to Sammy...and then he strangled him. To death."

Mrs. Cain wailed wordlessly, then cried, "My poor baby!" She tried to hug the air between them and did in fact put her arms around the small ghost, who returned the gesture.

"I know where he is, lady," Rory whispered, his throat tight with emotion. "I can take you to him." He slowly got up off the swing. "Come on, Sammy, you need to show us exactly where."

"Where is it? Where's my baby boy's grave?" Mrs. Cain asked, wiping tears off her grieving face with the hem of her apron.

"Well, it ain't exactly a grave," Rory said reluctantly, "but it's off in the woods behind your house about a mile."

"That close? All this time, he was that close?"

"Yeah," Rory sighed. He looked at the space between them. "Oh, okay. Sammy says you need a limb saw and prob'ly a shovel. Okay? And we should bring that Vampire Lady with us. We'll need her help; he ain't that easy to get to. That's why no one found him before now."

"Mona Lou? Okay." Now somewhat composed, Mrs. Cain nodded and stood. "I'll get everything together."

Rory sat there and waited, chatting idly with Sammy about *Star Wars* stuff. Mrs. Cain was gone more than fifteen minutes, but when she returned to the porch, she was dressed in rough clothes and had Mona Lou in tow, carrying a shovel and a bow saw. The goth girl looked intensely curious and asked Rory, "What's this about finding my brother? How can you possibly know where he is after all this time?"

"He's right here tellin' me," Rory said, patting the swing's seat.

Monu Lou shook her head. "Dude, you're seriously strange."

Rory fixed her with a glare. "Look who's talkin', Miss Vampire Lady. Does your skin sparkle in the sun, or what?"

She rolled her eyes. "Where are we *going*, Mom?" Mona Lou moaned.

Mrs. Cain's lips thinned as she looked out into the woods behind the house, and she tucked a stray lock of hair behind her ear. "We're going into the woods to find your brother, honey. We'll just follow Rory here."

"Shouldn't we call the Sheriff at least?"

"Not until we know for sure about... about Sammy," Mrs. Cain said, and sighed. "I'm sorry, Mona Lou. You're liable to see some things today you'll want to unsee, but... we need to know for sure. For closure."

Mona Lou stood up straight and squared her shoulders. "Okay, Mama."

Rory led them deep into the forest. The woods were moderately old-growth, so there wasn't much undergrowth to get in the way. He finally stopped after about fifteen minutes, pointing at a huge, spreading cedar tree with its lower branches lying flush with the ground. Quietly, he said, "That guy Junior Hickermon, when he was done, he...he pushed Sammy up under the branches of that tree there, so no one could see him. He's right up against the trunk, this side of it, under a bunch of needles and stuff."

Without a word, Mona Lou went to work on cutting away the lower branches of the tree. When it was pared back far enough to reach in, she looked to her mother. Mrs. Cain blinked at her for a long moment, then handed her the shovel. "You do it, sweetie, please," she said in a strained voice. "I-I just can't."

Mona Lou nodded silently and took the shovel from her mom.

Meanwhile, Rory turned his head sharply, tilted his head slightly upward with a confused look on his face, and said, "Who are — oh, really?" He then walked away from the big cedar for about a hundred feet, like he was following someone. Then he looked down at a slight rectilinear depression in the leaf litter covering the ground. "Oh, I see. Yeah. Ow. That musta hurt. *Who,* now? A girl, really? No kiddin'."

Rory looked over at the little boy with the dried red-brown smudge on his nose, then back at the scowling big boy, who, for his part, had a honker big enough to split wood and a big ol' bleeding gash on the right side of his head. "Sammy, dude, why didn't you tell me you had a friend out here?"

Sammy replied with a scowl of his own. "Rex? He ain't my friend. He's a mean 'un. Back when he was alive, he was about as bad as Junior."

"Don't you listen to that little pissant," Rex growled. "He's been doin' nothin' but moaning about being sad and missing his mama ever since he was left here."

Rory put his fists on his hips. "Now, that ain't fair, mister. He's not but seven years old. Or he was." He turned to go back to the Cains, and Sammy followed. Rex did not. To Sammy, Rory whispered, "All this today's about finding *you,* not this Rex kid. I don't like him, for some reason."

"Me neither. Imagine being stuck with him for 15 years and 43 days."

As they approached the Cains, Rory asked Sammy, "Rex, he's been here, what, more than 20 years? That much longer'n you?"

"That's what he says."

"Some girl attacked him with an ax? Really?"

"It was a hatchet. Says she split his head wide open while he was trying to 'get some,' whatever that means," Sammy said, his mouth twisting with disgust.

"Huh."

"He says the girl who kilt him is named something like...Ashley. Not that, exactly, but somethin' like that."

Rory stopped short and turned to look at Sammy, whose outline was starting to shimmer. "My —" He swallowed, his mouth suddenly dry. "My mama's name is *Ashling*."

"That's it! Prob'ly her, then," Sammy said as the shimmer ramped up. "An' if it was, then she did a good thing."

Suddenly, for just an instant, Rory saw Sammy as he would have looked like had he lived to adulthood: a tall, gangly man, handsome in a rugged way, with a kind smile. Then Sammy's form spiraled in and contracted to a point that veered to the left and slowly faded away, like the picture in an old TV set when you switch it off.

When Rory got back to Sammy's sister and mama, they were both crying, and Mona Lou was trying to call Sheriff Val Posner, cursing because she only had one bar this deep in the woods. A long bone with knobby ends lay on the ground between them, crusted with something dark. "That's a human leg bone," Mrs. Cain said through her tears. "That's my Sammy. Part of him."

"I know," Rory said quietly, sadly. Then he looked to Mona Lou. "I'd appreciate it if you don't tell Sheriff Val I was here," he requested. "Maybe just say you had a dream about this place, or that you got one of them anonymous tips, you know, and you got lucky." He turned away.

"Where you going?" Mona Lou demanded.

"I gotta get home. I'm late as it is." He paused, turned back, and added, "I'm glad you found Sammy. He's at peace now."

Then Rory turned and ran home.

***

Nine nights later, after all the business about finding Sammy had *finally* settled down, Rory was sleeping really well when someone booped his nose at two in the morning. *Again.* "Gosh darn it!" he exclaimed as he erupted out of bed, rubbing sleepy tears out of his eyes. "D'you have any idea what *time* it is?"

He glared at the two toddlers of indeterminate gender standing by his bed, holding hands and glowing gently. "You got no idea, do ya?"

They shook their heads no.

Rory groaned long and loud, so God would know just how put out he was. Then he said, "This is gonna be one of them recurrin' themes in my life, ain't it?"

The dirty-faced toddlers nodded gravely.

"Dang it."

AH! REAL MONSTERS

BY KASEY HILL

When I was younger, I had a recurring nightmare every single night. Therapists told my parents I was experiencing night terrors. They prescribed me medication after medication for antipsychotics, but none of them ever worked to stop the monster from appearing. My parents thought they were nightmares, but to me they weren't. They were so real that I could smell the creature when it arrived in my closet.

Each night, it started the same way. I would hear a scratching sound like nails clawing the inside of my walls, and then a chain would rattle. The scratching would stop as it reached my closet door, and I would hear the door handle jiggle. It would make the click sound and open only just enough for a hand to reach out. One by one, claws would emerge, and the hand would open and close slightly, tapping on the door. The door would creep open bit by bit as the chain rattled louder. The last I would see would be a head emerge from behind the door, and when it got to the eyes, the hollow eyes that were always misplaced, I would let out a scream, and my parents would come running. It would always be gone by the time they got there.

It was after about a month straight of walking me through my room, showing me there wasn't anything under the bed, showing me there wasn't anything in the closet, and not helping them schedule an appointment with my primary care doctor. He referred them to a sleep psychologist. It just wasn't one either. I was a special case, apparently. They hooked me up to leads and watched me in their office to see if I exhibited sleep paralysis. Stress is usually a factor in both sleep paralysis and night terrors.

Nearly all cases they examined with a definite diagnosis always had an episode in one of the night stays. I, however, did not.

So, the new doctors prescribed me anxiety medication along with some sleeping pills on top of the antipsychotic medications, packed me on my way back home, and told my parents to call if they needed anything. They explained that I hadn't exhibited any traits whatsoever while being monitored, but that did not mean I did not have the disorder. Upon my arrival home, that very night, the sleep demon returned to my closet, and my parents were awakened to my screams like normal.

After years of sleepless nights and my parents denying my fears, I was used to sleeping two or three hours at a time. They began sleeping with noise-canceling headphones, and it triggered a fight-or-flight response in me. Upon waking to the monster, I would leave my room, go downstairs to take my medication, breathe it out, and return to bed to sleep. The medications kept me doped up pretty much until dawn, so if the monster ever returned, I wouldn't know it.

This went on for many years until I went off to college and finally found peaceful sleep. However, nightmares of the nightmares still plagued my sleep until I met a man who talked me into hypnosis therapy. I could confront the monster in my dreams head-on and perhaps rid myself of the many years of the scratching and screams from a mangled, demonic face. Every time I heard a clinking sound of metal, it frightened me. Every time there was an odd scratching sound in the walls, perhaps from rats, it sent me to my bottle of anxiety meds. I couldn't even sleep in a room that had a closet. I wanted to live free of this...this creature…monster…thing.

So, I sat timidly in the hypnotherapist's chair and listened, letting the room's sounds overwhelm my senses. I focused first on the clock tick, then the air conditioner kicking on and off, and finally, I stared straight ahead at the hypnotherapist as he made notes in his book while glancing back at me often. The sounds began to churn together until I soon was drowning in a sea of sensory overload when he clicked his pen closed, and it startled me from my anxiety-induced state. He asked me if I was ready, and I just nodded, afraid to utter a word. He instructed me to lie back on the seat and get comfortable, then walked me through the steps to reach a hypnotic state. After twenty years of sleepless nights, I once again was lying in my bed as a child listening to the crawling sounds within my walls. Faintly, I could hear his voice, but his instructions were garbled as the sound of the metal chain clinked harder and harder, and the scratching grew louder and louder. And then all the noise stopped, including the sound of his voice. I watched in fear-stricken panic as my door crept open, as it always had as a child, but instead of being able to yell for my parents, there was nothing stopping this grotesque thing from opening the door completely this time. I was frozen in fear as his mouth came into view, seemingly stuck in a frozen agape fixation with a trail of blood leaking from it.

His face looked as it always had. His beady eyes scowled at me while a gaping mouth hole dripped and drooled, threatening to swallow me whole. His sharp talon-like fingertips looked twice as long as I remembered. My greatest fear had been that he'd tear the flesh from my body if he could get any closer than what he was to me. However, this time, no matter the force I exerted to scream, my voice didn't even make a croaking sound. Tears began to fall as the nightmare settled in, and I realized there was no escape from it. The only thing that my ears could register was the sound of the clinking of that terrifying chain.

He lumbered toward me, his steps over-exerting his strength as he pushed one leg in front of the other. I had nowhere to go. I was trapped in this nightmare in my own head. As he neared me and reached out to me with his clawed hands, another memory swiftly replaced this one. I was a toddler, and I'd wandered downstairs into the basement. It was dark and eerie, but as such a small child, the settings never bothered me. I remember hearing the chain and the claws. And right before me stood the menacing sight that had left me sleepless for years. He was chained in our basement, with mangled shorts as his only clothing. But I surprisingly had no fear of him. He would roll me a ball, and I would roll it back, playing a simple game with him. He stood from his seated position and walked over to me, reaching out for me to come closer. I remember being grabbed from behind as my parents snatched me from my playmate. They were yelling and screaming, and I watched him retreat like a scolded dog would when its master would raise a newspaper to strike it.

"NO!" Is all I can remember them screaming at my friend. "BAD!"

And I was toted away from the basement, and the door was forever padlocked. But why was he in the basement? And why did my parents have him there locked away?

The therapist managed to retrieve me from my memories. I bolted upright in my seat, sweat drenching my clothes. Wild-eyed, I stared around the room to realize I was back in his office while he stood over me mouthing words. He was speaking, but I couldn't hear him. I scrambled to my feet with him still trying to get my attention, but the only thing I could hear was the beating of my heart in my ears with the painful thump in my chest. I made it to my car and sat in the driver's seat, deep breathing, trying to calm myself down. I knew what I had to do. I had to know. I just had to know. So, I made my way to my parents' old house. They had relocated to warmer climates, and we were between renters on the property, so it was vacant.

Over the years, very little had changed in the house. My parents did some mild remodeling and updating, mainly just painting and new flooring, nothing serious. I grabbed a large flashlight and a crowbar from my trunk and headed inside the house. I set the flashlight down at the basement door and used the crowbar to pry the lock off it. Every renter we ever had asked about the basement, and my parents always told them it was off-limits due to its tendency to flood. There were never any questions asked, and no one ever tried to go down there. The lock clattered to the floor, and I grabbed the doorknob and twisted it, then yanked it hard from its place; however, it didn't budge. It hadn't been opened in so long that it had swelled in the door frame. A few yanks, and it gave in to my strength, creaking and popping open as I picked up the flashlight and shone it down the stairs.

I carefully walked down the steps one by one in case any of them were rotted. The basement wasn't unlike any other basements, being damp and dark. The mustiness of the cold floors settled in the air. I shone the light at the wall, and there they hung fetters anchored into the brick wall. An unfamiliar smell hit my senses, stinking like no other at first, and then it came to me. It was the smell that filled my closet every night. A scream came from behind me, and at the top of the stairs, there he stood. The monster from my nightmares, except they weren't nightmares. They had been very real occurrences. The door slammed behind him, and the rattling chains clanked on the stairs as he walked down them slowly. The anticipation and anxiety of what was going to happen next wracked my brain.

My hand shook with the flashlight, and my voice choked out, "Wh-wh-who ar-ar-rre you?"

He swallowed hard. A garbled, pitiful response leaked from his mouth. "You don't know me, little one?"

"I only remember you from my nightmares." I squeaked out.

"I was your brother..." he managed to get out.

Everything rushed back to me. My brother...the one who died before I was born...except he didn't die. They just told everyone that because he was born with deformities. They couldn't let anyone know he had been born mangled. There would be no way to adopt him out, so instead, they locked him away in the basement so no one could ever see him again. I shone my flashlight around the room. It rested on a small cage...this was purely bestial...it must have been where they kept him as an infant, and then, when he was old enough, they chained him down here. The real monster was not the one in my closet, but those I called mother and father and whispered I love you to at night. I was nauseated. I felt icky. My...my brother was tossed aside like garbage and left to die like a stray animal. I picked up a set of bolt cutters lying beneath the basement steps, walked to the wall the chain was fastened to, and cut it. I then walked to him, my flesh and blood, and snipped the lock loose from his metal collar.

"You're coming with me," I said as I reached my hand out for his.

He hesitated. I knew he remembered the words "no" and "bad" that screamed at him.

"It's ok. They aren't here to hurt you anymore," I said. "Come with me."

He grabbed my hand, and I led him out of the basement. He flinched from the light until his eyes slowly adjusted. I led him outside, where he stood in awe at the bright sun and green foliage. He inhaled deeply as if he had never smelled air before. I led him to my car and stuck him in the backseat with a throw blanket. I picked up my cell phone and dialed my parents.

"Heya, son! How are ya, sport?" Dad asked.

"I found him. My brother. The monster in my closet. The *abomination* in the basement. My nightmare, you hid. I found him, you sick bastards! And everyone is going to know what you did…what you did to him and what you did to me."

DOGS

BY SJ TOWNEND

Some people said she was a hero, you know, a superhero, one of those Average Joes who slip into a phone booth in their regular attire and come out five seconds later clad in bright spandex with their pants on top of their trousers and a cape billowing out behind them? Marjorie knew she was special, but she didn't believe she was *that* special. She certainly didn't think she was super.

Some sort of ability to help others, yes, but super, a masked crusader? No. No. No. She would not allow herself to have such delusions of grandeur, no alter ego of sorts. Marjorie didn't think of herself like that at all. And she couldn't pull off a mask, not over her half-moon spectacles and her blue-rinse perm. Marjorie, in Marjorie's opinion, just happened to possess a good heart and a rare talent. A special gift, if you like, which she had discovered quite by accident the first time. No one else, not a single soul she'd ever met, could do what she could do, so it had been her calling, hadn't it, in a way, that thing she did to animals?

And what she had learned she could do was kind and righteous. She didn't exactly feel she could sit back and rest on her laurels. No, she had work to do, work that had become a duty of sorts. And after the first time she became aware of what she could do, the power she held, and she went ahead and succeeded in changing a life, implicitly, she had to keep on doing it. She had to devote her life to the cause.

Luckily, she enjoyed what she did.

***

Marjorie lived in an odd little house, an old house, much older than her, herself at a ripe age, and the house sat at the edge of the common. You might have seen it, actually, in your youth, or while visiting grandparents and taking that post-lunch stroll your parents always insist upon.

But the house itself was not important, not especially, with its peeling paint and its moderately sized garden overgrown with wild violets and sunflowers that leaned too far toward the sun, but she was happy there. There was ample space for what she did, and she adored the view from her kitchen window, through the garden and out onto the vast stretch of green space that was the common. The peculiar little cottage was perfect for her. Yes, it was a little isolated, but she was content in her own way. And it wasn't as if her house was ever empty. Far from it. She had plenty of company. Her home was always filled with the sound of wheels rolling over wooden floors.

The first time she knew she might have been somebody special, a bit of a big deal, was when she encountered an unwanted dog, a dribbling mongrel, a black-and-white pup with hints of boxer and lashings of something far less pedigree. She spotted the pup tied up outside the butcher's shop, abandoned there, with a handwritten note that read: "Broken. Help yourself." The unfortunate mutt's back legs had given out. Poor chap. So she popped inside the butcher's to enquire.

"He's nothing to do with me," the butcher said. "The dog ran out from nowhere and into the road outside my shop. No collar or tags. The driver tore off without stopping. We tied the hound up out there a few days ago, but no one has come to his aid."

"Did you not think to contact a vet?" she asked. "The dog is injured, yes, but it doesn't appear to be anything life-threatening, and he's also significantly malnourished, all skin and bone."

"A vet? I can't even afford to pay my own dentistry bill," the butcher said, and he sneered at her, revealing a set of blackened teeth. "As if I can afford to take an abandoned dog to the vets!

Take the dog. Take him away. He's yours. In fact, I'll give you three pounds of sausages to be rid of him. It's bad for business, having him sat outside whining like that, with his back legs twisted at a strange angle." Something about the note had twisted in her heart like a stubborn knot. She had no medical skills and barely two pennies to rub together herself, but she couldn't have left the poor dog there, that poor shaking dog with its big brown eyes, so she untied the dog and placed him in her tartan fabric shopper cart, took the sausages that the butcher had wrapped in greaseproof paper, and then towed the injured dog home. "What shall we call you then, mister?" she asked. "I think you look like a Gus."

When they reached her home, the pair of them feasted like royalty on twelve plump pork sausages. And after their big meal, they fell asleep curled up together in her armchair.

At some point, she woke in the night, and she knew, she just knew, what it was that Gus wanted. It was obvious, really. What Gus had really wanted was for his hind legs to work again, but she didn't have that sort of superhero power, the ability to heal the sick—not quite—but she was special enough to give the dog a set of wheels instead, two lovely wheels with blue and silver spokes, and Gus took to them like he'd been born rolling, like he'd come out of the womb on skates. She watched him speed through the garden with a wild gleam in his eyes, kicking up dirt and barking at dandelions, and she laughed for the first time in what had felt like years.

Shortly after Gus came Bella, a regal Afghan hound with a long, flowing coat that trailed behind her as she limped along the path. "Hip dysplasia," was the first thing that the man who followed Bella to Marjorie's front door said, before even offering a hello. The dog had belonged to his grandfather, and Old Grandfather William had sadly passed away. The man claimed his own home was already too full with a child, a wife, and a fish tank. He simply couldn't make space for the hound. "Not with it having mobility problems, anyway, my house isn't equipped for such situations." And he hadn't had the time or the money, what with the holiday he'd just booked and his platinum membership at the golf club and all the paperclips he had to unfold and refold at work. His list of reasons was endless, and he'd already ushered the dog inside Marjorie's house and gone back out to stand on the doorstep to explain his misfortune before Marjorie had had a chance to give her opinion. "Plus, I heard from the butcher that this is the place for such dogs, the odd cottage on the far side of the common."

So, Marjorie accepted Bella into her home and introduced Bella to Gus, and there was butt-sniffing aplenty and some yaps and some woofs, and that evening, Marjorie held Bella gently in her arms. She reassured Bella that she was safe and welcome, and she had been brought to a place of much love. "Mi casa es su casa," Marjorie whispered and smiled as she ran a comb through the fine dog's lustrous coat, then petted the dog on her head. Bella, with her long, thin face and beautiful, big brown eyes, looked up at Marjorie and cocked her head, and Marjorie knew, she just knew, what it was that Bella desired.

There together, on Marjorie's sofa, Bella and Gus cuddled up with their snouts on Marjorie's lap. It was an awkward, cumbersome cuddle, what with Gus's shiny red wheels snagging Bella's long hair and taking up so much space, but with Marjorie's aid, and a bit of scooching about, they all managed to fit on comfortably, and once both dogs had nodded off, Marjorie wriggled out and smiled at the sight of the two wheel buds blossoming out like sprouting plants from Bella's grey hind, one on either side, and then she got into her own bed, where she stretched out properly to rest. The next day, Bella woke Marjorie with a happy bark. Bella was delighted to wake up with fully-formed wheels.

Bella, with a new lust for life, loved nothing more than chasing butterflies in Marjorie's garden, and Gus adored chasing

Bella. It brought such joy to Marjorie to watch Bella charge about, and Gus, now too, seemed over the moon to have such a playful friend.

After Gus and Bella, the dogs came in droves. Next came Billy, a one-eyed Chihuahua with a grumpy face and a sweet disposition, who had lost his mobility after an incident at the park with an overzealous goose. "Now, when I place him on the ground for some exercise, Billy just sits there like a sock that's lost its partner."

"I see," Marjorie replied as the prim lady at the door lifted Billy out of her designer bag and handed the pup to her.

"We heard about you from Mr. and Mrs. Brown, the things you do for dogs." And Billy's owner began to reel off countless reasons why Billy could not stay with her while also scrolling through text messages on her mobile phone.

"I'll take Billy," Marjorie said, politely interrupting the woman standing at her front door. "You don't need to justify your actions. I can see you must be busy."

And the very next day, after a large bowl of treats and a long, warm snuggle, Billy too woke up with wheels. What wheels! Billy, the smallest of the dogs, a pint-sized thing, had clearly wanted to be a large dog, a Great Dane or a St. Bernard, not a dog that could be slid into a handbag and paraded around like a doll, because the wheels on Billy sprouted out and kept on growing until they were huge. Gigantic. Picture a penny farthing being ridden by a mouse! Billy's wheels were so big that each resembled a spinning dinner plate melded into the flesh and fur of his left and right flanks, held in place with premium self-oiling steel axles. In fact, it would be reasonable to say that Billy had more wheels than a dog. More metal than flesh. But he was happy, so very happy, because now he could run around, and his little eyes, like raisins, shone with merriment.

Soon, the whole town began to take notice. Some whispered behind their hands— "What is she doing, the woman who lives in the odd cottage, collecting broken things?" Others, however, saw her house as a place of quiet magic, where lost and forgotten creatures found a second life. People left donations of kibble and sacks of used tennis balls, and the butcher sometimes dropped off delicious marrow-rich bones. Children would stop by on sunny afternoons to watch the dogs whiz past like tiny chariots. "Look! Look at the brindle one go!"

One day, a local businessman, a pompous man with a salt-and-pepper mustache named Cornelius Grigsby, paid Marjorie a visit. He stood at the edge of her garden with a stern expression on his chops and watched as Gus chased Billy in dizzying circles.

"Marjorie Blutherface," he said, for this was her full name, "I'm sorry, I should have let you know her *full* name sooner – not that her full name is of any *significant* importance, but you'll notice, it's not really a superhero name at all, is it? But don't let that put you off or deter you from reading on. Not all heroes wear capes or have names like Thunderstrike or Flow-Go-Waterleg or Velocity Man, do they? And a person like you, your name...it isn't exactly superhero material either, is it? But I see what *you* do when you are alone. I know what true powers *you* wield. These dogs are a menace. They're disrupting the town's peace with all their rolling about. You should take them somewhere quieter. Perhaps a home somewhere else? Somewhere far from here, far from our quaint, picturesque little town...a faraway place for the unwanted."

Marjorie's eyes narrowed. "These dogs aren't unwanted. They're loved. And what's more, they're loving life!"

Cornelius sniffed. "Loved or not, they don't belong here. They make people, myself included…feel uncomfortable. All that movement. The spinning wheels. These animals, part dog, part metal, and not quite whole, look utterly unsettling. You understand, don't you?"

But Marjorie didn't understand. Not one bit of what the man had said. All she saw were muddy-pawed creatures full of *joie de vivre* and jubilation. And something fierce rose in her, a force that had lain dormant since long before Gus had slobbered and woofed and licked into her life, an inner rage that had been resting like a sleeping tiger since her step father had dropped her off at the children's home and had told the duty manager he simply didn't have the time or the funds or the space to care for her now that her mother had passed.

"Come back tomorrow," Marjorie said. "And bring your friends. Bring everyone you know. I'll show you exactly how much these dogs belong."

The next morning, Cornelius arrived with half the town in tow, expecting to see Marjorie packing up her things. But when they reached the common next to Marjorie's garden, a curious sight greeted them all.

The night before, upset by Cornelius's visit, Marjorie had cuddled each of her wheeled dogs in turn, and she had stroked them all, and had stared deep into all of their playful eyes, before they had all fallen asleep, and she had known. From looking into their eyes, she had just known what they had each really wanted. And it made her sadder because she knew she could never give them back fully functioning hind legs. But she had been able to provide for them what they'd *nearly* wanted, if you like, the next best thing, because that's how her powers worked. And she would also give them a loving home, and as much fun as they could handle, and no pompous man in a ridiculous suit could ever tell her otherwise.

Cornelius gasped at the sight before him. A grand racecourse had been set up—complete with twists and jumps and ramps. The trees were decorated with lengths of pretty bunting. A lemonade stall stood pitched up underneath a leafy oak. Marjorie stood by her front gate with a marvelous grin on her face and her best lilac cardigan on. "Welcome!" she said. "Welcome, one and all."

Each of her twenty-three dogs had a freshly polished set of wheels which gleamed in the sunlight. Bella wore a tiny silk scarf around her neck, and Billy sported a yellow helmet with a purple lightning bolt painted on the side. Gus, the fastest of them all, stood there, tall and handsome, as proud as a knight preparing for battle.

Marjorie held up a checkered flag. "This," she declared, "is the First Annual Somerton Roller Dog Derby."

The dogs took their marks. Marjorie dropped the flag, and the dogs were off.

Bella soared over the ramps like a dancer in motion. Billy bulldozed his way through obstacles with unstoppable determination, with his pink tongue dangling out the side of his mouth. Gus darted through the course so fast that he was practically a blur. All of the other dogs on wheels gave it their very best, too. The crowd found themselves cheering. All of the crowd but Cornelius.

When the race was over, the crowd erupted in applause. "And now to announce the winner," Marjorie said through her loudhailer. "You are all winners! Each and every one of you, my fine fluffy friends!" And she gave each dog a treat. The ones that could still wag their tails wagged their tails with all their might, and the ones who weren't too tired did laps of honour, and the ones that were exhausted from all the fun and couldn't wag their tails simply tipped their heads back and howled like ecstatic wolves. The crowd dispersed with broad grins on their faces, chattering and giggling with mirth, until just Marjorie and Cornelius were left standing opposite each other on the common. Marjorie waved her dogs back inside and then turned to Cornelius with a triumphant smile.

"Do they belong now?"

Cornelius cleared his throat. "I still think this whole setup, what you have done here with this space, is an eyesore. I plan to ensure such a façade never happens again."

"Oh dear man, whatever has happened to you to make your heart so cold? Please, come inside for a cup of tea. Perhaps we can talk more."

Cornelius shifted from foot to foot and tightened his paisley cravat. "Well, there is another matter I wish to discuss with you, so perhaps refreshment would be a good idea." He stumbled over the edge of a ramp as he followed her back to her house.

"Careful there – maybe *you* would you be better off on wheels?" Cornelius wobbled. With a smirk on her face, Marjorie steadied him.

"Don't be ridiculous. I nearly broke a leg tripping over your stupid racecourse." He kicked the wooden plinth from its stack of bricks, and the pieces tumbled down onto the grass.

***

"The situation, you see, Mrs Blutherface, is one of a financial nature." Cornelius stirred his tea and helped himself to a gingernut while Marjorie poured fresh water into many small bowls for her dogs.

"There is always an ulterior motive." She sighed. "Go on. Tell me why you are really so in disagreement with my situation, with my precious babies and me."

"This patch of land, the common, your house and garden, we want to redevelop the entire area. I'm sure you're aware of the growing popularity of our town and our need for more high-end property?"

"I was not. But I think I have an idea of where this might be heading."

"You're sitting on a gold mine here, Mrs. Blutherface. I will make you a sizeable offer, to take your animals, this entire carnival act, and relocate it elsewhere, far, far away. I want to build here. A grand twelve-story apartment block. I'll make my money back on rental fees in under six months."

"But we're happy here, living next to the common, the dogs and me. And I'm too old and too ill to even consider a relocation." Marjorie reached for a biscuit from the pile stacked between them. Cornelius recoiled at the sight of Marjorie's hands, her fingers flexing slowly, like staggering knobbled twigs.

"Dear god, what is wrong with your hand?"

"Arthritis," she told him. "Rheumatoid arthritis. My hands have been like this for years. There's no way I could pack up and move house at my age, in my condition."

Cornelius dropped his biscuit back on the plate and shifted in his seat as if trying to create distance between him and her. "It's not contagious. I'm sorry if my hands have offended you." And she *apologized*. She apologized to *him* for *his* disgust at her painful affliction.

"I'm sure my team could provide help with packing, with relocating. In honesty, we just want you and your pack of beasts gone. But tell me one thing. How on earth could a woman with such a disability build and fix wheels for so many dogs?!"

The screech and burr of metal on wood caused Cornelius to jerk in his chair. Billy trundled over to Marjorie, perhaps sensing her distress, and placed his snout in her lap and looked up at his owner with his mesmerizing brown eyes and a twitching wet nose.

"Now, now, Billy, it's not dinner time yet. I'll feed you soon. Very soon. We have something delicious for dinner today. A special meal after all the fun and games. Scrumptious, buttery meat." Billy licked his lips as if he had understood her every word. Marjorie stroked Billy's head and returned her attention to Cornelius. "Oh, sir, I do not *build* the wheels. I know nothing of engineering or mechanics! I'd struggle to twist a screwdriver or bow a saw or arc a welding torch! But I would if I had to, even if it pained me, if there wasn't an easier way. Because who else would care for these poor creatures? And what sort of life is one led without compassion?"

"You hire a man in, I suppose. Tell me who it is. Who is in on this ridiculous set-up?"

"It's all me. I have a gift. I don't fully understand it, and it's not as honed as I'd like it to be. Ideally, if I were better at it, more gifted, then they'd all be healed entirely with four fabulous working legs. Then my pets could run and move and play as freely as you, but alas, I work with the powers I have been given. I do the best I can."

"Tell me how." Cornelius' voice grew louder. He leaned forward and raised a brow.

"It's not really something I can explain, but perhaps I could show you? The process might make you feel a little uncomfortable, but I think it would make everything more clear."

"Certainly, you show away."

Marjorie led Cornelius through to the living room and sat down on her sofa.

"Sit here, by me. Sorry about all the dog hair." She brushed down the spot at her side and, cautiously, Cornelius sat down.

"And what now?"

"I'll need to hold you in my arms and stroke your head, and you will look into my eyes and tell me what it is you need, what it is you want, and then, you must drift off. A couple of minutes of deep rest will do, if you think you can?"

"Fall asleep? At three in the afternoon? I can't. I have work to do."

Marjorie shrugs. "It's up to you. If you want to witness my power, that's the only way. I don't have another animal here right now needing help with which I could demonstrate, thankfully. My house is becoming rather full. I'll wake you up, don't worry. And if you can't sleep, just rest your eyes for a moment."

"And you're telling me all I have to do is tell you what I want, and that can be anything?"

"Of course. I'll do my best to accommodate your deepest desire. I'll get as close to fulfilling your wish as I can, as close as my powers will allow." And so, he agreed, and she wrapped her arm around his shoulder and began to smooth back his graying hair with a true tenderness, and then, and then, she brought her face kiss-close to his and stared deeply into his eyes. "What is it, Cornelius, dear? What is it you truly desire? You can want for anything, and I'll do my best, by the power vested in me, to help you achieve your dream. And then you must doze, and then you will wake, and then you may find that what you receive is pretty close to your request."

"I want to be rich, so rich, and I want this space, all of it. Your house. Your garden. The commons." But Marjorie knew this already. She just knew, just by looking into his cold eyes.

"Oh my. That is quite a large request, but I'll do my best." And so, she continued to stroke his hair, and as she did so, she said, "It's okay, it's all okay. You're a good boy, a very good boy, who's a very, very good boy?" And Cornelius tutted and let out a sort of grunt. "Now, please close your eyes, Cornelius. I'll wake you in three minutes." And thus, like a very good boy – although, you and I know he was not a very good boy – he did as he was told and he shut his eyes.

Three minutes passed, and when she sensed that his breathing had slowed slightly, his body felt softer under her arm, and she heard him let out a tiny moan like the sort of sound a sleeping puppy might make, accompanied by possibly a quiet fart, which all suggested to her that he had entered a state of significant relaxation, she patted him on the head. "Wake up, my dear. It's over."

Cornelius rubbed his eyes. "Nothing has happened. What madness. What poppycock and absolute nonsense. I'll have you removed from here on grounds of insanity. I'll have you committed. I'll have your dogs destroyed!"

"Have patience, my friend. Patience is a virtue. It has never not worked before," Marjorie said.

Cornelius stood up and swiped off dog hair from his suit trousers, and that is when he noticed the back of his hand glinting under the ceiling light.

"My hand! The back of my hand. It's hard. And golden! What's happening? Look! Look!" He hoisted his suit sleeve up and thrust his bare arm towards her, and the pair of them watched in awe as the gold colour spread up his arm. He tapped it with his other hand. "Gold, you've turned my left arm into solid gold!"

Marjorie's lips parted slightly, as if she wanted to speak but couldn't find the right words. And then, after Cornelius's nostrils flared and his cheeks grew red with rage, she managed to find some words. But they probably weren't the words Cornelius wanted to hear.

"The problem is, despite my power, despite this gift I've been blessed with, I've never been able to give people *exactly* what they want, just something of a close approximation. I'm sorry. So sorry," and there she was again, apologizing. Would you have apologized? I know what *I* would have said, and it would have involved words far too rude for this story.

Standing there, in the living room, with a golden metallic sheen rippling up his arm, towards his shoulder, up under his collar, his neck, his jaw, so quickly, spreading over his flesh like ink in water, Cornelius panicked. He bent over and tugged up the bottoms of his trousers. "My legs! They're turning to gold, too! My feet, they're so heavy! Weightier than lead!"

"I don't think they're heavier than lead, surely. Gold has a lower density than lead, I believe, but gold, I am sure you know, holds considerably more value, but I understand your concern." Billy, Gus, and Bella cowered behind her as she spoke, not sure what to make of the angry man who was standing in their home and shaking his hardening fists at their owner.

"What have you done to me?"

"I can't help you, I'm afraid. My powers, my look of love, only work on any individual once."

"I'm going to find a doctor, and then I'll be back with the police. You witch, you scoundrel."

Marjorie shook her head and stroked her wizened chin. "I prefer superhero, I think. Yes. Superhero is better than a witch. In general, I tend to only use my powers for good."

And so, Cornelius walked out of her house like a cranky robot, like a cat with each of its legs caught in a separate small cardboard tube, and twenty-three dogs rolled out of the living room, out of Marjorie's front door in Cornelius's wake and barked merrily. "Good riddance," they barked in dog language. "Good riddance, because now that he's gone, it must be dinnertime," Marjorie called her tribe back in with an ear-piercing whistle and dished out glorious dollops of prime steak into each of their bowls and patted each of their jolly heads.

And what became of Cornelius? Well, he made it as far as the centre of the common before his body transmuted, from toe to head, into pure, solid gold. He was lucky, in a way, because Marjorie was never one for causing harm. Once, a long time ago, back when she had dreamt of becoming a doctor, while watching her mother grow sick, before being dropped off at St Ursula's Home for Lost Souls by her mean stepfather, she had even stood in front of her bedroom mirror at midnight with a candle cupped in her hands and had repeated the Hippocratic Oath three times to her own reflection. She had never *murdered* or maimed anything in her life. All she had ever wanted to do was help.

There, from the centre of the common, with all the space he had wanted within his grasp, with all that lovely green space just inches from his half-unfurled sparkling fingertips, he remained, and each day, he watched Marjorie and her dogs as they rolled out to frolic on the common. And the dogs presumed that the gold statue of Cornelius, which had been erected in the middle of their play zone, was put there for the same reason that all statues of once-powerful men were erected, as a place for dogs to mark their territory. So the dogs that could, cocked a wheel slightly and left their scent at Cornelius's base, and the dogs that couldn't, well, they simply whizzed around him in circles and yapped like mad.

I see your smile, your cheeky grin, and I know why you're feeling gleeful. You've passed it, haven't you, on that long, long walk you took with your parents, after that fat Sunday roast. You've seen it with your own very eyes. Don't you recall? That statue of a man made from gold, which has long since mottled to brown and grey, that statue of a man which stands so proud and fierce in the centre of the green space. That statue of a man with a slightly angry stare set hard upon his face? Of course, you have.

DON'T LET THE BED BUGS BITE

BY MARIN MOOR

Thinking about her new life, Maria gazed out the window of the 6:55 pm Metro-North train to Cold Stream Manor. She couldn't believe it; they had waited so long. The planning, the sacrifices, the stress, and the enormous leap of faith had all brought David and her to this one moment. It had worked out! They would be living out the dream that many people in the City desperately long for but never achieve. They had miraculously found a little carriage house on the Hudson River close to Manhattan, and it was affordable. They had made it out of the rat race, and now they would be able to slow down, smell the roses, and enjoy the next chapter of their life together. They had so much to look forward to.

Manhattan was not what it used to be when they were young, just out of grad school. It had changed so much, and more importantly, it was ridiculously expensive to live there. Every dollar you made went towards the cost of living, and if you happened to be an artist, forget about "making it" unless you were a "trust fund kid".

After surviving for 20-plus years in the "race", she and David decided that they needed to change their lives and get out while they still had the energy. So on the weekends, they would often go up the Metro-North along the Hudson River looking for possible small towns to move to; they would stop for lunch and explore. They searched through all four seasons because they wanted to get the real feel for the towns. Summers could be crazy with tourists, but the winters could be serene, even "abandoned".

They made a list of requirements and priorities for the place of their dreams:

1. At most an hour and 15–30 minutes from Grand Central Station, as David would still be commuting.

2. Walking distance to the train, so as not to deal with 4-wheel drive/snowstorm stuff because they had no vehicle and no experience.

3. Cool bar and or restaurant in town; hopefully with some artistic culture to go along with it. Most importantly, though, not too trendy. They had had enough of "trendy" when they were living in Manhattan, and especially with the arrival of the millennial generation.

They just wanted a small place to chill out and enjoy the simple things, to relax at a slower pace. A little yard would be awesome for summer gardening. Privacy would be a needed luxury, of course, especially after all the years of being in every neighbor's line of sight. That being said, this is how their dream came true:

One late fall weekend, they decided to go just a little farther on their exploration and get off in a town they had never stopped at before. Actually, they had missed their stop to visit Maria's work buddy, Rita, and that's what led them to Cold Stream Manor. They knew nothing about it except what Rita had told them. She had lived on the Hudson for a while, nearby in Moss Landing, and had mentioned Cold Stream, Manor. She had described it as a small rural town with some farming and vast acres of surrounding forest. There was a very old, rundown mansion right near the downtown that had some folklore attached to the family's history. The town was, as Rita put it, "a little backwoodsy but with definite potential". It wasn't where the groovy were moving to or where the affluent bohemians from Manhattan spent their weekend getaways, so it might be less expensive and more appealing to them.

It was past Halloween, and the leaves were all over the streets in piles. The trees were golden yellow with intermittent red, and there was mist in the air. The days were getting shorter, and the temperature was dropping. Maria and David stepped off the train at Cold Stream Manor and stood for a minute surveying the view from the platform. They saw a small parking lot with very few cars and a couple of old pickup trucks filled with firewood. The trees around the station and as far as they could see were old-growth maple and buckeye; impressive and looming. The view directly west was the glorious Hudson River, showing off impressive cliffs on its opposite side. There were wispy clouds of mist hovering above the water. To the north, there was a winding road hugged by an old stone wall that disappeared in the distance.

The "Main" Street led down to the station area and ended at the edge of the river. Stores seemed mostly closed, and some looked vacant. Actually, nothing seemed really lit up except a Tavern with smoke snaking out of the chimney. They decided they would try it, have a late lunch, and maybe see what sort of people lived around here, locals or transplants.

They walked inside through the heavy oak door. Though it was only 3:00 pm, the inside was dark, and lanterns and candles were lit for most of the lighting, creating a sort of cabin/woodsy feel to the place. It was old and probably had a lot of history. It was called "The Muddy Toad". There were many empty round wooden tables, but they chose an old carved wooden booth to slip into near the front.

They noticed the place was fairly empty. The menu was Autumn fare; there was a stew with venison and a pot pie with roasted potatoes and sage-cooked sausage. You could tell this probably wasn't the place for vegetarians. A sign said they made their own organic Mead and they both ordered a pint. Maria ordered a grilled cheese with local bacon, and David had the stew; both were delicious, and the Mead was sublime with hints of blackberries and some spice they couldn't quite put a name to.

An interesting thing about the tavern was that the ceiling had wooden beams, which were covered completely with amazing carvings. Someone had spent hours painstakingly carving intricate designs/symbols into the wood, looking like planets or tiny creatures/bugs....toads? You couldn't see too well as the lighting was dim, the rafters were very worn, and the burning fireplace had deposited a little smoke in the air near the rafters. But you could sense a long story behind these carvings as if they were documenting something possibly; it was so fascinating. Maria had seen a plaque on the wall that indicated the place had been around since the 1800's. It said that most of the decor, including the wooden beams, had been shipped over from the original "Muddy Toad" in Wales by the family of owners who had settled here.

She wondered what the history of these symbols might mean, as it seemed to become almost its own pictorial language or message. She thought she might inquire with one of the locals. She told David she was going to have a closer look at the carvings and got up and moved over to a corner where there was no one around so she could peer upwards.

As she managed a better view, she definitely could make out the outlines of beetle or scarab-like biomorphic forms. Hundreds of them, of all sizes, were depicted moving all towards the same upward direction, almost suggesting a mission. There were also images of "toad-like" forms that had no limbs but instead wings. So strange, she thought; these too seemed purposefully directed towards the same goal. The hues were dark brown with patchy, deep red scarlet shading. It intuitively felt otherworldly and almost "dark," like something you would see in pictures of a book about ancient caves or hidden underground destinations. Maria walked back to David with a mind full of questions.

There was an old wooden bar up on the left with a group of what looked like "locals" standing around having a pint. All were men except one older, striking woman with long hair in braids and high muck boots; she was flanked by all the men. Every now and then, she would glance over at them with a curious smile and twinkle in her eye. The men around her ranged in age from 20's to 80's, and all looked like they could be "locals", dressed like farm or ranch workers but sort of dapper in a Barbour/European way. Their clothes were dated, and Maria suspected they weren't American. Rita had told them there were some very old estates in this area with dairy and sheep farms; possibly, they were farmers. It really didn't feel like they were only an hour and a half away from NYC.

Another couple of older men, in the same garb, were seated slightly in front of them but pushed into a dark corner. Their faces were lit up by the table lantern, and she felt that they kept looking at her and David in a weird way with a smile, and then they would resume their whispers. The whispers seemed to contain a strange dialect and tones she couldn't place; low, deep tones somewhat guttural. She thought it must be some old Welsh dialect. That being said, she thought maybe she would take this opportunity to ask them about the carvings and the history of such because she couldn't stop thinking about them.

Her love of art and folklore dated back to her studies of cultural anthropology in undergrad. Her thesis, which had been published, was on wooden sculptures of the Nigerian Yoruba tribe, in which the carvings represented their religious beliefs and cosmology. These artworks were not just decorative but gave visual form to divine and spiritual forces, which helped devotees achieve a state of receptiveness during ceremonies. She wondered if these symbols might have a similar function in Welsh history. She talked it over with David, who was not so keen on her approaching what he deemed as definite provincial, somewhat strange men. She chuckled and told him to lighten up. stood, then walked towards them.

Maria felt the old wood floors creak beneath her feet as she approached the two older gentlemen. They immediately stopped their conversation and stared towards her in sync as if a small lamb would naively skip towards a hungry wolf. She introduced herself at once and explained that she and her husband were eager to move into such a lovely town like this and escape the frenetic day in and day out of city life. They were desperate to find a slower pace and get back to the natural elements of life. These men didn't miss a beat and asked her to sit down for a minute, like the spider would say to a fly; David watched nervously as he downed his pint and called for another.

Maria at once brought up her fascination with the tavern and specifically the intricate carvings on the ceiling. She told them that she felt sure there must be a story behind such beautiful artwork and hoped they could shed some light on the history if they knew anything at all. The man on the left with a glint in his eye spoke. She noticed they both had stunning blue-green. He said his name was Arawn and his friend's name was Tegid, but added that he did not speak much English.

They told Maria that they had both been there over 70 years, as they had come over with their parents at a very young age. Both were descendants of the owners of the original Muddy Toad in the Welsh countryside. The secrets of the carvings, he said, were a little less interesting than she might think, mostly based on harmless folklore that dated back farther than any of their relatives remember. They were mostly just bedtime stories they had been told, which had been carried on for centuries.

The wood beams of the "Muddy Toad" reflected imagery from old Welsh fairy tales they had heard of as children. One of the tales was of a limbless flying toad, called "Llamhigyn Y Dwr" that was said to roam the countryside playing tricks on the fisherman and farmers. Other stories included tales of beetles and strangely shaped bugs that would come alive every midnight from beneath the earth to bring good fortune to those children who had done their chores. All harmless, he said, then chuckled and looked quickly at his silent old friend.

Maria felt disappointed by the unimpressive nature of this information. She was sure that there must be something more to this discussion than he was letting on because intuitively she felt that the carvings, albeit the whole place, were permeated with an underlying sinister secret. She noticed his friend kept looking at him in subtle ways, communicating silently. She wondered if they were hiding something because she felt a hint of foreboding behind their welcoming gaze, but she brushed it off, thinking she was just paranoid.

She rose and thanked them both for their time and decided to go back to David, as it seemed that the conversation had reached its completion, whether or not she wanted it to. She felt somewhat deflated from the rush of energy before as she made her way back to their table. At once, she thought she might look into the history of those bedtime stories herself.

After lunch, while they finished up their pints while waving for the check, that magnetic woman at the bar looked over and moved towards them. At that moment, you could hear a pin drop as the whole bar watched her move; it was eerie. She appeared to be in her 60's. She had a glow of perpetual youth. She had a long mane of black/black hair tied in braids. Her eyes were deep-set and large, brown. Maria thought she looked like not so much Welsch, but Eastern European, maybe some exotic North African. There was something unusual about her whole appearance that hinted at vast arid landscapes. She wore this remarkable long necklace of carved stones, which looked like scarabs and small toads; it looked like an artifact. The carved pieces were different hues of scarlet, greens, and blues, and were set in gold brackets connecting them all in one gorgeous display of magic; quite a statement that this woman probably could only wear with such grace. Maria couldn't keep her eyes off the piece of jewelry; it almost looked like a talisman.

She introduced herself as "Kirke" and had a slight accent as well that they couldn't quite place. She said she was curious as to our presence, as not many out-of-towners stop here, gravitating toward the more artsy towns like Broadmoor or Moss Landing. They looked at each other and smiled, telling her they had missed their stop and decided to investigate this area, looking "off the beaten path" where it might be more affordable, and added their current mission of scoring their "forever home" away from the city. Maria's friend Rita had hailed the town as some hidden gem on the Hudson.

Kirke smiled at their candor and, not missing a beat, said, "Well, how about that? It just so happens that I'm a realtor and know of a place you might like. I could take you to see it right now, as it's just down the road and within walking distance of the train station. It's a little carriage house on the grounds of an old farm estate that's been in my family for generations. The town is actually named after this estate: Cold Stream Manor." Maria and David just stared at each other in surprise; they couldn't believe their luck. They both turned back to the woman at once and said, "Yes, we would love to see it," with disbelief at such serendipity.

So they settled up and thanked one of the owners, who was one of Kirke's cousins, she told them. It was around 5:30 pm when they walked out, and the light had faded with a heavy sky. They walked down the hill towards the river. As they walked, Maria asked Kirke how her family acquired the estate. They were both eager to hear the backstory that made way for their incredible luck in meeting her.

She said when her grandfather came over from Wales, he was hired to manage the farm on the estate, as he had a long history of farming. When the owner passed, he left everything to her grandfather. The estate had a working farm that her grandfather had restored with money he and his brother had made from the Muddy Toad, as well as from sales of locally raised meat from their farm. At this time, though, from decades of neglect, the Manor house was in need of repair, and things were so expensive that Kirke had decided to sell off the little cottage to help with some of the expenses.

As they approached the end of the street at the station, they turned north on the road that they had seen before stepping off the train. There was an old stone wall on the right side, and Kirke explained that it was the beginning of the estate boundary. The entire estate was surrounded by this stone wall built by hand over 200 years ago. There was an elaborate wrought-iron gate that was ajar; it looked old and worn with age and use. Kirke slipped through, and they walked along the gravel road till they came up to the carriage house on the right. It was set back off the road, nestled between large winterberry bushes starting to bloom.

Maria and David looked at each other, and at once they knew it would be perfect for them; it looked like a setting for a fairy tale. The cottage was constructed of stone, but inside, the floors were wood, and the ceiling had the same wood beams as in the Muddy Toad. There were large fireplaces in each room and gorgeous views of woods and fields from the windows. The window in the kitchen permitted a clear view of the original mansion in the far distance. The cottage needed a little love, but it was in much better shape than they had anticipated from what Kirke had intimated.

Outside the back window was a stone patio and a small garden area with some interesting statuary covered with moss and vines. Inside, there were a couple of pieces of old wooden furniture that went with the cabin-like ambiance they'd felt in the Tavern. Kirke saw them admiring the pieces and told them her great uncle was a revered craftsman back in Wales and was famous for intricate wood carvings based on symbols found in the mythos of Welsh folklore. She showed them the necklace she was wearing, which had been in her family for 6 generations. There were symbols carved in lapis stone and garnet; Maria was mesmerized by it. Kirke added that the family continued to preserve and honor their heritage in any way they could.

The furniture that remained included some beautiful chairs that flanked a butcherblock old farm table in the kitchen for breakfast. The master bedroom revealed a stunning wooden-framed bed that mimicked and was covered with the same intricate carvings as the Tavern. To say it was magnificent would be an understatement. Maria couldn't believe how gorgeous it was. It looked like a museum piece. The wood was dark brown walnut with hints of a red tint in places. She felt that anyone lucky enough to sleep there would feel like royalty. Kirke saw her admiring it and said that if they were interested in the place, she would make sure the pieces were moved back to the mansion, as they took up quite a lot of space. Maria said, "Oh yes, of course", even though that's not what she was really thinking.

At the end of the tour, Maria and David said goodbye to Kirke and left confident that this would be their new home. Kirke gave them her number and email. She would email them the contract and finalize it as soon as they wanted. It was perfect, and there were no concerns or apprehensions on anyone's side. David and Maria felt blessed, and within three weeks, everything was smoothly settled, and they were on their way with plans and visions of their new future. A graphic designer by day and painter by night, Maria had already started to work remotely so she would be ready to move immediately. They had given notice straight away, so they would only lose one week, and that leaves us back to Maria's final commute and first night at their new dream home and life.

She had gone to the Fairway before she had boarded the 6:55 PM train, wanting to purchase a couple of special items for their first night at the cottage. She had splurged and bought some fresh oysters and a bottle of champagne, some brie, and a baguette; she was determined to memorialize this occasion. She even had bought a couple of pillar deep red candles to put in the old brass candlesticks she had owned for decades, thinking they would fit right into the atmosphere for the evening. The movers had dropped most of their belongings off the day before in boxes: Kirke had let them in. So all she had to do was arrive and enjoy her first evening, get everything ready for David's arrival, then they would toast to their "Forever Home".

As she arrived at the station, Maria hoisted up all her bags and stepped out onto the platform. The weather was cool and wet, most of the leaves were in soggy yellow piles, and the trees were bare. It was the beginning of December, and there was a definite chill in the air. They would have a fire tonight for sure as part of their celebration. She looked around, and again, there were not many vehicles at all. She could still make out in the distance the Muddy Toad with its amber glow from the windows and smoke curling out of the chimney. She almost felt like going up there to see if Kirke was there to buy her a drink in her excitement, but decided against it as she wanted to start getting things sorted and phone her friend Rita to tell her she was getting settled.

She walked down the foggy road along the old stone wall towards the gate to Cold Stream Manor. It was dark outside and beginning to drizzle slightly. She didn't mind the weather, as it would add to the ambiance of the crackling fire she would make upon arrival. As she walked down the road toward the cottage, she could see a light on inside and could smell smoke from the fireplace. She smiled while thinking Kirke must have made a fire earlier and left a light on for her so she would be sure to find her footing; she was a gem. She felt so excited at that moment about her new life and was very grateful. This was what she and David would be coming home to. This was their new life, closer to nature, finally, after so many years surrounded by concrete.

Entering the cottage, she savored the sweet smell of wood burning and felt the warm air embrace her. Seeing the boxes piled up in the living room, dining room, and kitchen, she knew the unpacking would be quite an undertaking. The fireplace glowed with the embers of a previous larger fire, and she put another log on. She went into the kitchen, put down the bags, pulled out a corkscrew, and uncorked a bottle of local wine Kirke had left on the table with a little bouquet of purple asters. As she did, she looked out the kitchen window towards the Manor house. It was the only room where you could get a glimpse of the great mansion.

She noticed that the manor had many lights on. She could barely see through the large windows except for the subdued glow of light, but there was definitely something happening there. The light from the windows strobed out into the darkness surrounding it. She could make out subtle shadow movements moving in and out of the glow. Maybe Kirke was having a dinner party, she thought. She poured herself a large glass of wine and, with a sip, decided to take stock of their purchase by strolling around the place in admiration.

She loved the kitchen; it had the feeling of being both well-used and well-loved. She imagined families eating dinner of homemade beef stew in the winter with big chunks of baked bread to dip. The bathroom had a fantastic old clawfoot tub still in amazing condition. There was a window where you could look out while in the bath and see a little garden area, complete with blooming sage and a large urn filled with an old-growth rosemary plant. She moved through the living room, dining room, visualizing where they would put this or that piece of furniture, then the study, and lastly, the bedroom.

As she opened the door to the bedroom, she was shocked and let out a small gasp. The gorgeous wooden bed that she had admired so much still remained. She felt sure that Kirke had not made a mistake but had not had time to move it out. But as she approached the bed, which was neatly and elegantly made up with sheets, blankets, and pillows, there was a note to her from Kirke. The note said, "Welcome to your new home! The bed is a gift if you want it, as it has served so many previous tenants eternally happily: enjoy, Kirke". Maria was elated. She adored the bed and immediately decided to call David to fill him in on the generous gift.

He was also surprised and shocked by her generosity; he felt the bed must be a rare antique and worth quite a lot of money, as it was in excellent condition. *Why wouldn't she want to keep it in her family?* he asked. Maria told him to stop overthinking and just accept the generosity. She obviously saw how much I adored it, and maybe the estate is filled with stuff like this.

He chuckled. "You're right."

They chatted a little more about how lovely Maria found the place upon her arrival, including the bottle of wine and flowers. She said she was going to call Rita to say hi before she turned in to fill her in on the great bed score. David made his goodbyes and told her that he probably won't get in till late, so don't wait up. She said no worries, hung up, and decided to eat a little something, prepare a plate for David, and then take a long, hot bath before turning in; she felt tired all of a sudden.

She poured another glass and slipped into the hot bath filled with lavender salts. She had some candles burning and could see the glow from the fireplace in the living room illuminating the hallway that led to the bathroom. It was so quiet, she thought to herself. The rain had subsided, and all she could hear was the silence; not even crickets were chirping; probably too late in the season for them. She was so used to incessant, frenetic noise and commotion living in the city. The only way to get some quiet was to wear earbuds. She chuckled to herself and savored the moment, fantasizing about the future and how much more at peace they would be up here; they would have the time and space to just breathe.

Within the silence, she began to ruminate over that fateful day that led them to this moment. She couldn't help but go back to the discussion that she had had with that local man in the Muddy Toad. She was still convinced that there was more to the pictorial imagery than what he brought forth. She picked up her phone from a section of floor near the tub and decided to Google the name he had said about the toad imagery: Llamhigyn Y Dwr. Yet what she found was nothing harmless at all. Llamhigyn Y Dwr was described as a malicious creature from Welsh mythology and folklore that lived in swamps, ponds, rivers, and lakes. It was said to be a giant, limbless frog or toad with a bat's membranous wings (sometimes even a bird's feathery wings) and a long, reptilian tail with a large stinger at the tip. Its favorite prey were fish, poor sheep who wandered too close to the water's edge, or even fishermen.

Yikes, she thought. That made more sense considering the dark feelings she intuited about the carvings. Although getting really sleepy, she did a deep dive on the scarab/beetle imagery in Welsh tales and couldn't find anything. The Google searches went directly to Egyptian use of scarabs in burial rituals symbolizing rebirth, resurrection, and transformation. They placed the scarabs on the mummy to help ensure the potential for the deceased soul to become whatever their heart desired in the next life. There was even some hint of "offerings" or "sacrifices" to ensure the successful elevated rebirth. Maria suddenly felt so exhausted that she couldn't go any further, but would look into this more tomorrow.

As she rose from the bath and slipped on her robe, she could hear something and was not sure if she had imagined it or not. Her mind, now groggy, was a little anxious from what she had been googling. It was a faint sort of scratching noise, then it stopped, but then it started again. She could not make it out too clearly; not only was the wine hitting her hard, but she was exhausted from the day's activities and the excitement. She guessed it might be coming from the bedroom. 10 minutes later, she heard it again, but a little louder now, sort of a scraping, creaking wood sound, but very subtle. She determined it was a mouse stuck behind a closet in the bedroom, trying to move around, and at that, she emptied the tub and walked back into the kitchen to close things up.

She had a couple more nibbles of the treats she brought and put out a plate for David. She put one last log in the fireplace and went into the bedroom with her glass to call it a night. She put her sweats on, slipped into the gorgeous bed, and began to read her book. She stopped and took a moment to sigh again at the intense satisfaction she was feeling, and with a broad smile, she took her last gulp of wine. She felt utterly relaxed, even a little dopey; must be very strong wine, she thought, and decided to turn off the light.

She felt herself immediately slipping into slumber. It was as if all resistance to sleep was gone, as a true relaxation she had never felt before took over her. The last thing she remembered before she drifted off to sleep was that faint scratching noise louder again; it seemed to be rising up all around her. However, as she made an effort to come back to consciousness, she almost felt unable to move, almost paralyzed, and so just let deep sleep envelop her. She made a fading mental note to buy a mousetrap tomorrow.

She wasn't conscious of the movement happening all around her. The bed's wooden carved scarabs and flying bat-like toads had come alive and began to glisten in the firelight, glowing greens, purples, scarlet, and blues like vibrating opals. With faint scratching noises, they were crawling in hordes away from their places within the design on the bed. They traveled deliberately down towards Maria and under her covers and sheets towards her skin.

There were hundreds of them. The flying creatures assisted in moving the bedding away to get a clearer pathway to the body.

Maria was unconscious and completely paralyzed by the wine Kirke had left. The creatures covered every inch of her body so you could only make out her outline, and then, all at once, began to devour her bones and all until nothing was left. It happened instantaneously in a flash of green-blue light, and all at once, Maria was gone.

Epitaph

When David got home to the cottage, it was well past midnight, so he tried to be very quiet not to wake Maria up. He walked into the kitchen and noticed from the window as Maria had that there was something going on in the manor. At this time of night, he thought and questioned their newly acquired neighbors. There was a bright glow coming from within the manor. He could faintly see many figures in the tall windows that looked like they were possibly dancing, waving their arms in the air, celebrating. They obviously had no concern if anyone was looking in. Oh well, he thought, to each his own; something great must have happened for such a festive occasion. He went into the bedroom to see Maria, but she was not there. The bed was certainly gorgeous; he was in full agreement with her. There was a note in red ink on the bedside table from Maria, a glass, and the rest of the wine for him. It said:

" ....was lonely, so I went to sleep at Rita's.
Good night,
Sleep tight,
Don't let the bed bugs bite........xo"

He smiled and yawned, finished the bottle, and climbed into bed.

PUERITIA SOMNIA

BY NEMO ARATOR

previously published at RIC Journal, May 2024

The oldest dream I can remember is from when I was a little boy, about five or six years old: the dream about the witch and the forest labyrinth.

My memory begins as I was walking toward a huge, dark, tangled mass of trees and bushes. I was walking down a path along the fence-line between a flax field and a pasture; the town was somewhere behind me; I didn't look back. I entered the trees and followed the path onward. It wove and wound through the thickets in such subtle contortions that I quickly lost any sense of direction.

But on I went. Indeed, it seemed I was being drawn forward, and fast: I seemed to be floating at a speed set between walking and running. The grass and twigs and leaves were tramped flat underfoot; the route was well-worn by whatever deer and cattle and schoolchildren like me who found their way here and couldn't help but go onward, for the foliage grew densely on all sides.

The path forked in places, which I picked at whim, for each seemed to lead endlessly onward – except some, which ended suddenly, whereupon I would have to turn around and go back, like all the others before me. Occasionally, I noticed doors seemingly embedded in the greenery, deadwood amid its living brethren. Most of them were closed, and I left them so, simply took note, then carried on.

As I wandered the endless trails, I noticed the trampled grass underfoot had become woven into a thatched carpet; it seemed the forest path had somehow become the long, meandering corridors of a mansion-like house. But it seemed there was no way out, and I would never find the way back into my own head.

There became an urgency to my passage, for it seemed as if I lingered anywhere; something started to accumulate in the air, as if I were being followed by a cloud, a miasma of noxious vapors, and it was catching up with me. I remember stopping once to see what would happen. The mist gathered like a presence, gaining density until it was able to coalesce into shape, and that's when the dream became a nightmare: it was the crone, the old hag.

Bone-white crazy-face, blazing eyes, her hands were claws, like the talons of some horrible bird; it didn't become real until I saw it. I screamed and fled, bolting down the pathway as fast as I could, mind crazed with blind animal fear. I ran and ran, and sometimes it seemed I lost her, but as soon as I felt safe, there she was again, popping from the woodwork like some hideous cackling jack-in-the-box. And on I ran, but she was always right behind, the sour stink of her breath on my neck; it seemed she was everywhere.

Somehow, I found my way to the downstairs of my parents' house. I barely recognized the rooms for all the trees and bushes; the furniture was mired in undergrowth. But I knew where I was now. I ran upstairs and down the hall to my parents' bedroom. The floor was covered in moss and leaves fallen from the huge branch that had burst through the main window. I ran into the bathroom and locked the door, and then I realized I had cornered myself. The hag would follow me here, and there was nowhere else to hide. I could jump out the window, but it was a two-story drop to the cement pad below. I got into the shower and closed the curtain.

Then I looked up and saw not the ceiling, but a round hole of light some distance above me, as though I was standing at the foot of a well. And then I realized that I was. And it was while I was staring into that light that I somehow started floating up into it. Floating up into the light and back into myself, and that was how I escaped. I woke up, lying in bed, and the sun was shining through the window down upon me. And then I started shaking with cold, trembling relief: I escaped just in the nick of time, bare seconds before she would have caught me.

***

I remember that dream so vividly, mainly because it was my first nightmare, the first time I ever woke walloped by post-dream terror and trembling. Notable also that this happened within the first year after we moved into the big white stucco house on Third Avenue, the house in a hollow between two churches. Before that, we lived in a small bungalow across the street from the school, but my memories of that place are few. This new house was very spacious and possessed many fine features otherwise. I suspect something in the architecture inspired these dreams, for it seemed to suggest more than was readily apparent.

The next dream I can remember occurred about a year later. I was lost underground, dreaming my way through an endless series of caverns and limestone passageways, trying to find my way out. I had a brief lucid moment when I recognized something from before, and then I realized that I was again lost in the house of the forest: the layout was the same, but this time, the trees had been transposed with rocks and tunnels. And then I was going helplessly onward, because there was nothing else I could do.

At some point, I found another little boy crouching by the wall, hunched over like he was sick. At first, he didn't seem to notice me. I must have asked if he was okay, because then he said, "I can't see anything. I don't even have eyes."

And then he turned his face to mine, and I saw smooth pockets of skin where his eyes should have been.

I continued onward without him, eventually finding my way into a long rectangular chamber with a dinner table at one end, and a pair of couches around a fireplace at the other. This, I immediately recognized as our living room, despite the dank limestone walls and the moss coating the upholstery. The table was set for dinner, but the food was covered in dust and mold. The fireplace was likewise full of dead cinders, like a pile of old bones, gray and ancient, cold. But I was relieved; once again, I found my way home.

Then I heard voices echoing from down the corridor: strange chittering buzzing voices. They were coming this way, and I knew immediately that I had to hide. I ducked behind the lump of sofa, which, in the dream, was a slab of rock, and I cowered there, trembling, hoping they wouldn't find me. The fireplace burst into flames when they entered the room, and I could hear the skitter-scatter click-clacking of their many feet. They were laughing and dancing, running back and forth across the room. The firelight cast their shadows upon the wall: weird inhuman shapes, leaping and frolicking. They were making these horrible sounds like a kind of singing: a hideous piping warble.

When I dared peek around the couch and saw them, I almost cried out. They were gint insects the size of small children. They scurried around the room, climbing the walls and crossing the ceiling as easily as they did the floor. It took me a moment to realize they were playing a game of catch, tossing something back and forth amongst themselves. At first, I thought it was just a lumpy leather ball, but then I got a good glimpse as it passed through the light; with horror, I saw that it was the severed head of the boy I met earlier in the cavern passageway.

I ducked back behind the couch and just crouched there, quaking, terrified. After a while, I resolved to escape before I was found. Remembering how I got away in the previous dream, I waited until the fire died down, then hobbled over to the fireplace, climbed into it, and started crawling up the chimney. Up the long dark tunnel and emerged back into the daylight of myself.

***

About a year later, I awoke one night to find myself standing at the top of the stairs: I opened my eyes and saw the steps descending into the darkness of the ground floor.

My body was poised as though I had been about to descend at the moment I awoke, but I also had the impression, based on muscle fatigue, that I'd been standing there for quite some time. And I stood there awhile longer yet, my body like a statue of itself standing upright. I felt the eternity of that moment, the house still and silent in the night all around me. I remember not being at all alarmed to find myself like this; in those blurry first moments after waking, I felt only a calm acceptance of the situation. I was probably dreaming about something right before that, but my mind was like a blank slate, wiped clean by the opening of my eyelids. And I looked down the stairs into a seemingly denser darkness than was here upstairs.

And then I realized something had gone down the stairs ahead of me. It had swooped past, and it was the speed and suddenness of this thing that startled me awake. I stood there listening, my head tilted slightly. Whatever it was, it seemed to have been subsumed by the shadowy silence below. The idea of going down there to investigate filled me with dread. My whole family was asleep. Nobody would wake up if something happened; they were too far gone; for we are a people who sleep soundly, and with their doors closed.

My fear grew the longer I stood there; I thought I felt an immanence rising from the darkness, an atmospheric gathering, condensing, coalescing in the air, slowly growing into a manifest presence. I had a vision of a huge swollen mass occupying the entire living room downstairs, like a humongous puffy worm beetle, something with a human face embedded in its piebald side, and a gleaming smile. It was that hour of the night when anything could happen.

I went back to my room, closed the door, and got into bed. I didn't roll to either side or onto my belly, as I might have done; instead, I lay on my back, so I would be ready in case something came through the door. However, it was more likely to come from the closet, which seemed so similar to an elevator with its folding doors; that thing downstairs would just slither into the fireplace and emerge up through there. I lay there terrified, waiting, wondering, listening to the darkness and the silence, a silence that became so loud I thought I could hear it subtly contorting, as though that emptiness was trying to shape itself into something, but not quite being able to, and eventually I drifted back to sleep.

***

A strange thing happened one night sometime either before or after that; I am not sure exactly when it was. For reasons unknown, the bed in my room was moved from one side of the room to the other. This must have been done chiefly for the sake of variety; I don't remember being troubled by this; it didn't seem to have been inflicted upon me. Nonetheless, I awoke in the middle of the night, floating over the spot where my bed had previously been and was now just empty floor space. I was just barely awake enough to say that I was at all; I remember turning over, and that's when I became conscious enough to realize that there was nothing beneath me, but not conscious enough to be alarmed or even perplexed by this.

By some miracle, I was floating upon thin air, suspended at an elevation slightly higher than that of the mattress; it should be impossible, and yet it was so. I fell immediately back asleep, unconcerned about either falling or how or why this could even be. I merely forgot about it, and I don't think it ever happened again (or if it did, I was unaware); perhaps it was just a dream or a hallucination, something that happened to someone who wasn't even really awake.

***

It turned out I was sleepwalking more often than that; I just didn't know about it. Apparently, it started after we moved into the new house. They said that not long afterward, my parents, and sometimes even my sister, would hear various little noises in the house at night, which, at first, they thought were just the usual sort of house-settling sounds. Occasionally, they heard a soft thudding sound, which my dad joked was the thing that goes bump in the night. But if it wasn't bogies, it might be intruders; however, when they went to investigate, they found it was just me, sleepwalking.

It was really spooky, they said, the first time they found me walking around in the dark, like a little robot zombie, making obscure gestures and performing incomprehensible actions. I was unable to open doors or climb stairs, and so, my somnambulant self was confined to roaming the open areas of the second floor, where I could move safely and unobstructed, sometimes walking into things. That thudding sound they heard was the sound of my head colliding with a door or wall.

After the first few times, they became accustomed to this, perhaps annoyed, and when it happened, they guided me back to bed. If I ever woke, I was invariably confused, but with a sleepy child's blithe compliance, I'd go back to bed and immediately drift off once I was under the covers, and they'd go back to their room and do the same. They didn't tell me about this for a long time, and I remember even as a boy I found it rather disturbing that my sleeping self was going about and engaging in activities I had no recollection of.

After a couple of years during which this condition persisted, they took me to see a doctor. He checked me over and said I was healthy. He said it probably had something to do with the move; I missed the old house, and the sleepwalking was a metaphor of something, trying to find my way in the dark. However, it was to be considered a good sign that if I couldn't open doors and abstained from stairs, then I still had at least that much survival sense, even at that level of operation, and thus wasn't much risk to myself or anyone else.

The doctor recommended bunk-beds, if my parents could afford the expense, because their son was not as likely to wander around the house at night if he had to climb down a ladder first. So, that is what they did, because it seemed worthwhile, and would be a nice gift for the kids.

***

For my part, I thought getting bunk beds was a great idea. Several of the other kids at school had them, and this was much to my envy. Now I had one, and not just me, but my little sister too. I started sleeping on the top bunk immediately, of course, which was just brilliant: if anything under the bed was going to grab my ankle and try to drag me under, well, ha-ha, I'm way up here.

But one night, I awoke and saw the moonlight pouring through the window, lighting the space of the wall between the bedroom door and the closet door; it perfectly framed the shadow of the tree in the backyard and its restless branches shifting in the wind. Those branches crisply etched shadow like a web of veins or shattered glass. Within that shifting juxtaposition of lines, there seemed to form or become perceptible a vaguely anthropomorphic shape: a tall and narrow upright bearing, but vaguely insectile and skeletal, like a praying mantis wearing a tuxedo.

As soon as I thought this, it seemed to crystallize itself completely and step forth bodily into the room. I heard a faint metallic sound, a subsonic screeching squeal, not unlike the unoiled hinges of an opening door. And there it was, this thin being hunched over; it was so tall its head almost touched the ceiling. It stood looming over my bedside and stared down at me, lying on the top bunk, frozen with abject terror. I stared back at it, hypnotized by those cold black eyes and the feeling of intrinsic malignity that comes from being faced with something so utterly alien. And that's all I remember. The overwhelming fear must have blotted out my memory, and I was mercifully granted the black release of sleep and forgetfulness.

It was also while lying in the dark of the top bunk that I first had visions of those beings who dwelt in the world below, and they beckoned me down to come join them and partake of their sinister delights. But also, I knew this vision was a window on Hell, if there ever was such a place, and those beings were the damned: they were demons, tempters, corrupters, deceivers, urging me to commit their same sins and taste of that knowledge. They came to me then, and they've been with me since.

It was around this time that I started researching black magic, Satanism, and the occult, and my impressionable young mind was so saturated by these topics that it opened a window whereby they could approach me. And that was what they wanted me to do – go all the way to the ultimate. I would be eternally stained, forever exiled from the Kingdom, but among the elite who had done and known what it was like. This vision was recurrent for many years, and like the one before it, was chiefly just a molten static picture held: the beings never actually did anything except watch me and radiate menace.

The only other vision I remember from sleeping on the top bunk was of a castle on a misty mountain, a dreary scene of gray and green. I was always on the ledge overlooking the drawbridge in this dream, and two or three huge gray snow leopards were up there with me, reposed with regal calm; their vigilance served with a certain feral indifference. They sat so still they looked like statues, but I knew they were alive because one of them turned its head and looked at me. I always had an erection during this dream, but I don't know why, and since it was before I started masturbating, I was afflicted with this pleasant tumescence, but knew not how to alleviate it. These visions ceased when I shifted to the bottom bunk a couple of years later.

***

As I grew older and lazier and less fearful of oneiric phenomena, I started sleeping on the bottom bunk. I remember dreaming I had awakened one morning and lay in bed groggily, half-asleep, half-awake. The bedroom door was ajar, and I could hear the voices of my mother and sister talking in the hallway right outside my room, just out of sight, but I knew they were there because I could hear them talking. And they were saying exactly the sort of things that they would. Upon waking later, I remember marveling at how accurately a dream could mimic reality, and I thought it actually was them.

However, in the next moment, I turned my gaze from the slightly ajar bedroom door to the wide-open closet door; instead of hanging garments, I saw that it now opened onto a vast desolate plain – a barren wasteland suffused by a yellowish haze of drifting smoke and mist. Merely by looking through the doorway into that desert realm, I was somehow drawn wholly into it, my vision telescoping forward until I suddenly found myself standing on the edge of a great black hole on a plateau in this wasteland. It was boiling and bubbling deep down within, like the pit of a cauldron, and drifting out with great noxious billows of a miasma-like steam-cloud.

And then I saw another entity was here, a tall, spindly creature like a giant insect, like a praying mantis wearing a wizard's cloak. It started chanting and waving its arms and dancing – yes, it did a crooked little dance, jumping and floundering like a broken puppet, all the way around the rim of that great black hole. It was calling out to some force or agency it sought to summon, and it seemed to be working: I could feel it rise, the swelling immanence, like a rapid shift in the barometer, something was coming and it was gonna get here fast…

Dimly, I realized this whirlpool conjuring was something happening on another planet or in another dimension, and this mysterious being was a black magician who had brought me here as an offering to whatever it had summoned, which would be a horrible doom for me. Doubtless, this bastard would get some magical powers in reward. I was yanked back into my body and popped up in bed, eyes open, heart pounding, panting, frightened. That was a close call, I thought, and here it was potently established that dreams are a type of astral travel and there can be danger in these things.

After that, I inexplicably moved my bed back to the other side of the room and started sleeping on the floor. I don't know why I did that, except perhaps as some kind of protective gesture. Sleeping on the floor took the pleasure out of sleep, and I was no longer able to remember my dreams, though I continued to dream vividly for many years. I remember some nights I would awaken, lying on the floor with the pale moonlight pouring through the window, and I remember being awash in that light.

TACOS

BY A.M.F. TAYLOR

It wasn't unusual for their parents to leave them alone. What was unusual was that shortly after they left, there was a knock on the door.

Before Anthony could stop her, Amy ran past him and flung open the door.

The creature on the other side was tall. It definitely wasn't human, although it wore clothes, including a familiar fuzzy pink hat on its head. Dark hollow eyes swam in skeletal sockets, and the nose was more of a snout. Wiry gray-brown fur covered the creature from head to toe. It even had furry pointy ears and a tail that curved to the side and moved through the air in slow rhythmic pulses. As Anthony stared, the skin of the mouth stretched wide, revealing sharp, pointed teeth and too-long canines.

Amy shrieked and slammed the door. She had probably been hoping for a cupcake delivery or a surprise visit from Grammy. Their parents had gone to pick up tacos for dinner, and it was too soon for them to be back. Neither Anthony nor Amy would ever have expected *that* creature to be there, although Anthony would have at least checked the peephole before opening the door.

Anthony stepped forward and locked the door, sliding the chain in for good measure. Amy's dark eyes widened in fear.

A deafening silence followed the slamming of the door. Anthony and Amy stood staring at one another, breathing heavily. They pressed their bodies against the door, trying to be soundless. As if the creature didn't already know they were there. As if they could somehow hide. As if the creature they had just seen couldn't break down the door with half a thought.

Of course, they knew what it was, even though they had never seen one before. They had heard of them. Been warned against them countless times. Never go outside during a full moon, never even look out a window. Anthony's eyes flicked to the calendar on the kitchen wall at the other end of the apartment, just visible from where they stood. Even from this distance, he could see the full moon marked not this Thursday but next. Over a week away. So this *thing* on their doorstep shouldn't be there. It shouldn't be possible for it to be there.

But it was there. It was there with its teeth and claws and clothes. Anthony didn't need to look through the peephole to know it was still there. He could feel its presence.

Then they heard a light tapping on the door. Not a knock, just a rhythmic clicking as if the creature had begun to drum its claws on the other side of the wood. An impatient drumming, as if it were waiting for them to make the next move.

Anthony held his breath, but the drumming continued.

Click, click, click, click, pause.

Click, click, click, click, pause.

Click, click, click, click, pause.

Anthony stared at Amy, his heart hammering. When his heartbeat grew to such a clamor that he couldn't hear the drumming anymore, he swallowed. He inhaled loudly, gasping in air he had forgotten to breathe. Amy stood frozen.

He had to do something. Say something.

"Can we help you?" Anthony choked the words out, his voice barely a whisper. But at the sound, the drumming stopped.

"Yes." The voice on the other side of the door was low and grumbly. More of a growl than anything else.

"It's not a full moon," Amy said, her voice shrill. "You shouldn't be here." Her frizzy brown hair seemed to stand on end, adding exclamation points to the frightened features of her face.

"True." Anthony could hear a hint of a smile in the voice this time. As if this were all rather amusing and not at all terrifying. He exchanged a look with Amy as the silence continued. Their parents always reminded them that the creatures were temporary. They were fleeting, animalistic versions of real humans who would wake up the following day with many, many regrets. It didn't mean the creatures weren't dangerous. They wreaked havoc and caused death and destruction everywhere they went. But when the full moon was over, they were human again. Their parents had tried to explain that the creatures deserved to be pitied. It wasn't their fault. They couldn't help it. And so Anthony and Amy had learned to forgive them.

But the creatures never spoke. They never knocked. They took what they wanted. They never asked questions or thought about what they did. They didn't have any concept of right or wrong, and they couldn't help their behavior. That was how it had always been.

That was why Anthony and Amy spent each full moon night huddled in their room, music blaring against the cacophony of disaster outside their window. There were shadows in the darkness and faraway snarls, but that was the extent of what Anthony and Amy knew of full moon nights. Their imaginations had to fill in the gaps. They were told stories and legends, but most of that felt faraway, too. The creatures liked to be outdoors, so inside was the best place to be. There was always a babysitter in the living room, keeping guard against a world full of monsters. That adult stood between them and the door, and that had always been enough.

But this? This wasn't right. And Anthony thought this might be even more terrifying. As the silence on the other side of the door continued, he tried to remember to breathe. This creature was waiting for something. It was waiting for Anthony.

He was four years older than Amy, so he felt responsible for her. He needed to make a decision. The tension in the air was so thick, he couldn't take it anymore. It was up to him.

Anthony grabbed the dark red umbrella leaning on the wall next to the door and raised it in his hand as if brandishing a sword. Then he pushed Amy aside, unlocked the door, and swung it open.

The creature stood there, its lips pulled back in what could have been a snarl or a grimace or maybe a creepy attempt at a smile. But these creatures did not smile. They couldn't smile. Smiling was a human thing, and Mom and Dad always said the creatures were not human. They would be human again, but on one night every month their humanity vanished in a flurry of teeth and claws and blood.

Anthony and Amy knew to be careful.

Anthony swallowed, stepped in front of Amy, and stared into the creature's eyes. He pointed the umbrella in a menacing way, trying not to notice how it wobbled in his hand. Anthony recognized the hat, somehow still on the creature's head. It was the only thing not changed by the transformation. The striped blue and white shirt was split and torn, and the skirt with the buttons Amy always admired was in pieces, but still somehow stayed around the creature's waist. The thing even had her pink purse, the one with the gold clasp, over its left shoulder.

"What do you want?"

"To explain."

So much was familiar about this thing in front of them, but not that growly monstrous voice. Not at all. Anthony heard Amy whimper behind him when the creature spoke.

"May I come in?" Her voice was like razor blades, searing up through an unwelcoming throat.

Anthony resisted the urge to look at Amy. He squared his shoulders and stood tall. How was he supposed to answer that question? This had never happened before. Their parents hadn't prepared them for this. They had never left them alone during a full moon. Never. Mrs. Peterson would come sometimes, or even Mr. Seward. A neighbor or teacher, or someone they trusted, would always stay with Anthony and Amy on those nights when their parents weren't safe.

Anthony swallowed, not taking his eyes off the depthless black eyes of the creature. His shoulders sagged a little then, as if in defeat. He tossed the umbrella back in the corner. There was no point.

"Sure, Mom," Anthony said, stepping aside.

The creature made a weirdly human gesture of smoothing out the tattered skirt and trying to smile again.

Anthony cringed, still avoiding Amy's eyes. He didn't know if this was the right thing to do, and he couldn't deal with Amy's questioning looks.

The creature filled the hall, its ears brushing the ceiling and its tail swishing behind. It walked upright on its hind legs, a disturbing mix of human and canine features. It made its way to the sofa and sat, motioning for Anthony and Amy to sit as well.

The creature stank. It smelled like blood and despair, and Anthony couldn't bring himself to do as the creature suggested. He stared at the furred claw patting the sofa, inviting him to take a seat. No. Anthony sat in an armchair facing the couch, still feeling like he was too close to this predator. Amy tried, too, even going so far as to take a step toward the couch while turning her head away and wrinkling her nose. She hesitated, then stayed where she was, standing, immobile and staring. Their mom loved to bake, and she always smelled like vanilla and sugar. She smelled comforting and wonderful, like home. She kept the house tidy, played the violin, and loved to knit. Anthony couldn't reconcile this awful thing that smelled like decay with his own thoughtful, sweet mother.

Maybe this was a trick. This thing couldn't be their mom, could it? Anthony and Amy had never seen her in this form; their parents had always tried to conceal this darkness from their children as much as possible. He squinted at the hat on her head. He knew that hat. He knew those clothes. Anthony shut his eyes, hoping that when he opened them again, things would be different.

But when he opened them, the huge hairy beast still sat on the floral couch where they watched television, did homework, and read books. Where they laughed and wrestled with Dad and built forts out of pillows.

"Hurts to talk like this," the creature said, gesturing to her body with her claws. "But need to explain." She paused, swallowing. Her voice was heavy and slow, filled with weighty pauses. "Things are changing. It's been happening more and more, not only when the moon is full."

Anthony and Amy stared at the creature sitting on their couch, pretending to be their mother. They watched her tongue dart out as she shifted her position.

"Except changes aren't complete. I remember who I am. Sort of. Your father doesn't always change with me like he used to." There was a wistful look in the black eyes. "I've been changing more frequently."

Anthony couldn't take his eyes off her mouth. The teeth were razor sharp and longer than his little finger. He noticed something pink and stringy caught in her back teeth, and he cringed. Anthony and Amy had never even wanted to know what their parents did when they changed. But now here was their mother, a huge beast in a mockery of her familiar clothing, trying to pretend everything was fine. That it wasn't weird, she was not a human right now. That she could sit there, on their couch, like some unwanted houseguest. Anthony thought of what his mom, his real mom, would do if there was a guest in the house. Offer her tea and cookies? Anthony shook his head. The last thing he wanted to do was think about what this thing wanted to eat.

"Things are changing," she repeated. Anthony stared. She had whiskers, fur, and a long tongue. Anthony suddenly thought of his Uncle Joe's dog, Willie. Would his mother like to be petted as Willie did? Her belly rubbed, and her ears scratched? Anthony stifled a burst of nervous laughter, covering his mouth as if to cough. He could feel Amy's attention on him, questioning and panicked. He did not meet her eyes. The creature continued to talk in her grating, disjointed growl, explaining how things had slowly begun to change and how she didn't know what would happen next.

Next?

Anthony then realized what her true fear was and why she had come to them like this. She had come in this form because she was scared. Even in her horrifying, endlessly dark eyes, Anthony saw concern, confusion, and worry.

He swallowed, his throat dry as he began to understand what she meant.

"You think you might stay like this?"

She looked at him, her eyes pathetic. She nodded slightly, and Amy whimpered again.

"Are you…safe like this?" Anthony's voice was low, and he saw his mother's furry ears flicker toward him as she listened. "You always said it wasn't safe for you and Dad to be around us during the full moon." The idea that he had something to fear from his parents had always seemed so far-fetched. But staring at this thing in front of him, Anthony understood. He understood because he felt that fear now. Before, it had always been the *idea* of fear. He knew he *should* be afraid. But right now, in this moment, his terror was all-consuming.

The creature cocked her head, reminding Anthony of a confused puppy. This shouldn't be a difficult question for a parent. Yes, she would always keep them safe. Yes, everything was fine. Yes, there was no reason for children to worry about their safety, certainly not from their own parents.

She raised a furry hand equipped with sharp claws and adjusted her hat. Anthony waited for her answer, his fear rising with each moment that passed. He stared as her shoulders lifted in a shrug.

Anthony stood quickly then, reaching for Amy's hand, ready to drag her toward the door. They couldn't outrun her, but they could get away. Maybe they could hide. They could go to Mrs. Peterson's apartment across the hall. She had a steel door with bolts, and if they got there, maybe they would be safe.

"It's okay," the creature said, watching them with curiosity. "I'm still trying." She swallowed, wincing. "To figure all of this out." She paused, casting a guilty look at the floor. "Difficult." She gestured at her throat, at the words she kept forcing through. Anthony squinted at her, but did not sit again. But they didn't run yet either. Anthony felt Amy's hand in his own, and he gave it what he hoped was a comforting squeeze. "I'm safe to be around," the creature said. Then she paused. "Now."

Anthony swallowed. What did *that* mean? Why had she paused? Wasn't she *always* safe to be around? Why? What was different about now? Perhaps it was simply because of the timing, because it was far enough away from the full moon. Maybe as it loomed on the schedule, her full transition became more imminent and her behavior more unstable. That was probably what she meant.

"Because it's not the full moon yet?" He heard the hope in his voice and saw the creature's eyes narrow. Her eyes dropped again, and even her ears drooped. The shake of her head was almost imperceptible. Anthony didn't understand. He glanced at

Amy for help, but she didn't meet his eyes, just stood staring at the creature that was their mom, yet was not their mom.

A few moments passed as Anthony tried to decide which question to ask next. Why was she safe? When wasn't she safe? How would this ever work? He pushed his free hand into his face, sliding his palm over his eyes and then down to his chin. He swallowed, trying to think of what to say.

But she began speaking first.

"I'm safe now," she said, speaking slowly and carefully but still staring down at the faded rug. "Because I'm not hungry."

Anthony let the words hit him. He let them soak into his brain. He tried to organize them in a way that made sense. She's not hungry now. She doesn't want food. But if she were hungry, she wouldn't be safe. They can't be near her when she's hungry.

That's fine, it would be okay then. They would just keep her fed. That couldn't be that hard, could it? He tried to think about what a werewolf would eat. Maybe they should move out of the city, find a farm, and raise animals for their parents to eat. That would be okay.

Anthony's thoughts raced, trying to solve this problem. They could all stay together as long as they kept Mom from being hungry. They could do that. He could handle that.

He opened his mouth to reassure her, to reassure everyone, but then he closed it. Something tickled at the back of Anthony's mind.

Why?

The small question startled him, then began to take over as dread filled him.

He glanced at Amy, who returned his gaze with terrified eyes. She squeezed his hand, but it wasn't comforting. It was a warning.

Why?

Why did she have a full belly?

Their parents had left together, going out to pick up tacos from Bob's on the corner. They were supposed to bring back dinner. Perhaps their mom had eaten some tacos before she changed forms. That's probably all she meant. Anthony felt sick, unable to convince even himself, his stomach suddenly churning, a dead weight lodged there. He looked back at the front door, desperately wanting another werewolf to knock. Another werewolf who could explain everything, and it would all make sense.

He waited a beat, hopeful, as if merely by wishing it to be so, he could make his father appear at their door.

When his eyes came back to his mother, she wouldn't meet his gaze. The next question caught in Anthony's mouth. His tongue was dry, his throat scratchy. He opened his lips as if to speak, but nothing came out. Anthony stared, looking at the blood flecked on the ripped shirt and the matted fur around her snout. Matted with blood and gore, he realized. Her revolting smell hit him again, nearly knocking him off his feet. That smell. He knew what that smell was. He focused on that stringy pink thing stuck in her back teeth. Something that might look like flesh if he looked hard enough. He didn't want to look hard enough. Anthony suddenly felt dizzy with the realization of why she was here alone.

Still, he couldn't ask. His mouth refused to form the words. Amy realized, too, but somehow she was braver and could ask it.

"Where's Dad?"

ABOUT THE AUTHORS

Nemo Arator

Nemo Arator is a student of surrealism. He seeks gnosis through dreams, intoxication, and objective chance. This story is from his forthcoming book To What End.

Krista Farmer

Krista Farmer is an author who lives and works in Washington state. She's had work published in Swords & Sorcery Magazine, Bewildering Stories, and others. You can find her on Instagram: kristafarmer_

Mawr Gorshin

Mawr Gorshin was born Martin Gross in Timmins, Ontario, in 1969. He moved to Taiwan ROC in the summer of 1996, where he's lived ever since, teaching English as a second language. In his spare time, he has composed and recorded music (classical and pop), which can be found on the Jamendo website, under both his original (the classical music) and pen names (the pop music). Over the past fifteen years or so, he has focused on writing, much of which can be found on his blog, 'Infinite Ocean' (poetry, prose, analyses of literature, film, and music--mostly from a Marxist or psychoanalytic perspective--and writing on narcissistic abuse). Below are his blog, Facebook links, and Jamendo link:

https://www.jamendo.com/artist/362453/mawr-gorshin
https://mawrgorshin.com/
https://www.facebook.com/mawrgorshinwriter/
https://www.facebook.com/mawr.gorshin

Megan Guilliams

Megan Guilliams is an Independent Fiction author who specializes in Urban Fantasy, Horror and Dark Romance. She is a Franklin County native who lives in Virginia with her husband and two children. When she's not writing Young Adult and New Adult Fiction, she enjoys painting. Filling the walls of her home with colorful lowbrow art and Pop art, Megan enjoys bringing her book's characters to life. As a young child, Megan dabbled in short stories, often entertaining her peers. While Megan doesn't hold any specialized degrees that led her to her writing passion, she currently has over thirty novels published on Amazon and Kindle. You can find more of her work in the year to come, as well as read her story "Kroak" in Nature Triumphs: A Charity Anthology of Dark Speculative Fiction, "Love, Lies and Bleeding" in The Devil's Playground: A Horror Charity Anthology for Drug Addiction, "The Christmas Wraith" in Last Christmas: A Holiday Horror Anthology, "She Bitch" in Piece by Piece: An Anti-Valentine's Day Collection of Short Stories, Poetry and Prose. "A Taste of Heaven" in Beauty in Darkness, a Literary Tribute to TS Woolard, and "The Lights" in Confessions from the Think Tank, Volume 1. A Kid's Space Camp Charity Anthology. Concept by Editor Rob Tannahill. All Published by Dark Moon Rising Publications. You can also find her poem "Leon" in Sleeve of Hearts, Poems, edited by Lindsey Goddard, and brought to you by the Weird Wide Web. Other published shorts by Megan Guilliams include: "Over Easy" in Dark Harvest, an Ecohorror Anthology, published by Twisted Dreams Press, "House of Shadows" in The Stranger at my Window, published by Baynam Books Press, and "But... I Jest" in Tales From the Lark Side: A Horror Comedy Anthology, published by Weird Wide Web and edited by Lindsey Goddard.
https://www.amazon.com/stores/Megan-Guilliams/author/B0CTP2D7XD

Kasey Hill

Kasey Hill is a critically acclaimed, versatile writer from Franklin County, VA, known for her work in several genres, including urban fantasy, horror, thriller, paranormal romance, and metaphysical/New Age topics. She has
authored both fiction and non-fiction, with a particular interest in Wicca.

Her fiction often dives into the supernatural and the macabre, blending mythological elements with modern storytelling. She has published multiple novels, poetry collections, and short stories. Notable works include her Guardians of Light series in the mythology fantasy genre and her poetry, which has received recognition for its depth and emotional resonance. As she grows in the horror genre, she has a particular penchant for Southern Gothic/Appalachian Gothic storytelling, such as her Adult Horror novel Devil's Claw and her Young Adult horror series, The Whispering Spirits, featuring The Haunting at Foxwood Village and Dark Coven. She has several Horror short stories circulating for anthologies and Ezines, featuring her unique style of worldbuilding.
www.kaseyhillauthor.com
www.facebook.com/kaseyhillauthor
www.instagram.com/kaseyhillauthor
www.tiktok.com/kaseyhillauthor
www.amazon.com/stores/Kasey-Hill/author/B00O2WT210

Joshua Ladd

Joshua Ladd is an author and editor who loves drumming up stories while hiking near his home in Colorado Springs. He is co-editor of the fiction anthology Into the Deep, Dark Woods (WordFire Press, July 2026), and his short stories have appeared in numerous anthologies. He can be reached at joshualadd@joshualaddwrites.com.

Floyd Largent

Floyd Largent is a former archaeologist who never woke a sleeping god or unearthed an ancient evil (alas). Currently a full-time writer and editor, in the past year, he has published or had accepted for publication six poems and 30 short stories, in venues including Altered Reality, Bewildering Stories, Bullet Points, Chewers, Dream Theory Media, Exquisite Death, Freedom Fiction Journal, Masticadores International, Suburban Witchcraft, 5-7-5 Haiku Journal, and more.

Paul Lonardo

Paul Lonardo is a freelance writer and author with numerous titles, both fiction and nonfiction books. Paul has placed short fiction and nonfiction articles in various genre magazines and ezines. He is a contributing writer for several publications, and he is an HWA member. Visit Paul's author website at: www.thegoblinpitcher.com

J.T. Lozano

J.T. Lozano is a psychological horror author who hails from Mission, a small border town in deep south Texas. He is the youngest in his family, which consists of four other siblings: two brothers and two sisters. Although J.T. resides in Mission, he was born in Monterrey, Nuevo Leon, Mexico, and moved at the age of three. J.T. began writing in 2007, using poetry as a form of self-expression, and wrote his first story shortly after that. In the following years, from which the writing bug bit J.T., he has written well over 30 poems and has written and published half a dozen books, but the numbers continue to rise each year. The ideas constantly fill his head, and if you ask J.T. how long he plans to write, he will simply answer, "I'll keep writing as long as you keep reading."

Marin Moor

Marin Moor is the pen name of Mary Martha Collins is a writer and artist based in New Jersey. She studied painting and cultural anthropology at Sarah Lawrence College, received an MFA from Hunter College and spent 25 years living and working on the coast of Northern California, where she ran a successful concrete fabrication business that earned national press coverage. She has recently returned to writing after nearly a decade as a full time caregiver for her parents. "Don't Let the Bed Bugs Bite" is her first published essay. She is currently at work on a memoir.

K.R. Moore

K.R. Moore is an author that likes to bring joy and look at the positives of life. Channeling them within his writing into the craziest, most bizarre ways possible with fun at every turn. When you pick up a book from Moore, you can expect to go on a journey with unforgettable casts of characters with comedy and oddity always close by. In addition to self-published works, he currently has 27 short story pieces published in magazines such in Nat 1, Bookzine, BarBar and many more. One of said shorts was showcased at the Art Museum of South Texas.
He is an ace in Fantasy, Sci-Fi and Romance but even explores other genres as well. He works hard to come up with memorable adventures, magic systems and more in his ever growing Bizarre Short Stories anthology series. You can reach out to him on Instagram, Threads and TikTok as @Penname.exe.

Charis Negley

Charis Negley is a Colorado Springs-based historical fiction and spec fic writer originally from Wilmington, Delaware. When she's not reading or writing, she enjoys crocheting, listening to classical music (particularly Tchaikovsky), participating in community theater, and drinking coffee. Her work has previously been published in Curious Blue Press, Siren's Call, and Pawsitively Creepy.

Pip Pinkerton

Pip Pinkerton was born and raised in Oakdale, Minnesota. Pip is a wanderer and a dreamer. He loves writing short stories, poetry, and screenplays. A former theatre student and current guitar player, Pip currently co-manages a record shop. When he is not writing or jamming, he is spending time with his trusty rottweiler Shrimp. Pip has been published on the Monstrous Femme website, as well as with HorrorAddicts.net, Wicked Shadow Press, Sometimes Hilarious Horror, Theaker Quarterly Fiction, J. Manfred Weichsel, Pawsitively Creepy, and Ink'd Publishing. He has upcoming work to be featured in anthologies by Red Cape Publishing, Xpress Publishing, and Alien Buddha Press.

https://www.amazon.com/stores/Pip-Pinkerton/author/B0DZTYJVZ6

Jason Rogers

Jason Rogers is currently a high school English teacher in a juvenile detention center. He focuses mostly on screenwriting, but his days in high school offer a lot of inspiration that needs to get out somehow.

Neil Sanzari

Neil Sanzari is a weird fiction author. He attended NYU's Tisch School of the Arts, and the School of Visual Arts. Neil worked as a graphic artist in the advertising field in New York City for many years until he was displaced by the tragic events of 9/11. And now he lives with his wife, Celia, at the Jersey Shore writing short stories, and creating comic books. And he is currently working on a novel.

Michael Errol Swaim

Michael Errol Swaim is a horror and fantasy author. His first horror publication can be found in issue three of the e-zine Carnage House, and his stories and poems also appear in The Horror Zine, Flash Phantoms, Mocking Owl Roost, the Weird Wide Web podcast, and multiple anthologies by publishers such as Hellbound Books, Dark Moon Rising Publications, and Wicked Shadow Press. He is a member of the Cherokee Nation and lives in Northeast Oklahoma with his wife Mandy, his kids, and his cat, Wolfgirl. His first extreme horror novella, Absorbed By Excrement, is available from Amazon.

A.M.F. Taylor

A.M.F. Taylor likes to write creepy stories. She lives in Pennsylvania with her husband, two boys, a quirky calico cat, and an extraordinarily lazy pitbull mix.

https://boiledpotatoesblog.wordpress.com/

SJ Townend

SJ Townend is a single mother of two young children, a teacher, and an author of dark fiction. She has stories in publications from Vastarien, Eerie River Publishing, Dark Matter Magazine, and a few other places. Her first horror collection, Sick Girl Screams, introduced by Robert Shearman, is out now (Brigid's Gate Press) and her second horror collection, Your Final Sunset, is coming in 2025 (Sley House Press).
Twitter: @SJTownend
Blue-sky: https://bsky.app/profile/sjtownend.bsky.social

D. Winchester

David Winchester is a veteran of the US Navy. As a lover of science fiction, he joined the submarine service because he knew it was the closest he'd ever get to being in a spaceship. After that, he spent a decade and a half turning the wind into electricity, then spent a year living in a van. He is currently in Germany with his wife, where he writes on a variety of projects, including web novels and short stories. You can find out more on his website, https://caffeineforge.com/

www.ingramcontent.com/pod-product-compliance
Lightning Source LLC
LaVergne TN
LVHW091116080826
845145LV00008B/1942